Fraud at

Snowfields

by

Daniel Klock

www.fatherchristmasbook.com

Published by
Dr. Daniel Klockenbrink
Heinrich-Hertz-Str. 11
28211 Bremen
Germany

For more information, news, the author's blog, and more visit:

www.fatherchristmasbook.com
www.daniel-klock.com

First Edition October 2013

Also available as Kindle eBook edition, October 2013.

ISBN: 148109145X
ISBN-13: 978-1481091459

Fraud at

Snowfields

The White Christmas Organisation

www.fatherchristmasbook.com

Prologue

Bluerorcs! Six, seven, a dozen? He cannot tell because the tiny, bright-blue explosions of light keep blinding him. Will, running as fast as he can. Flashes of blue, flashes of yellow, brilliant flashes of blue and yellow together like fireworks—he is as frightened as he has ever been. He keeps running, followed by Bluerorcs, his legs pumping and his boots hitting the ground hard—*thump, thump, thump.*

Then the thumping gets louder and changes into a persistent banging.

'Aren't you ever going to get up?'

Will heard somebody yelling and sat up abruptly.

'Mum's called you twice already!'

He realised it was his sister Lucy shouting at him through the bedroom door. And he was sitting in his bed, safe at home. He wiped the sweat from his brow. Only a dream—or rather a nightmare he thought, the pictures still quite vivid in his mind.

'Okay,' he muttered. Then louder, 'Okay', so Lucy could hear him and would stop thumping the door to pieces. 'I'm awake, I'm coming.'

He shook his head. What a strange dream that had been. It had felt so real. Actually it still felt real, as if he really had been chased by those strange creatures through some dark tunnels. Again he shook his head to clear away these strange memories, and hurriedly got up to wash and dress himself.

'Morning, Will,' his mother greeted him when he rushed into the kitchen. 'Didn't you hear me? You must have slept like a rock! Now hurry! You've hardly got time for breakfast.

Quickly now, or you'll miss the bus and Mr Walker won't be pleased if you're late.'

This was Mr Walker's week for late duty and as he was Will's favourite teacher, he did not want to get on the wrong side of him, so he gulped down his breakfast, brushed his teeth —well, sort of, he really just wet them perfunctorily—grabbed his bag, and raced towards the bus stop. He was just in time to catch the bus. Breathing hard, he settled down in a seat and sighed in relief: no detention today...

Chapter 1

All through the day at school, Will had a slight headache. Not that it mattered much—in two days the holidays would start, and none of the teachers expected much concentration from their classes. In fact they themselves were not concentrating on the lessons too much, either, but were already making plans for Christmas and thinking of all the preparations they had yet to make.

As the lessons were rather boring, Will could not help but think about his strange and rather vivid dream throughout the day. It had not really felt like a dream at all—not like any dream he had ever had before. Perhaps more like a memory? But really, Bluerorcs, what kind of a word was that? He shook his head and muttered under his breath, 'That's crazy. Such things don't even exist in science fiction books.'

'Yes, Mr Burns, you would like to add something? Hm?' Will heard Mr Walker call him. He snapped to attention.

'No, sir. Sorry, sir.'

But Mr Walker had already turned his attention towards Ben and James, who had started elbowing each other. 'Boys, really!'

Finally even this school day was over, and the bell released Will. He did not feel like lingering with his friends as he sometimes did, but caught the bus straight home, still slightly bothered by his dream.

'Hi, Mum, I'm back,' he called as he entered the hall and tossed his bag into a corner. 'No homework,' he added, before she could pester him.

'Hello, dear,' she called back. 'How was your day?'

'Oh, Mum, what can school be like? Just the same as every other day,' Will replied as he walked into the kitchen. There he stopped abruptly. He was suddenly surrounded by a waft of delicious aromas. He knew them so well: his mother was baking Christmas biscuits at last. Will's mum had lived in Germany when she was a girl, and since no one in the family much liked mince pies anyway, she kept up the German tradition of making specially spiced biscuits every December. Suddenly his dream was completely forgotten as he found his mouth watering in response to the promising flavours.

'Oh well,' his mother replied, still with her back to him. 'I thought that just before Christmas you would be doing something special, something nice.'

'No, not today. Today was the same as always. But tomorrow is the last day before the holidays, so we'll have breakfast together in class and some Christmas decorations and stuff like that. And Mr Rupert said he wants to read us some Christmas tales and sing some carols with us.'

'Oh, that's nice,' replied his mother.

'Yes,' said Will. Then he grinned. 'Much better than maths, anyway.'

His mother smiled. 'Of course. I can remember my school days as well.'

Will laughed.

'Now that you are home, could you help me with the biscuits?'

'Sure,' replied Will. 'Just let me get changed.'

'Of course. Go on then'

Will went to his room. He took off his school uniform and got into more comfortable clothes. As he hung up the uniform, he thought his mother was right. It would be nice to have a festive breakfast instead of some boring history or maths lesson. And he had to admit to himself—although he would never have said this in school or to his friends—that he still liked Christmas stories and carols. This was his favourite time of the year and he had always felt something special about it. Somehow there was just ... something ... about Christmas that made him feel more real, more himself, something others did not seem to feel so strongly. He had always wondered about this, and was still thinking about it when he went back into the kitchen.

'Oh, there you are,' his mother said. 'Could you knead the dough over there, please? You're stronger than I am.'

'Okay.' Will went over to the side, where a lump of dough was sitting on the worktop. He started kneading it, inhaling deeply—cinnamon, vanilla, almond.... Mmm, the smells of marzipan, cardamom, coriander.... He was well-practised in picking out all the different aromas. He stole a bit of the dough—didn't it always taste even better before it was baked?—then he mixed more flour into the rest of it. He smiled as he listened to the carol on the radio. And he had to think about his seemingly extraordinarily strong feelings about Christmas yet again.

'What are you smiling at?' asked his mother.

'Oh, I'm just happy it's Christmas.'

'You've always liked Christmas very much,' his mother observed.

'Well, it's such a nice time. Everybody's really friendly and happy, there are the presents, the Christmas trees, the decorations everywhere—I think that's all just wonderful.' He pointed at the ball of dough in front of him. 'Is this enough?'

'Let me see.' She came over and looked at the dough. 'Yes, that's fine. Now you can roll it out. The cutters are over there.' She pointed to the sideboard.

'Okay.'

Will started rolling out the dough using the large rolling pin. When he judged that the dough had the right thickness, he went over to the sideboard and fetched the cutters. He first selected one that was in the form of a Christmas tree—one of his favourites.

'Isn't Lucy here yet? I haven't seen her, and I thought she only had school this morning.'

He started pressing the cutter into the dough.

'No. Yes.' His mother laughed when Will looked confused. 'Your sister finished school early, but she went over to visit her friend Laura, and I expect it will be some time before she'll be home.'

'Oh. Yes, those two can talk for hours.' Will rolled his eyes. His mother laughed again.

Will continued pressing the cutter into the dough until he had used up all the space. He placed the biscuits on a baking tray. Then he rolled the rest of the dough back into a ball and flattened it again with the rolling pin. This time he selected a cutter in the form of a star. He enjoyed the work and listened to the carols still playing on the radio.

When he had finished up all the dough, he placed the rest of the biscuits on the baking trays and said to his mother, 'I'm finished. Do you need help with anything else?'

His mother looked at the baking trays and nodded approvingly. 'The biscuits look very nice. Thank you. I can do the rest. Off you go.' She smiled.

Will smiled back, washed his hands, and left the kitchen. He went up to his room. His eyes fell on his bed. Underneath it were the presents he had bought for his parents and his sister. Now that he was twelve, his belief in Father Christmas was beginning to weaken. When he had been a young child, he had, of course, firmly believed in Father Christmas. But then, over the years, he had been told Father Christmas was just a myth, a fairy tale for children. Later on he had learned that the usual appearance of Father Christmas—the image of a nice, jolly and rather corpulent man with a bushy, white beard, and a magnificent red robe—was supposedly just a clever marketing campaign by a well-known soft-drinks producer. He grimly remembered what a tremendous disappointment that had been! After all, he had always been most firm in his belief in Father Christmas. He just could not imagine Christmas without him. All those years he had always been most diligent in writing his letters to him, spending ages so the writing would be very clear and easy to read. And he always had them ready by the end of autumn so they would reach Father Christmas in good time. But then he learned his parents were supposed to buy all the presents, gift wrap them, and place them under the Christmas tree while he was sleeping on Christmas Eve.

And everybody seemed to confirm this: the shops, the television, his friends at school, and even his parents. He could still remember the long and heated discussions he had had with his friends when the first of them had been told Father Christmas did not exist. But in the end he grudgingly had to admit that they seemed to be right. There were, for example, all the people attacking the shops and buying lots of toys, electronics, and just about everything else you could think of right before Christmas. There were men in Father Christmas costumes in the shops and shopping malls, virtually at every street corner, ringing bells and shouting, 'Merry Christmas'.

But, in spite of all the evidence, Will always had a nagging feeling there was more to it, more than just a fabricated story and a marketing gag. There were some things that just did not fit. For example, he sometimes thought his parents looked vaguely puzzled when he opened his presents on Christmas Day—as if they were surprised by the presents he unwrapped.

He always got what he had asked for in his letters—well, he thought somewhat sheepishly, as long as he asked for sensible things like a model railway or a backpack, and not a fully functional moon rocket or a living elephant. Sometimes, though, his parents had looked vaguely disturbed by the things he received, as if they could not remember buying them. And, now that he thought about it, he'd often felt the same way about the presents he had given them. Sometimes they looked grander than they had when he had bought them or were more the colour and shape his parents liked.

But because just about everybody had told him Father Christmas did not exist, he had always dismissed this as a trick of his imagination. In the last months, though, he had sometimes thought about it, and more and more aspects seemed not to fit the explanation. He suddenly realised they would make rather a lot of sense if Father Christmas really existed after all. Or was it really just a children's tale? Was he not too old for this, and was he just making things up, willing them to be true?

Well, nothing he could do about it anyway. He would not be able to prove the existence or the nonexistence of Father Christmas. And, of course, he would not hear the end of it from his sister if he brought up this topic yet again. He just could not believe that others did not see or feel all the hints and clues he could see and feel. And that nobody else wondered about this.

Oh well. He would just enjoy Christmas like he did every year. He went to his computer to check his e-mails. There were none. So he picked up the book he had been reading. It was, of course, a good Christmas story. He went downstairs to the living room, sat down on the sofa, and started to read.

As he read, he turned to musing. What *did* make him love Christmas so much. He remembered when he was very little, he had had a dream. His parents had told him Father Christmas comes down the chimney on Christmas Eve and leaves the presents in the stockings and under the Christmas tree. In his dream, Will woke up in the middle of the night on the twenty-fourth of December. A noise had disturbed him. He was only five but he crept down the dark stairs, missing the third one from the top that creaked—he knew that because he had already been caught trying to get ice-cream in the middle of the night—and there in the living room was Father Christmas—no mistake. The old man winked at him, sat him on his knee, whispered a message Will could never quite remember, put his finger to his lips, and was gone. Will thought hard, still wrapped up in the magical presence that had just left. But there were his presents, as promised. Did he get the Lego he wanted? Was the model car there? It did not look as if he had got the jet plane he wanted—the parcels did not look big enough. Dare he open the presents? No. His mum and dad would not be pleased. Christmas was always a special day in the family. He was only a little boy but he still appreciated the ritual. Get up, long breakfast, open presents, one at a time, dinner—ooh—turkey, stuffing (that sometimes tasted better than the turkey) baked potatoes, vegetables (forget those!), Christmas pudding, crackers, funny hats, jokes. Then Dad, snoring on the sofa, Mum in the kitchen, he and Lucy sharing, bickering. Tea-time. Christmas cake, biscuits (no mince pies), trifle. Supper: pork pie, cold turkey, ham, salmon, crab paste, goodies that never came round again until next year.

So Will crept back to bed and waited for the next day. But his dream of Father Christmas kept him warm through the night, the whispered words always a kind of promise, just out of reach.

Will grew older. Christmas stayed the same. One year he stayed awake all night, creeping downstairs in the early hours (missing the third step, of course) but he never saw Father Christmas again. And yet, somehow, the remembered presence and scent of the old man seemed to linger in the Christmas paper, in the presents, in the essence of the day.

Will could feel it creep over him again as he fell asleep over his book.

In the early evening his dad came home. They had supper and then spent the rest of the evening in the living room watching television or, in Will's case, reading. He finally went to bed. Before he eventually dropped off to sleep, he thought yet again about Father Christmas and how he could not believe the old man did not exist.

Early next morning Will was woken by the alarm clock. He got up and stumbled into the bathroom, still quite sleepy. After he had washed himself, he was a bit more awake and remembered this was the last day at school before the Christmas holidays. This woke him up quite a bit more, and after getting dressed he very nearly bounced down to the breakfast table, where his mother was just putting out his cereal.

'Good morning, dear,' she greeted him.

'Morning, Mum.'

'So lively this early in the morning?' she asked, raising her eyebrows.

'Indeed. Today's the last day before the Christmas holidays!' Will announced.

'Oh, that's why. I wish you'd treat every day at school like this.' She grinned.

Will grinned back. 'No way!'

His mother laughed.

'Eat. Eat and get yourself off to school, you!'

'No. No breakfast today. We're going to have breakfast at school, remember?'

'Oh, right. I forgot.'

Will was actually five minutes early for the school bus—he could not remember that happening before. Oh well. It was Christmas after all.

His way to school was uneventful, and at the beginning of the lesson with Mr Rupert they put up Christmas decorations in the classroom. The girls had prepared paper-cuts for the windows in the shapes of Christmas trees, reindeer, and Father Christmas with his large, well-filled sack, riding his sleigh. The boys hung up red and green garlands as well as stars made out of golden foil along the ceiling and walls. The school had provided a small Christmas tree that stood in a corner of the classroom. The students had already decorated it with self-made hangings two weeks earlier, and had put a large, golden star on its top.

When they had finished with the decorations, they prepared breakfast. They pushed all the tables together so they formed one large table. Everybody had brought something for breakfast like marmalade, chocolate spread, or rolls, and they put it all in the middle of the table to share. Mr Rupert sat down in their midst, and they started to eat. After Mr Rupert had eaten a couple of rolls, he fetched a large book with a bright, glittering white cover that looked like ice. The title was printed in red letters on it. It was a story about a boy joining the workforce of Father Christmas.

Some of the boys started to snigger. The workforce of Father Christmas indeed! Did their teacher think they were still babies, believing in goblins and elves and other little Christmas helpers? And then a boy who actually worked for Father Christmas, manufacturing presents, riding sleighs, popping down chimneys? Will listened curiously. The whole story had an almost familiar feel about it. The sniggering grew louder and one of the boys pointed at Will's rapt expression. Two boys were now actually laughing out loud. Irritated, Mr

Rupert closed the book and suggested ending the morning with singing Christmas carols. The girls sang with quite a bit more enthusiasm than the boys—well, except Will of course, though he did try not to show it too much. He realised some of the laughter had been directed at him for being so interested in the story, and he certainly had no intention of becoming the target of some prank afterwards. But inwardly he enjoyed himself very much. It was the best day at school in a long time.

Finally Mr Rupert ended the prolonged breakfast and sent them home. Will said good-bye to his friends and went home on the school bus. When he got off together with Henry, who lived a few houses down the road, he wished him a Merry Christmas and went home. He opened the door and entered the hall.

'Hello! I'm back!' he called.

'Hi, dear. I'm in the living room,' his mother called back.

Will put down his rucksack, took off his jacket, and went into the living room.

'Hi Mum. Breakfast was great, very Christmassy. It really put me in the mood for the holidays. By the way, when will Dad be home?'

'It's a normal working day for him, so not before five, as usual,' his mother replied.

'Then he wouldn't want to put up the Christmas tree today, would he?' Will grinned.

'No, I don't believe he'll be in the mood for it this evening.'

'Well, tomorrow is only the twenty-third, so I guess it's early enough.'

'How gracious of you.' His mother raised one eyebrow.

'I sometimes have my moments.' Will answered cheekily.

They both laughed.

***

The next morning Will took advantage of the fact that it was the first day of the school holidays and slept until ten o'clock. Finally he got up and went down for breakfast.

'Hey, sleepyhead!' his sister called when he went into the kitchen.

Will just grinned and replied, 'I'm sure you only got up ten minutes before me.' He looked at her pointedly. 'You're even still wearing your pyjamas.'

His sister turned slightly red. 'So? They're comfy,' she replied, and busied herself with her cereal. Will laughed. He sat down and grabbed the cornflakes. After he had munched through them, he went into the living room. 'Morning, Dad.'

'Good morning, Will.' His father looked up from his newspaper, smiling. 'Ready to go and get the Christmas tree? Come on then.'

Will did not need to be asked twice. He followed his father to the shed where the tree had been kept for the last few days so it would stay fresh in the cold. They picked up the tree, still packed tightly in a net, and brought it inside, where they placed it in the stand in the usual corner of the living room. Then Will held the tree, trying to keep it straight, while his father was lying on the ground twiddling around with the screws of the stand to get the tree standing upright.

After some grunting his father declared, 'Okay, it's fast now.' He got up and stepped back a few feet to look critically at the tree. 'Let's see if it's straight.'

But despite their best efforts, it was not.

His father sighed again. 'Every year it's the same. Why can't they invent a stand that's easy to use and will get the tree straight? Always this fiddling about with those stupid screws.'

Resigned he ducked under the tree again.

'Okay, Will. I'll loosen the screws, and you'll hold the tree once more.'

They went back at it.

'Well, it's fast again. Let's see...' His father got up.

'Hmm. That doesn't look too bad. What do you think, Will?'

Will stepped away from the tree and looked at it critically.

'Yes, I think it's good. It's straight. It looks good.'

'Okay,' his father said, 'then it's your turn.' He smiled and turned away from the tree.

'No,' Will disagreed, 'not yet, actually.'

'Oh?'

'You've got to put the lights on it first,' Will said, and grinned at his father.

His father groaned exaggeratedly. 'Oh no, I forgot. That's even more fuss than that stupid tree stand.'

Will laughed and whined, 'Ooooooh, please, Daddy. Let's have a tree with lights this year, ooooh, please!'

His father shot him a scathing glance. 'Get those lights, you plonker!'

Laughing, Will went and fetched the lights from the next room. They had brought them down from the attic already with the rest of the Christmas decorations at the beginning of December. He laid the lights out on the floor and sorted them so they were lying in a straight line without knots in the cable. Then he inspected the single lamps and changed the ones that were broken. After everything was sorted out, he nodded in satisfaction and handed the chain to his father, who placed them on the tree. He had to correct their positions several times until he had distributed them evenly and finally was satisfied.

Will watched from the sofa. His father turned to him. 'Well, Christmas fanatic? What do you think?'

'It looks great!' Will beamed nearly as brightly as the lights on the tree shone.

His father laughed. 'Good.' And he fixed the lights securely in their positions. 'Okay son. Now it's definitely your turn.'

'Sure!'

Will went looking for his sister Lucy. He found her in the kitchen with their mother, helping her cook lunch.

'Oh, here you are. Do you want to help decorate the tree?' he asked her.

'No!' She shook her head vigorously. 'You can do that boring work on your own. Not that you would mind anyway.' She laughed.

'No. Actually I like it, as you well know.' Will smiled.

'Have fun. We're busy.' His sister waved him away.

'I definitely will,' he called back over his shoulder while he left the kitchen. He heard his mother laugh, but he did not know whether this was because of his last remark or because of something Lucy had said. He suspected the former, but hurried back into the living room.

He looked at the tree once again: so pure at the moment, with just the lights bathing it in a soft, golden glow. After he had looked at it for a while, he went back into the adjoining room and fetched the boxes with the tree hangings and decorations. There were so many, he had to go several times. After he had them all in the living room, he opened them and spread out the smaller boxes and bags that were inside, containing the different ornaments, toppers, baubles, tinsel, garlands, and everything else. He arranged them around the room so he could see them all and could choose the ones he wanted.

While he was doing this, he did not notice that his father, who was sitting at the table again, looked up from his paper from time to time and smiled, seeing how much pleasure Will was getting out of his work. Unaware of this Will unconsciously hummed carols under his breath while he rummaged through the boxes and bags, trying to choose exactly the right ornaments.

Like every year he had already started a month earlier to plan what the Christmas tree should look like. He had decided on a traditional tree this time, mainly in red, with big baubles, some wooden ornaments, rich bows, crimson faux fruit, and some silver tinsel. All in all he did not want to put too much decoration on it, but did want to use fewer and larger pieces, and keep it rather plain but stylish. He selected the biggest red baubles and arranged them around the tree. Then he added some smaller ones. After that he selected a few bells with fine, silver designs on them, and placed them between the baubles. Next came wooden ornaments like angels, small sleighs, and bright parcels.

Will stopped after he had arranged the wooden ornaments around the tree. He stepped back a few paces to have a look at what he had done so far. He looked at the tree critically from different sides and found several flaws that definitely needed correction. So he stepped up to the tree again and relocated those ornaments that did not please him yet. He next placed red bows on the tree, followed by the fruit. Finally he put strands of tinsel here and there, and stepped back to examine the tree again. He looked at it from different angles, walking here and there. He nodded, picked up a few red baubles in the form of birds, with silver decoration and silver tail feathers, and added them to the tree. Finally he walked over to his father, who looked up from his newspaper.

'I'm finished!' Will declared.

His father nodded gravely, got up, and went over to the tree, having a good look at it.

'Well done,' he said finally. 'That looks really good. Nice and traditional, all in red as it is. And it isn't so overburdened as the ones you the see in the shops and malls these days. I like it! Good work.' He smiled at Will.

Will beamed. 'Do you think we should add a topper?' He eyed the tree.

'Hmm.... No, I like it as it is. It looks more natural without one. No, don't put one on it.'

'Yes, that's what I thought,' Will said.

Just then his sister came into the living room.

'Well, how... Oh.' She interrupted herself in mid-sentence and stopped right where she was. 'Why, it's beautiful,' she said finally, still gazing at the tree. 'Very nice, brother dear.'

'Why, thank you, sister dear,' Will said half mockingly, but he had to grin when he heard this unexpected compliment.

'No, I mean it!' said Lucy, looking directly at him. 'It's really very nice—nearly the perfect Christmas tree. It shows taste,' she added a bit grudgingly.

Now Will really was surprised. Was this his sister talking to him? Praising him?

Lucy looked at the tree again. Finally she turned away and headed back for the door. 'Beautiful,' she said not quite under her breath, but Will was quite sure that she had not meant him to hear it.

'Oh.' Lucy turned round just before she reached the door. 'I actually came to see how far you had got, and to tell you lunch will be ready in twenty minutes—well, fifteen now.'

'That's fine,' Will said. 'I'm nearly ready. I just have to clear away the boxes.'

Lucy nodded and left.

Will packed the smaller cartons back into the bigger cardboard boxes and took them into the adjoining room. Then he and his father went into the kitchen, and they all had lunch.

***

Later in the afternoon, they all sat together again, drinking tea. Will enjoyed some of the delicious Christmas biscuits they had baked just the other day, while his mother leafed through the Christmas cards they had received that morning. She selected one of them and put the others aside.

'Listen to this one,' she told them. 'Merry Christmas, hope you are fine and so on... then this: Kids like our clever Ken enjoy new books, reading interesting new knowledge!' she read from the Christmas card.

Christmas was, unfortunately, also the time when you heard things like this, thought Will. It was not too hard for him to guess who had sent this card, even if she had not mentioned Ken in the sentence. Only Aunt Peggy would write something like that on a Christmas card—always looking for yet another way to praise her prince-son Ken, who was, in Will's opinion, just a stupid, oafish git who always pestered his doting parents. He enjoyed a joke nearly two minutes after everybody else, of course, and only if it was not too witty. One could say Will did not like Ken. The 'books' his aunt referred to probably had titles like *Where Is My Cow?*, *Harry the Hare and His First Day at School*, and *Billy the Badger Goes Shopping*. He shook his head.

On Christmas Eve they were all together in the living room. Will's mother and his sister sat on one side of the corner sofa, Will on the other side. His father was in the armchair. They played a board game and then chatted for a while, talking easily and, on the whole, enjoying a nice, quiet evening together in front of the magnificent Christmas tree. It was getting late, so finally Will and Lucy got up to go to bed. Their parents stayed up a while longer and finished the bottle of wine.

***

Will opened his eyes. He saw it was already light. Immediately he realised it was Christmas Day! He looked at the alarm clock next to his bed: 9:17. Definitely time to get up. He jumped out of bed—something he only did once or twice a year, and certainly not on a school day—and, still in his pyjamas, bounded down the stairs and into the living room. There he saw his stocking hanging from the mantelpiece. It was full to the brim! When he went over to examine it more closely, he saw he was not the first to be there. His sister was already sitting in front of the fireplace, also still in her pyjamas, and had the contents of her stocking lying all around her. His parents were sitting at the table, his father leafing through a magazine, his mother drinking Christmas tea. Will could smell it from where he was standing. Both were smiling at their children.

'Good morning, Will,' his mother said. 'I hope you slept well.'

'Yes, thank you,' he replied, and added, 'Morning, Dad.'

'Good morning, Will. It seems to me that Father Christmas was quite generous this year.'

'Yes, it seems so.' Will looked yearningly at his stocking, which was threatening to tear itself loose from the mantelpiece, it was so full and heavy.

His mother laughed as she saw this. 'Go on then!'

'Morning, Sis,' he said to Lucy as he hurried past her.

'Morning, Will,' she said, her attention focused on her presents.

19

Will reached the mantelpiece and carefully took down his full stocking. He went over to a clear space on the carpet, where he got down on his knees and emptied his stocking, carefully pulling the presents out one at a time. When he had emptied the entire stocking, he had four small parcels, one large Father Christmas figure made out of chocolate, several chocolate coins, and a few other bits and pieces lying in front of him.

He carefully opened the presents. In the first parcel he found a book he had wanted very much for the last few months. The other parcels also contained things he had wished for and had put in his letter to Father Christmas (out of habit he still wrote them every year although he would never have admitted it). He looked up and saw his parents watching him and smiling.

His mother said, 'Well, are you happy? Got everything you wanted?'

'Yes! That's great! Exactly what I wanted.'

His mother's smile became even broader. 'And what about you, Lucy?' There was no answer. 'Lucy?' Will's mother called louder. 'Lucy?'

'Hmm?' Lucy slowly raised her head. 'What?'

Will's mother laughed. 'I asked you whether you are happy with your presents.'

'Oh.' Lucy beamed. 'Yes! They are marvellous!'

Will's mother laughed again. 'That's fine then.'

Will's father laughed too.

Will and Lucy were occupied with their presents, and their parents quietly enjoyed their tea. Soon it was lunchtime, and they sat down at the table to enjoy their traditional Christmas meal. In the afternoon they gathered around the Christmas tree and opened the larger presents Father Christmas had placed underneath it.

Later in the evening, Will lay in his bed, thinking happily about his presents and the pleasant day he had had with his family. Just before he drifted off to sleep, he could not help but think again about how some of the presents had seemed more grand or more to the liking of the one who received them than would have been possible if they had just been bought in a shop. So perhaps it was Father Christmas who had brought these presents after all...

Chapter 2

On Boxing Day Will slept quite late and it was well past eleven when he finally got up. He washed and got dressed, then he went downstairs. Halfway down he saw his father coming out of the living room.

'Morning, Dad', he said brightly and then he noticed the odd look on his father's face.

'Yes, morning... Morning,' his father said, seeming a bit preoccupied. 'Er, I was just going to get you, in fact. We've got a visitor who wants to speak to you.'

Will was surprised by the mysterious expression on his father's face while he said this. 'A visitor? Today? And he wants to see me? A relative or what? Maybe Aunt Peggy?' He feverishly hoped it was not her.

His father shook his head. 'Oh, no. No, it's not a relative. Not at all...'

Will was really curious by then, especially as he saw his father's puzzlement. 'Who is it then?'

His father scratched his head. 'The answer to that is not quite so simple. It's best if you just have a look yourself.'

Now it was Will's turn to shake his head. Why could his father not simply tell him who this visitor was? He opened the door to the living room, by then bursting with curiosity. He saw his sister sitting at the table, staring wide-eyed at their guest. His mother was sitting on the couch and talking to the visitor. She interrupted herself and looked up as Will walked into the room. Her face held an odd expression, similar to Will's father's. But Will did not really look at her. He gazed at the visitor. And indeed it was one of the weirdest persons he had ever seen in his life.

The stranger wore green-coloured trousers, a green shirt, a brown waistcoat, and a bright-red overcoat. He was looking at Will, and Will saw he had sparkling green eyes. His face had a merry look, and tiny wrinkles at the corners of his mouth and eyes suggested he laughed quite often. He started to smile when he saw Will, and then he got up in a fluid movement, extending his hand and walking over to him.

'Will! Will Burns! How nice to meet you. I want to wish you a very merry Christmas', he said, grinning and shaking Will's hand vigorously.

Will noticed his own mouth had somehow fallen open, and so he quickly said, 'Er, thank you very much, Mr, er... Sorry, but who are you?'

The man held up his hand. 'My fault, my fault. My name is Conrad Chevalier, but please just call me Corny, like everybody else.'

'Mr Chevalier came in this morning, and he said he has important things to talk to you about.' His mother had got up and was standing next to Will, a proud smile on her face. 'Your dad and I were a bit surprised when he knocked on the door, but what he wants to talk to you about is really stunning. It took a bit of persuasion for us to believe it.'

She laid a hand on Will's shoulder, steered him to the couch, and made him sit down. His father sat down next to Will's mother on the other side of the corner sofa, taking her hand and sharing a smile with her. Then he looked at Will and smiled at him proudly. Will felt totally confused, wondering what this curiously-clad man could want from him. Mr Chevalier took a seat right in front of Will and looked at him gravely.

'Now, Will, I know you must be quite confused by all this, and very curious about why on earth I came to visit you on

Boxing Day. Trouble is, every time I have to do this, I'm not quite sure where to start.' He winked at Will, confusing him all the more.

'Well, I know you have just finished the current term at your school, right?'

Will just nodded, feeling mystified.

'Now, I have come today to tell you about a different school. One that would be happy to have you as a student in March, when the next school year begins there. When I say school, it is not just a school but more of a college or even a job-training facility. This school chooses twenty young people each year who are allowed to enrol. And... Hrumpf.' He cleared his throat and announced, 'We are happy to inform you that you are one of those students who can start there in March next year.'

He beamed at Will, who felt he should respond somehow. 'Oh, that's good, but... Er, I'm afraid I have no idea what school you're talking about.'

Mr Chevalier's grin faded a little, and he smacked his forehead. 'Of course. My fault, my fault. Sorry. You obviously wouldn't know about it, would you, because it is kept secret. A big secret, in fact. The school I'm talking about is Snowfields. It is the training centre for the direct helpers of Father Christmas. It is the foremost place to learn all about Christmas, the production and delivery of the presents, and where you get the high qualifications needed for this tricky business.' He was positively beaming again. He stood.

'Today I have the great honour to inform you that you qualify for this school, and that you have been chosen to undergo all the necessary training that will allow you to belong to the top of the business one day!' With this he reached into his waistcoat and pulled out a scroll bound with a gold ribbon and sealed with a blotch of red wax and presented it to Will.

Will was stunned. He stared at the scroll, then at the man holding it in front of him, who was grinning so hard his face was in danger of splitting right in half. Will looked at the scroll again. He heard Lucy shouting, 'What?' but he ignored her. He glanced at his mother. Her face shone with pride. He turned to his father. There was a happy smile on his face too. Will looked back at the stranger who was still holding the scroll in front of him. He slowly shook his head and a grin finally spread on his face, too.

'Very, very good! It was a great idea and it was well presented. Brilliantly. For a moment you really had me there. But in the end it was just a bit too grand to believe. A bit over the top. Nevertheless it was great fun—playing a joke like this on me. Whose idea was it? Yours, Dad? And this gentleman who helped you so excellently, is he a colleague...from work? I...believe I...'

While he was talking, he looked at his parents. But then he stuttered to a halt, because their smiles were slowly fading, and they shook their heads. Something was wrong here. Even Lucy was silent. Now, of course all this could not be true—that much was obvious to him. But why had they not all joined in, laughing with him now that the fun was played out? He had a feeling he was missing something. Will looked at the stranger again: his grin had faded quite a bit, too, and he was also shaking his head vigorously.

The man looked up to the ceiling and moaned. 'Why? Why don't they ever believe me? It must be these modern times. The young have become so distrusting. Too much rational thinking, too little imagination in their heads. Ah, well, it's not the first time.' He sighed. 'Will, listen. I really am what I've told you I am—an emissary of Snowfields. I really have been sent to invite you to our school. And this scroll I've got for you is genuine, and no joke at all.'

Will felt uncertain. He turned to his parents, who were nodding at him encouragingly. He said to the stranger, not quite so sure of himself now, 'Well, this joke has gone far enough. There's no need to push it any further.' But there was more than a little doubt in his voice.

His father cleared his throat. 'I think it would be best if we show him your...your means of transportation, Mr Chevalier.'

The stranger's face lit up again. 'Yes! You're right. My fault, my fault. That should help him believe me. It always does the trick. Let's go!'

He seized Will's hand and pulled him along. His parents followed. Before Will knew what had happened, he was through the door, and the stranger was dragging him onto the snow-covered terrace.

Will was dumbstruck. He absolutely could not believe what his eyes were telling him was in front of him. There was a real sleigh standing on the lawn at the back of their house! A sleigh! Not a small sledge for children, like the one he had that was standing inside the garage, the ones you rode down the snowy hills on just for fun. This was an actual sleigh—the kind you sometimes saw in films, drawn by horses. And this one was large, made out of brown wood that was so smooth and highly polished it gleamed and shone in the sunlight. There were red ribbons and bows tied here and there to the railing all around it. And—he rubbed his eyes and pinched himself really hard in case he was still fast asleep and dreaming wildly, but they were still there—four great and proud reindeer stood in front of the sleigh. They were large animals with glossy coats in different hues of brown. All of them had impressive antlers and bright-red tack with tiny, golden bells. Then there was a squeal and Lucy bounded past the others towards the reindeer.

'Oh! Aren't they cute? Look at them!' She ran straight up to the nearest one and started stroking its nose.

27

Conrad stood beside Will, once again a broad grin on his face, and he laid a hand on Will's shoulder. 'Quite impressive, isn't it? Of course,' he added in an offhand way, 'it's not our newest model, the Executive High Motion, but the Wood Voyager Supreme, which is standard for delivery service. But I am quite fond of it because it's tough and never lets you down when you need it. You know, the newer ones always give you a bit of trouble when you get into atmospheric turbulences.'

Will wanted to answer, but he had to go looking for his voice first. He found it hiding in a dark place in the corner of his throat, brought it up, and got hold of it again.

'I... I can't believe it,' he said. His brain ran the last sentence past him again and marked a word in red. 'Er, turbulences? Does it fly? Really fly?'

'Oh yes, of course it does.' Conrad laughed. 'And the feeling is really indescribable. It's breathtaking when you are flying over a snow-covered city that is bathed in the warm glow of all the Christmas lights. Or when you are flying over a white beach in a tropical region, where palms are growing and the blue water is so clear you can see the rainbow-coloured fish trailing lazily through the water.' His eyes sparkled, and his face mirrored the joy of flying.

Conrad went over to the reindeer and patted the nearest one lightly on its head. It responded by rubbing its nose on his arm. Will gave them a closer look. They were proud animals. They were standing there quite calmly, their heads held high in the air, and only once in a while one of them would toss its head and paw the snow restlessly. Even all the fuss Lucy was making did not disturb them.

'Come on over and have a closer look,' called Conrad.

Will carefully walked over to the sleigh, almost afraid it might disappear when he reached it. He gazed at it. The wood was velvet-smooth and so highly polished he could almost see his face in it. The skids were of shining silver, nearly fiery where the sunlight hit them. He stretched out his hand carefully and touched the wood. It was real. A feeling of deep wonder overcame him.

Conrad's voice right next to him made him jump: 'I know exactly what you'd like. Let's take a short trip round the chimneys, okay?'

Will could only answer with a weak nod, not trusting himself to speak.

'What about you, young lady?' Conrad asked Lucy. 'Would you like to join us?' He smiled at her invitingly.

But Lucy shied away, looking rather afraid. 'Oh, no. No, thank you. I'd rather watch for now. Thank you very much.' Prudently she stepped away from the sleigh.

Conrad nodded understandingly. 'Okay.' He turned back to Will and helped him onto the sleigh, climbed up in front of him onto the driver's seat, and took the reins. He gave them a light shake, and the sleigh started moving with a slight jolt. They had only gone a few feet when Will felt they were lifting off the ground. In the next moment, they were completely in the air, and went right over the top of the nearest bush. They rose higher and higher. Now they were level with the balcony, then they were going round the chimney of the house. They were still rising, and Will gripped the rail so tightly his knuckles turned white.

Conrad turned round. 'All right there, Will?'

Will just gave a slight nod. He was busy looking down at the rooftops that were passing by underneath. A slow grin crept onto his face and grew wider and wider, threatening to split it in two. His grip on the railing lessened to just a good hold-on.

Conrad looked back at him. 'Ah, I see. Now you know what flying is like. Brill'nt, isn't it!'

Will forced his gaze away from the wonderful sights below long enough to grin at Conrad. 'Yeah, it's fantastic. I've never felt anything like this in my life.' He looked down again and saw that they were passing over a couple taking a stroll through the snow. 'But won't people see us up here? What will they think?' He gave Conrad a concerned look.

'No, no.' Conrad laughed. 'There's no chance anyone will see us if I don't want them to. Nobody except you and your parents are able to see the sleigh, because I spelled it.'

'How—' started Will.

But Conrad interrupted him. 'I can't explain to you how we do it just now. But this is one of the things you will be learning at Snowfields. It's taught in Basics of Magic there.'

'Magic!' Will gasped. 'You... How... Magic really exists?'

'Of course it does!' Conrad snorted. 'How do you think Christmas would work without magic? There just would be no Christmas without magic! All the deliveries on time, the fulfilment of the individual wishes, all of that wouldn't be possible. Look, you've even got the popular saying "The Magic of Christmas". That wasn't just made up out of nothing.'

Every time Will got a grip on himself again, it felt as if the rug were pulled out from under him, and he was left feeling dumbstruck once more. He still could not believe all this was happening. Then he concentrated on his surroundings again and realised the sleigh was slowly losing elevation. A moment later they had landed on the lawn at the back of the house again, without even the slightest bump when they touched the ground. Conrad got up from the driver's seat and then helped Will out. When he got down from the sleigh and tried to put his weight on his legs, he was glad of Conrad's hand, because the flight had somehow turned his knees into jelly.

'Don't worry. This happens to almost everybody when they fly with a sleigh for the first time,' Conrad told him, giving him a slap on the back, which very nearly sent Will face-down into the snow. They walked up to his parents, whose eyes were filled with wonder at having just witnessed the miraculous flying sleigh. His father laid a hand on Will's shoulder, and they all went inside into the living room again.

When they had sat down, Conrad gave Will a serious look and said, 'So, Will, after this small demonstration, I hope you believe me and the things I've told you. I really was sent from Snowfields to present you with the invitation to our school. I'd suggest you read this first, and then I'll tell you more about it.'

He offered Will the scroll again, and this time Will took it.

'In the meantime... Would it be possible to get a cup of tea?'

Will's mother jumped up: 'Oh, I am so sorry, Mr Chevalier. I should have offered you one right away, but I'm afraid all these unusual events this morning and all the quite unbeliev-able things you've told us quite distracted me. I'll bring you one right away.' She hurried into the kitchen.

Will untied the gold ribbon that bound the scroll and looked at the seal. It was of red wax, and imprinted in it was the image of a Christmas parcel with a garland of holly around it. He remembered he had seen the same image on the sleigh.

'That's the official logo of our organisation,' said Conrad when he saw Will looking at the image. Will broke the seal and unrolled the scroll. It was made of heavy parchment, and the writing was in black ink—very clear and handsome.

Snowfields
Official Training School of the Christmas Service
Part of the White Christmas Organisation (WCO)

Dear Mr Burns,

It is my honour to inform you that you have been accepted as a student at Snowfields Training School.

Together with this scroll, you will receive all necessary forms and information, including a list of the things you will need to bring with you, as the school will not provide them. Our emissary will be pleased to help you if you have any questions. Please feel free to write to me if there are any problems or if there is anything you do not understand. Means to reach me will also be explained by the emissary.

Also enclosed you will find a form we need to enrol you as a student. Please complete it with your personal details and send it back as soon as possible. Your first term will begin on the first of March. Instructions on how to reach the school are enclosed and will also be explained by our emissary.

I must request that you will not mention anything about the school, Snowfields, the Christmas Service, the White Christmas Organisation (WCO), or anything else about the related aspects to anyone except your parents, brothers, and sisters (not even other relatives!) unless you know they are members of the mentioned institutions. You can recognise a member by a badge showing the logo of the White Christmas Organisation, which is also printed on this scroll and all the other documents which are enclosed. This logo is only visible to members of the organisation.

I am looking forward to welcoming you personally at our school.

Merry Christmas.

Star Dustfall
Snowfields

Will read the letter twice before he let it sink onto his knees, and he looked up. In the meantime his parents had laid the table and were sipping tea together with Mr Chevalier. Will handed them the scroll wordlessly and started looking through the other papers that had fallen out when he had opened it. There was the form and the list of things he was required to have, the instructions on how to reach the school, a list of the subjects of the first term, and a paper with the heading 'Main Facts about Snowfields, Top School of the Christmas Service'.

He peered closely at the paper where the subjects were listed. He would never have dreamed that subjects like this even existed. There were, for example, Basics of Magic, and Handling of Letters to Father Christmas, but also some quite ordinary subjects like Logistics, Warehousing, and Material Procurement. There also was a short definition next to each subject.

'Basics of Magic,' he read, 'provides the knowledge of all the necessary magic that is needed for the day-to-day work and the delivery of presents. You will be trained in special abilities, mainly for coping with problems and to guarantee uninterrupted business. This subject will be taught by Miss Star Dustfall.

'Handling of Letters to Father Christmas: This subject may sound a bit odd and not very important, but it is in fact one of the most vital departments of our organisation. You will be taught how the letters have to be interpreted, how the wishes have to be judged, and, most important, how it is possible to make nearly everybody happy on Christmas Eve, even if the wish expressed in the letter is impossible to fulfil. The teacher for this subject will be Mr Quill Parchmentinus.

'Logistics: One of the major problems our organisation has to cope with during the whole year is logistics. Material has to be provided for the production of presents, unfinished products have to be transported between different depart-

33

ments, the finished products have to be stored until they are needed (this will be taught in a special subject), etc. This subject will be taught by Mr Getius Thingsmoving.

'Warehousing: This subject deals with the storage of all goods used in production, and especially of the finished products. The training will involve learning about the management of the space, the different methods of storage, optimal indexing of the goods, providing optimal access to the goods, etc. This subject will be taught by Mrs. Storia Itaway.

'Material Procurement: The materials used in production have to be obtained, they have to be stored until they are needed, the necessary amounts have to be judged, contracts have to be negotiated, etc. All the necessary qualifications for these tasks will be gained in this subject. It will be taught by Mr Argius Contractus.'

Will was fascinated. All this sounded really interesting, just amazing. He looked up and saw that Conrad was watching him, and when their eyes met, Conrad smiled and gave him a wink.

Will asked, 'So, you really want me to join this school? Me? To learn all this? And you said Father Christmas really does exist?'

'Yes, indeed. All this is true, and you were chosen to join this school from a lot of other young people. You've got all the necessary qualifications. And, I can tell you, you'll really like it there—I myself was a student at Stardust College and, though it was good, I would have given nearly anything for the opportunity to go to Snowfields. It really is the best place the Organisation's got. All doors are open for the graduates of Snowfields, many of whom are working at the top levels of the organisation. You've got a bright future lying in front of you, Will!'

Will looked over at his parents, who had finished reading the letter.

His father said, 'Well, what do you think, Will?'

'I... don't know. All this sounds so...so absurd. Father Christmas, a Christmas Organisation, a school for Christmas.' A smile spread on his face. 'But it's the best thing I've ever heard, and even if this is a dream, I want to live through it until it ends. What do you think?'

His mother smiled. 'I am glad you think about it like that. Your dad and I have been talking about all this since Mr Chevalier arrived this morning and told us what he wanted. And, although it took him quite a bit to convince us he was telling the truth, we think you've got a great opportunity here, one you shouldn't miss.' She laughed. 'I would have given anything to work for Father Christmas if anyone had asked me when I was young.'

Will looked at his father, whose enthusiastic nod said he was feeling the same.

Will looked at Conrad, who had been sitting there listening to the conversation without interrupting. Finally Will squared his shoulders and said, 'Right, then. I would like to go to your school.'

Conrad jumped up. 'Excellent! I assure you, you won't be disappointed. It will be far better than you can imagine.' He grinned eagerly and rubbed his hands together businesslike. 'Let's get cracking! I will tell you a bit more about the school and the village around it, about the way to get there, and all the other things you'll need to know. But most of it is also explained in your letter.'

And Conrad started to talk. Will listened, fascinated. He learned that the school was set in a lovely village, and was dedicated to training staff for the White Christmas Organisation. School and village both belonged to this organisation, and all the people and other beings who lived in the village worked for it. There were factories where presents were produced, warehouses where they were safely stored away until Christmas, research departments where new presents were invented and new technologies for all the other departments were researched. There was even a faculty where magic was researched, because as humans became cleverer and their technologies more advanced, the organisation had to keep up, to be at least one step ahead, to hide its activity and its existence. The school had one new class each year, and there were approximately two hundred students there at the moment.

But then Conrad stopped. 'That's all I'll tell you about the village and the school. All the rest you can find out for yourself when you are there. There are only three more things to add. First, don't forget to send back your acceptance letter in the next few days. You'll find the address and the details that are requested in your letter. The second thing is how you'll get to Snowfields. This one is rather easy. On your first day, you'll get your things together, go out, and look for a street lantern. Just an ordinary street lantern. Stand directly under it and say the following words: "Calling Cloudy's Transportation Service. Transport required". You'll find this also referred to in the letter. And the third and most important thing is that you and your parents have to be really careful not to mention anything to anyone about Snowfields, the organisation, or what you will be learning and doing there. Don't speak to anybody about it. Not unless you are positive they also belong to the organisation or are connected to it. That's extremely important!' He held up his finger in warning while he said this.

'I think I've told you everything you need to know for the moment. As I've said before, the main details are all mentioned in the letter. If you've got any problems, just let us know. There are details in the letter on how to get in touch with us.'

Will nodded.

'Well, that's about everything you need to know for now. I'd best be on my way then.' Conrad grinned. 'I've got to invite another one to the school today. Thanks for the lovely tea. And Will'—he winked at Will again—'I'll see you in March at Snowfields then.' With this Conrad got up, shook hands with Will's parents, gave Will a friendly slap on the shoulder, and shook his hand too. Will's father led their visitor out into the garden, and stood there with Will and his mother to watch Conrad leave. Conrad got onto the sleigh, shifted around until he had found a comfortable position, and shook the reins. He took off, flew a last curve above the garden, waved once more, and was gone.

Will and his parents were left standing in the garden, looking at the tracks the sleigh and the reindeer had left in the snow. These were the only signs that all this had really just happened. That, and the letter Will was holding in his hand. He looked at it again, to reassure himself once more that it was real.

***

Christmas was a never-ending topic in Will's house until the end of the holidays. Even Lucy seemed enthralled by the idea of a real Father Christmas and there were endless musings about what Will would learn, be allowed to do, and whether he would get to see the Man himself.

Halfway through the first week of the term, Lucy stood by herself at the railing of the playground. She was finding it hard to come to terms with what she told herself was really too fantastic for a twenty-first century girl to accept completely. Two boys from her class approached her. She saw them coming from out of the corner of her eye. In actual fact, she rather fancied the taller one, Robert. He smiled engagingly.

'Penny for your thoughts, Lucy?' he said, nudging his friend surreptitiously.

'What? Oh, hmm, I was just thinking about Father Christmas...' Lucy was flustered. Robert had never spoken to her before although she had tried a number of ways to make it happen.

'I don't believe it!' said Fats, Robert's friend.

'Halfway through January and you're thinking about Father Christmas? He might come again in December if you still believe in him then, you nutcase.'

He gave her a rude push and she hurt her back against the railing.

Lucy saw red. 'There *is* a Father Christmas,' she yelled. 'Will's going to work for him.'

Horrified, she clapped her hands over her mouth.

'Wow,' said Robert. 'I always knew there was something peculiar about Will. Now you too! What a pathetic family.'

The bell for lessons intervened. Lucy, in tears, dodged the two boys and ran for her classroom. Still horrified about her lapse she waited for Will after school, but his teacher had dismissed the class early and Will was on his way home.

Robert and Fats had not wasted much time. Gareth and Jonas, the two boys in Will's class who had ridiculed him before, had been told the story about Lucy and the looks they directed at Will during the last lesson disconcerted him. He did not particularly like the boys but he could not fathom what their sly looks and nudgings could mean. Out of school, he decided not to wait the next twenty minutes for the bus and began to walk home. The pavement was a bit slippery but Will watched his step and walked quite confidently. There was a sudden shout behind him.

'Hey, Father Christmas boy.'

Puzzled, he turned to see Robert suddenly sliding full-length along the pavement. Fats bumped into Robert and fell on top of him. Gareth and Jonas collided with each other and ended up on the groaning heap of boys. Will shrugged and went on his way.

When Lucy got home, she had scared herself into not saying anything to Will, telling herself nothing had really happened. And nothing did. As yet.

At the beginning of February, it snowed hard. Lucy was relieved nothing had come of her outburst. In the lunch break at school, Robert and Gareth saw a new opportunity to torment Will. He was standing alone in a sheltered alcove trying to learn the verses he had to recite that afternoon. Not that he was putting much effort into it. After all, soon he would be going to a *real* school, the school and centre of training of Father Christmas himself. While he was rehearsing, he did not see Robert and Gareth beckon over Fats and Jonas. They worked out a plan to bombard Will from four sides with slushy, icy snowballs, at the same time pinching his book and giving him a thorough wetting—and beating—if they could get away with it. They positioned themselves and just as Robert was getting ready to lob the first snowball, he yelled, 'Well, lookee here, it's the little pansy that still believes in Father Christmas. Shall we show him what happens in the real world?' He drew back his hand but was suddenly smashed in the face by a mass of snow and slush. Half-blinded, he glared at Gareth, who shrugged and immediately pointed at Jonas. Soon all four were engaged in a furious snowball fight, only broken up by a teacher, who narrowly escaped losing his glasses to a badly-aimed snowball. Will gave the whole episode no notice. School was school.

February was drawing to its end. Word was, Will was leaving the school. Robert and his friends felt thwarted. They were determined to get Will, somehow. They saw their chance when Will was on his way home, walking jauntily, full of anticipation of what lay ahead. There was a shout behind him, 'Hey, Father Christmas boy.' He'd heard that one before. He turned, and this time they were very close—Robert and his gang. Will hardly had time to blink before they were on him. Jonas punched him in the eye before Robert tripped him up and Gareth kicked him in the stomach. Fats was about to sit on him and squash the breath out of Will when he suddenly started screaming like a banshee and hurtled off down the road. Jonas and Gareth collided heads and fell down, their eyes rolling upwards. Robert tried to punch Will but somehow ended up punching himself and lay splayed on the pavement, stunned and out of it for a while.

'What the...?' A figure appeared suddenly before Will, pulling him upright.

'Sorry. My fault, my fault. Unfortunately I'm rather late this time.'

Bewildered, Will looked up. He knew this figure, clad in green, with a brown waistcoat and a red overcoat.

'You?' was all he could manage.

Conrad gave him a wry smile. 'Yes, me.'

'Sorry,' said Will immediately, 'I didn't want to be rude. But... what are you doing here?'

'Helping you, of course,' replied Conrad while he brushed some snow from his clothes.

Will put a hand to his left temple, that had started to throb.

'Er, thank you,' he said, still bewildered. 'But how did you know?'

'Well that's my job, of course,' Conrad replied.

Will could only look at him, not understanding in the slightest what Conrad was talking about.

'Oh,' Conrad finally said. 'I didn't tell you, did I? My fault, my fault. You see, Father Christmas always warns us that faithful believers like you are especially at risk from louts like that bunch.' He looked a bit uncomfortable. 'Sorry I was a bit late, but you've really been keeping me on the hop so far, and I've still got my other duties to fulfil.

'Oh, take this.' He suddenly offered Will a small piece of steak. 'Hold it over your eye. It's supposed to help.'

Still bemused, Will did as he was told.

'Try not to get into any more trouble before the term starts —my wife gives me grief if I stay away too long and you are quite accident-prone. ' Wearily Conrad looked up and down the street. 'I'll walk you home,' he said, 'just in case I missed a bully or two. They won't get you again.'

'But how... where...?' Will did not know what to ask first.

'Oh, my fault, my fault. I haven't told you yet.' Conrad said. 'It's quite simple. I'm not just acting as an emissary for Snowfields, but my main job is with the security service of Snowfields. I'm a field agent, assigned to watch over members of the White Christmas Organisation who are at higher risks. And as I told you, you've got a rather high risk rating. But here we are.'

They were approaching Will's house and as he turned to ask Conrad something more, the emissary—or agent or whatever—just vanished. But somehow Will could still feel his presence. He felt protected and safe, rather honoured in fact, and was glad to have escaped his tormentors so lightly.

When his mother saw his black eye he had to explain he had been in a bit of a fight. Lucy could not help overhearing and burst into tears.

41

'That's all my fault,' she sobbed and told them what had happened in January.

'Lucy! How could you?' her mother scolded. 'You know we must all keep Will's new life secret.'

'Oh, Mum. It doesn't really matter,' said Will.

'Those boys have had it in for me ever since the Christmas breakfast at school. I think I gave myself away a bit then, even before we had ever heard of Snowfields. I'm sure they think I'm a bit loony. Anyway, I'll be gone in a few days and they'll find someone else to pick on. And Lucy, just make sure you stay out of their way, and they'll forget all about you.'

Will could soothe his mother quite a bit when he told her about Conrad's intervention and how he seemed to be watching over Will.

Chapter 3

Finally the great day arrived. It was the first of March. A couple of days ago Will had already packed all the things he was going to take. Everything fitted into a small suitcase because, as he had been told in the letter, he was going to get most of the things at Snowfields, and he only had to bring personal items.

The suitcase stood beside his desk, and lying on the desk was the paper with the instructions on how to get to Snowfields. Will had read it well over a hundred times since Christmas, especially in the last few days. He was so excited, and could hardly wait to get started.

He got up at eight o'clock and went down to have breakfast with his parents for the last time in quite a while. During breakfast he reflected on this, and his excitement was slightly dampened as he thought about going to live in completely new and foreign surroundings without his family for the next several months, until he would see his home and his parents again during the summer holidays. Nonetheless he looked forward to going to Snowfields.

They did not talk much during breakfast, only the usual things you say in a situation like this: 'Are you sure you have packed everything?' 'You will behave yourself, won't you?' 'And let us know how you're doing!' 'Did you pack everything you'll need? Not forgotten anything, have you?'

At a quarter to ten, Will got ready to leave, took his jacket, folded the paper with the instructions for the journey, and put it in his pocket—though by then he knew every word by heart. He picked up the suitcase and went down the stairs, where his parents were waiting for him in the hall. He embraced them one last time.

'I hope you'll have a good time there,' his mother said, 'and I'm very proud that you were chosen to go to this school.' She turned her head slightly and rubbed her eyes, where a bit of moisture glistened. His father patted him gruffly on the shoulder and gave him a last quick hug. Then he took Will's suitcase, opened the front door, and went outside. Will took a last look around the hall, turned, and followed his father. His mother came last; she closed the door, and together they went along the path through the front garden, reached the street, and turned left to where the next street lantern was standing.

Will stood directly under the lantern and looked up and down the street to make sure nobody was watching. His parents took a few steps away from him, for none of them really knew what to expect. Will looked at his watch: 9:58. *Time to get on with it*, he thought. He took out the paper with the instructions, picked up the suitcase, and waved to his parents one last time.

'Bye then, see you in the holidays,' he called.

His parents waved back to him and his mother called, 'Bye Will, have a great time!' Then, still looking at them, Will said the spell as it was written in the instructions.

His mum and dad vanished from his sight. In fact everything vanished from his sight. He felt a slight tingling all over his body. Then it was over—it had not even taken a second—and he could see again. At least he hoped so, for all he saw was white.

He was in a room with white walls, a white floor, and a blue ceiling. Then he realised it was not a ceiling at all, but he was looking at the clear blue sky. And the whole room was bathed in bright sunlight. The walls and the floor looked a bit uneven. He touched the wall next to him, and it felt quite...

well...fluffy. A bit like wadding. He suddenly realised he was not standing in a room at all, and in fact he was not even on the ground any more: he was surrounded by and standing on— a cloud. He actually was inside a bright, fluffy, white cloud!

But before he could think about this any more, he heard a voice: 'Ah, yet another one. Hello, there. Hello? Yes, I mean you, Will. Mr Will Burns in fact, if I was informed correctly.'

Will was completely confused. How could anybody be up here? Well, he was up here, so he supposed somebody else could be, too. But how could that somebody know his name? He turned around—, and found it rather difficult to believe what he saw: a rather small, figure behind a light-brown desk. The figure was totally green: green arms, green face, green eyes, and even green hair. In contrast to this, it wore a bright red robe, golden gloves, and a golden top hat with a red band. Obviously it was standing on something so it could reach over the desk.

The strange figure waved at Will: 'Come on, I don't bite. And we don't have the whole day, you know.'

Will started to walk over to the desk. With each step he felt the 'ground' was quite springy under his feet.

'You're also headed for Snowfields, are you?' the figure behind the desk went on.

Will nodded as he reached the desk.

'I thought so—well, of course I also received a memo saying you people would be coming through today.'

The figure made a face. 'The memo also said we should behave ourselves and welcome you properly.' It snorted. 'As if we were ever impolite to a customer!'

Then it noticed that Will was staring at it quite blankly. Its eyes narrowed.

'I know what you're thinking. You're thinking I'm a goblin, aren't you?'

'No, no, I certainly...' stuttered Will.

'Well, you better had, because that's what I am. Everyone working here is a goblin.' It smiled. Then it smacked its forehead, nearly throwing off its top hat. 'But I'm forgetting myself again. Please excuse me.' Then it bowed deeply, smiled, and extended its hand. Will tried very hard to ignore the fact that it had six fingers. 'I am Lektrin, your obedient valet. Before you make any embarrassing mistakes, I am a boy-goblin. We wear the top-hats and the girl-goblins wear the pointed hats. Sharp hats, sharp tongues – get it?'

Will, feeling slightly bemused, shook the offered hand and said, 'Er, I am Bill Wurns—er, I mean Will Burns.'

'Right then, Will. Welcome to Cloudy's Transportation Service, the easy way to travel. Just find yourself a street lantern, say the words, and we'll pick you up and take you anywhere you want. That's our motto,' he added with a slightly embarrassed grin, and pointed at the badge that was pinned to his robe. It said 'Cloudy's'.

'So,' he went on, 'you want to go to Snowfields then? A fine school that is. Just give me a second to find the correct form for you.'

He shuffled through the papers on his desk. Some fell to the ground, but the goblin ignored them.

'Ah, here we are: Will Burns.' He peered closely first at the form, and then at Will. 'Yes, it's you on this photo, so you've got permission to use Cloudy's Transportation Service.'

He ripped something off the form and handed it to Will. It looked like some sort of credit card.

'That's your transportation card for Cloudy's Transportation Service. Just show it to the staff when you want to use the service and we'll take you wherever you want. Now, if you'd please go through the gate here, and my colleagues will help you. Thank you for using Cloudy's Transportation Service, and don't forget to collect your "miles and a lot more".'

Lektrin looked down at his papers again, then he seemed to notice those that had fallen to the ground. 'Damn,' he stepped down from whatever he had been standing on, and started to pick up the papers, muttering under his breath.

Will went towards the opening in the wall next to the desk, still wondering what Lektrin's last sentence was supposed to mean. But then he saw a poster hanging on the wall (*Hanging on a cloud?*,—Will could not help wondering) and read, 'Remember to collect your miles with our miles-and-a-lot-more-programme, and receive our attractive bonus gifts for free.' He shook his head and went through the opening.

Now he stood in a quite large, circular room. Again the floor and the walls were white and fluffy, with the blue sky forming the ceiling. In the walls were well over a dozen openings, leading into tunnels which stretched away farther than he could see. In the middle of the room were several desks. Sitting behind them were more goblins. They too were completely green, clad in red robes, and wearing golden hats with red bands. Several of them were talking to customers.

Will looked around. There was a small man with glasses, wearing a long, black coat and a bowler hat. Beside him stood a black briefcase, and leaning against it was a black umbrella. The wood at the handle was formed like the elaborate head of a parrot. Will continued to look around the room, but then he quickly looked back at the umbrella. For what had looked like an ordinary wooden parrot's head had suddenly moved. He stared at it, and the head stared back. Then it gave Will a sly wink and started talking to its owner, who calmly answered.

Will shook his head in wonder and looked at the next customer, who was even weirder: a rather small figure wearing a large, conical helmet and a dark-red and golden cape. His face was hidden behind an enormous beard. This was not too bad by itself, but then Will noticed the small axe at his side, and he could not help but think that what he was seeing there must be a dwarf—a real dwarf!

By then one of the goblins had seen him standing in front of the entrance and was waving at him. 'Hey, Mr Burns! Over here! How can I help you?' she called.

Somehow everybody here happened to know his name, Will thought. He walked up to the desk. When he reached her, the goblin bowed deeply pointing her hat towards Will and said 'Lektra, your obedient valet.'

'Er, your colleague gave this to me and said to go in here.' Will handed Lektra the transportation card.

'Ah, you're one of the new ones, right? Just a moment. I've got the memo here somewhere.' She shuffled through the papers on her desk, and quite a few of them fell over the edge and out of sight. 'Oh, bother,' she muttered. She flashed Will an apologetic smile. 'I'm very sorry about this hold-up. Normally we'd do this with our computers, but we've had this brilliant new system installed—"Doors", it's called. When they installed it, they said it was the most advanced system, and it would only crash very rarely, about once in ten years. Well, the ten years were over after two hours, and for the rest of the day the system crashed every two minutes. We then turned back to ordinary paper.' She snorted. '"What do you want to do today?" is the motto of this stupid Doors programme. Well, I know what I want to do with this programme, but it wouldn't be appropriate to say this in front of a customer... Ah, here we are.' She pulled a sheet of paper out of one of the stacks, which wobbled precariously and started to slip, and then the papers drifted towards the others already lying on the floor. The cloud. Whatever.

'Let's see,' Lektra went on. 'Yes, Will Burns, student at Snowfields. Oh, you are going to Snowfields. That's nice. I heard tell that the school is just fantastic. Well, wait a moment, I think....' She looked around the hall. 'Yes... Lektrius,' she called.

Another goblin looked up from serving a customer. 'Lektra, my dear, what can I do for you?'

Will noticed that the customer the goblin over there was serving was, to his relief, a perfectly ordinary human. In fact it was a girl, and she looked to be about Will's age. She had rather long, blond hair, and wore a long, black coat. She looked in the direction of Lektra, and when she spotted Will a quite relieved look replaced the former slight confusion on her face, as if she were glad to see another human up here, too.

'You've got another one for Snowfields there, Lektrius?' called Lektra.

'Yeah, that's right,' came the answer from Lektrius after he had consulted the papers on his desk.

'Then the two of them could go together, couldn't they? Mine is also for Snowfields.'

'Yeah, no problem. I'll wait for you.'

Lektra turned back to Will and grinned. 'Fine then. You've already met a school friend there. I'll just finish your papers, and then we'll send the two of you on your way.'

With this she started a real fight on her desk: forms in all colours fluttered about, and her weapons were an army of stamps and an arsenal of quills, pens, and pencils. After a few minutes, she seemed to have won the battle and, again smiling apologetically, handed Will his transportation card back, together with a small piece of red paper.

'Sorry about this, but without the computers we've got such a lot of paperwork up here, I sometimes wonder if we really are a transportation service or rather some sort of paper works. What you do now is go to the tunnel over there, where it says "Transfers" on the sign. Just walk into it. The rest will happen automatically. The red card is your ticket. You received one hundred and twenty miles for this trip. Thank you for using Cloudy's Transportation Service.'

'Thank you,' said Will. 'Goodbye.' As he started to walk over to the indicated tunnel, he noticed that the girl had also finished at the desk and was heading towards the same tunnel. They met in front of the entrance and looked at each other.

'Hello. I'm Will. Will Burns,' he said with a tentative smile.

'Hello. My name's Annabel Winston,' she said, and smiled back at Will. 'Are you new to Snowfields as well?'

'Yes. I still can't really believe this is happening, and that I'm really going to this school.'

She laughed. 'Nor can I. I was ever so surprised when Mr Chevalier came to our house at Christmas to tell me I was accepted at Snowfields—even though I never applied to it. I hadn't even heard about the place before.'

Will nodded. 'That's exactly what I thought.' He looked into the tunnel. 'Well, I guess we'd best go on inside.'

Annabel nodded back and together they stepped into the tunnel. Then Annabel gave a small squeal, and Will let out a low grunt. The floor had looked exactly like the one in the other rooms—white and fluffy. But when they had stepped into the tunnel, the floor suddenly began to move them along. Will got over his surprise and turned to Annabel.

'I think it must be something like the moving pavements they've got in the big airports.'

'Yes, I suppose so. But they could have warned us now, couldn't they!' Annabel said indignantly.

'I'd guess they just forgot we wouldn't know about it.'

Annabel said nothing to this, but still eyed the moving floor suspiciously.

As they were travelling quite fast, it took them only a moment to reach the end of the tunnel. There the floor slowed down, and then stopped completely when they reached the opening into the room at the end. They picked up their suitcases that had travelled with them, took a few steps into the room, and looked around. They seemed to be in another reception area: four other tunnels led away from the room, labelled 'Express', 'Executive', 'Standard', and 'Functional'. There were four counters as well, one beside each tunnel.

Behind each counter small squares of cloud floated several inches above the ground. Sitting at the counters were four goblins, all clad in red robes and wearing golden top hats with red bands, and they had the usual stacks of papers in front of them.

When Will and Annabel entered the room, all four goblins looked up expectantly. The one sitting next to the tunnel labelled 'Express' called, 'Miss Winston. Mr Burns. If you would come over here, please, and we'll have you on your way in no time at all.' The other three goblins turned away, looking rather bored.

Will and Annabel walked over to the counter. The goblin bowed to each of them, saying, 'Lektro, your obedient valet.' Then he started on his papers, mumbling, 'Now, let's see. Will Burns and Annabel Winston. Where did I put this memo again... Ah, here we are! Could I see your tickets, please? The red cards, please.' Will and Annabel handed him their cards. 'Thank you. Ah, yes. Destination is Snowfields, service is express, status is priority, special arrangements... Oh, you've got the grand tour. That one's great! You'll certainly enjoy it. The grand tour is my favourite way of going to Snowfields. It's perfect if you want to get a first impression of the place. But you'll see that for yourselves. Now then, if you would hand me your luggage, please—thank you.'

51

Lektro put their suitcases on one of the small squares of cloud floating about two inches above the ground behind his counter. Then he took out what looked like a small stick and touched both of the suitcases. A bright label appeared out of thin air on each of them that indicated 'Snowfields' in large golden letters. He gave the cloud a light tap with his stick, and it silently drifted away through a small opening in the wall behind the counters. Will stared at this in amazement, and then looked at Annabel. This was magic—the labels had just appeared out of nowhere! Annabel looked back at him and nodded equally surprised.

Lektro ignored this. 'All right, we'll handle your luggage. Now let's get the two of you on your way.' Lektro handed them back their tickets. 'Just walk through the gate here beside my counter and your journey will begin. Thank you for using Cloudy's Transportation Service. Always your obedient valet.' Once more he bowed deeply to each of them in turn.

Will and Annabel walked through the gate. Behind it was another corridor and again, just as soon as they stepped into it, the floor began moving, taking them along. But this time they were prepared for it. Finally the floor stopped, and the room they stepped into was by far the largest they had seen so far. Will immediately saw it had only three walls. Where the fourth wall should have been, he could only see blue sky. Dozens of sleighs stood all over the hall, each with reindeer in front of it, and they formed neat and orderly rows just like in a car park, or rather—a sleigh park. Some of them were large and were pulled by four or even six reindeer; the rest were smaller and had only two reindeer. On one side of the hall was an enormous sleigh, and it was pulled by no less than twelve reindeer.

Before Will and Annabel could take in anything more, they were greeted by yet another goblin (green, red robe, golden pointed hat with red band). 'Miss Winston, Mr Burns? Welcome. I am Lektrissara, your obedient valet.' She bowed to them both deeply. Then she pulled out a memo from inside her robe and glanced at it. 'Ah, yes.' She looked up again, gave Will and Annabel an inviting smile, and made a sweeping motion with her hand. 'Would you please follow me? Sleigh number sixteen is reserved for you.'

They followed her to a sleigh, and when they had reached it Lektrissara indicated for them to climb up onto it. Then she left, but not without a 'thank you for using Cloudy's Transportation Service', which was immediately followed by the inevitable bow combined with 'your obedient valet'.

As soon as they were seated the driver of the sleigh said, 'Hello. My name's Lektrorius. Your obedient valet!' He bowed to them both too. 'Please make yourselves comfy. I'll fly you over to Snowfields. This is your first flight?' he added rather as a statement than a question.

They both nodded—though Will thought briefly of his flight with Conrad. But that had only been a short one, just around and above his home, and did not really count.

'Right then. I can assure you, you're definitely going to enjoy this! I've never met anyone who didn't like flying. And the view is just unbelievable. There's no need to worry,' Lektrorius continued when he saw their rather apprehensive smiles. 'This is an absolutely safe way of travelling. So just enjoy the view, snuggle into the blankets if you get cold—and here we go.'

He shook the reins, and the four reindeer stepped out of the row of sleighs, pulling the sleigh towards the open wall— and right over the edge, as if there were solid ground and not thin air out there. Lektrorius pulled on the reins again, and they moved faster and gained height.

After the first few moments, Will got a bit more confident and loosened his rather tight grip on the rail of the sleigh. He looked around. They were high up now and level with a few puffy, white clouds. He could hardly see the ground, and then only intermittently when there was a break in the clouds, and he could not make out many details, only a small town, a dark forest, and a small lake. Behind him the opening to the sleigh hangar was getting smaller and smaller. Then they were so far away that all he could see was an unsuspicious-looking cloud. He turned towards Annabel. She still looked a bit shocked, but seemed to be coming round as she gazed at the clouds. A look of wonder lit up her face.

'They look so beautiful when you are this close to them,' she said dreamily. And she was right, thought Will. The clouds shone, brilliant and unspoiled, in the bright sunlight. They formed delicate figures of pure white in an otherwise blue sky. And every light touch of the wind left minor changes here and there in the structure.

'Yes,' said Will while reflecting on this. 'And the world looks so tiny and unimportant down there.'

Annabel just nodded, and they sat in silence, watching the scenery in wonder, totally spellbound by the beauty all around them.

They finally came to an enormous cloud, and Lektrorius shook the reins again so the reindeer slowed down. Will swallowed. It seemed as if they were heading right into the cloud.

Lektrorius turned to Will and Annabel. 'We are now going through the main passage to Snowfields,' he told them with a grin, and pointed towards a huge opening that had appeared in the cloud.

They entered the opening and went down a tunnel that led them continually downwards. It was lit by the sunlight that filtered through the cloud, and this gave the whole tunnel a rather mysterious appearance. It was much wider than it was high, and they passed quite a few other sleighs that were coming up it. After a short time and a few gentle curves, they reached an opening. The moment they left the tunnel, Annabel gave a small squeal of pure delight.

'Oh, that is just beautiful.'

Will was also quite taken by the sight.

They were soaring high above a valley surrounded by mountains on three sides. They could not see the tops of the mountains because clouds lay like a ring around them. The mountain range opened at the far side of a village, and there stood a dark-green forest, split only by a road and a small river winding their way through the trees. The river was fed by a sparkling waterfall that cascaded down one of the mountains, then it flowed through the village with gentle, elegant curves before it led off into the forest.

The village consisted of houses of very different sizes. Some were so small Will could not believe there was enough room for anyone to live in them. There were normal-sized houses—those formed the majority—and there were a few very large ones that looked like warehouses.

Lektrorius shook the reins once again, and took them right above the village. There he flew them round in a wide circle and let the sleigh sink lower so they could get a good look at the buildings. Will could now see that the houses were all built in the same style, but each had its special touches that made it quite unique without disrupting the overall appearance. They were all made out of red brick, had golden window frames, and brown doors. The roofs were laid with light-brown pantiles. Between them were neatly-paved streets. Tall golden lanterns were placed at short, regular intervals.

Then Will noticed something that only the warehouses and the very large houses had: right in the middle of the buildings there were no pantiles, but flat roofs laid with beige tiles with marked areas on them. Then Will understood—these were landing areas for sleighs, several of which were parked in marked corners at the sides of the platforms. While he was watching, he could actually see one landing on a platform on one of the warehouses.

He saw people moving in the streets, but could not make out any details. There were also vehicles of all sorts, mainly carts and sleighs. Spaced throughout the whole village were quite a lot of small gardens and green areas, with lawns, beautiful trees, flowers of every colour, ponds, and fountains.

It was by far the loveliest and most picturesque place Will or Annabel had ever seen in their lives. Lektrorius turned around smiling at his two passengers.

'Great, eh?' he asked them.

Will could only nod in agreement.

Lektrorius guided the sleigh into a curve and headed for the southern end of the village. There stood a very large building, or rather a complex of several buildings, surrounded by a large park, which included the gently curving river that passed through the grounds on its way into the forest.

'That's your school over there,' said Lektrorius, and pointed towards the complex. Will peered over the side of the sleigh and looked in the direction Lektrorius was pointing. As the sleigh flew in a wide circle along the front of the school, Will could see it had a magnificent façade of the same red brick as the other buildings he had seen. Windows with golden frames glinted in the sunlight. In the middle of the wall was an elaborately carved door, very tall and made out of brown wood polished to a perfect sheen. But before he could make out any more details, they had gone past and were flying over the rest of the school buildings. 'Look at those lovely towers and turrets over there,' said Annabel, 'and that structure with the glass roof right at the back near the forest looks really out of place—more like laboratory or factory.'

They reached the other side of the complex. The façade was similar to the one at the front and there was also an extensive lawn edged by trees and bushes. Then they were over the main house again, flying lower and lower, and Will could see that the school also had a small landing platform. Lektrorius headed straight for it and landed the sleigh on it with hardly a bump.

'Well, here we are,' he told them. 'I hope you've enjoyed the flight and the view of Snowfields. And that you'll have a good time here. Perhaps we'll meet again sometime.'

He grinned, got down from the sleigh, and helped Will and Annabel down. Then he took off his top hat, bowed to them each in turn, and politely said, 'Thank you for using Cloudy's Transportation Service. Always your obedient valet.'

He hopped back onto his sleigh, shook the reins, and was gone.

Will and Annabel looked around the surrounding roof until they saw a door in the wall next to the platform. They looked at each other, and Will shrugged his shoulders. 'Let's go then.'

And they walked towards the door. They were still a few yards away when it suddenly opened, and a woman stepped out onto the platform. She was of medium age, not very tall, and quite slender; she had blond hair and wore red-rimmed glasses that formed quite a contrast to her long, rather plain dark-blue dress. When she saw Will and Annabel, she stopped, smiled, and nodded to them both.

'Hello, you two. Welcome to Snowfields. Miss Winston.' She looked at Annabel, extended her arm, and shook her hand. 'And Mr Burns.' She also shook Will's hand. 'I am Miss Dust-fall, and I want to wish you both a successful time here at Snowfields school. If you'd please follow me, then I'll take you down to where the other new students are waiting.'

She turned round and went back inside. Will and Annabel followed her. They went down some stairs, and she asked them about their journey. While they were talking, Will thought he rather liked her. They came to the foot of the stairs, went down a few corridors, then two shorter flights of stairs, and reached a great foyer. Then they walked along another shorter corridor and came to a large double door made out of clear and milky glass forming a tasteful pattern.

Miss Dustfall opened the door and said, 'Please wait inside. We'll continue when all the students have arrived.' Then she left.

Annabel stepped into the room, and Will followed her. It was quite large, with rows of tables and chairs. There was a fireplace at each end of the room, and a merry fire burned in both of them, but there was none in the large fireplace opposite the door. Two girls and three boys sat at a table not far from the door, and looked up when Will and Annabel came in.

A red-haired girl waved at them and said, 'Hello. Are you new here?'

They both nodded and walked over to the table.

'So are we,' the girl continued. 'We arrived here only a few minutes before you, and were just getting to know each other. My name is Bianca—Bianca Lane.'

Will and Annabel introduced themselves.

'My name's Wesley Limerick,' said the dark-haired boy sitting next to Bianca. He was quite tall and muscular, though he seemed to be a bit shy.

The boy sitting next to him had straight, blond hair, wore blue-rimmed glasses, and was small and slim. He jumped up to greet them. 'Hello, nice to meet you. Fredorgius Bagshot is my name, but please call me Freddy. Everybody does.'

He grabbed Will's hand and shook it vigorously while he went on talking: 'I believe we'll have a great time here at

Snowfields. Corny made it all sound absolutely fantastic. We'll be helping to arrange Christmas every year, and we're going to work for...for Father Christmas himself!' His voice was filled with awe. 'Just imagine it. I can't wait till we start. There must be such a lot for us to learn. I—'

Will held up his free hand to stop Freddy. He rather felt as if he were drowning in words. 'Freddy,' he said. But that had no real effect—Freddy just kept on talking. So he said it louder: 'Freddy!'

This worked. Freddy broke off in mid-sentence, an embarrassed look spreading over his face.

Will laughed. 'Freddy, it's really nice to talk to you, but before we continue, could you please let go of my hand? I'm going to need it in future.'

Freddy looked down and realised he had been shaking Will's hand the whole time. 'Oh, I'm so sorry. I'm just a bit excited that I'm finally here at last, and when I'm excited I tend to babble without end, and I—' He realised he was doing it again and clamped his mouth tightly shut.

Will laughed again. 'That's quite all right. I believe I'm at least as excited about all this as you are, and I hope they'll tell us more about everything soon.' He turned to the third boy, who so far had been sitting still and quietly at the head of the table.

'Hi, I'm Will,' he said, and extended his hand.

'Hello. Richard Loxley.' And that was it. He completely ignored Will's hand.

Annabel turned to the second girl, who smiled at her. 'My name's Wendy. I am so glad to meet you and Bianca, 'cause before I got here, I thought there'd be mainly boys.' She grinned when she saw Annabel's understanding smile. 'I see you know what I mean.'

Will and Annabel sat down with the others, and they talked about their expectations. They had only been sitting there for a few moments when the glass door opened again, and another student came in. She looked around, and when she saw them sitting at the table, she came nearer and asked, 'Hello, are you new here as well?'

They all nodded, and she laughed nervously. 'Good. I'm feeling a bit lost right now.'

Freddy also laughed. 'Don't worry about that, we're all feeling much the same way.'

The others grinned or nodded.

'Oh, sorry, I didn't introduce myself. My name's Sabrina Bluetonic.' She held up her hands. 'Don't ask me how my parents got that name, I never understood their explanations at all.'

The others all introduced themselves, and Sabrina joined them at the table. Will noticed she had nice, deep-blue eyes that formed a perfect contrast to her long, blond hair.

Freddy picked up the conversation again. 'So, what do you think?' he asked. 'Will we be allowed to help Father Christmas as soon as next Christmas?'

'Well,' said Bianca, 'from what I've heard so far, I think the organisation is quite extensive, and Snowfields is just a small section of it. I'm not even sure that Father Christmas is here, and I'm quite certain we'll first have to finish this training before we'll get to do any real work for the organisation.'

Wesley added, 'And there'll surely be tests and exams we've got to pass before they'll let us do anything outside the school.'

'Yeah,' said Sabrina, 'and of course we'll not be helping Father Christmas directly, or even be anywhere near him. Those positions will be reserved for the best senior members of the organisation. We'll probably not even see Father Christmas for quite some years.'

Freddy looked a bit disappointed.

Then the door opened, and a rather good-looking, relatively large man, probably in his mid-forties, entered the room and smiled at them.

'Hello.' He walked over to them. 'I'm Argius Contractus, one of your teachers. I hope you all had an interesting journey here. I bet you enjoyed the sleigh ride, eh?' He smiled as some of them nodded shyly. 'I bid you all a very warm welcome here at Snowfields, your new home for the next few years.' He made a wide, sweeping gesture with his hands. 'You'll like it here, although,' he winked at them, 'there are also loads and loads of things waiting for you to learn.'

The students grinned nervously.

'Now then.' Contractus clapped his hands. 'I hope you have already made yourselves known to each other?' He waited for their nods. 'Good. As I told you, my name is Contractus. I'm the master for the acquisition of the basic materials we need here, and I'll be your teacher for that and for the basic processes of our production of presents. But furthermore I'm your guide at Snowfields. I'll show you around, and help you get settled in and started in our school. And I'll be there for you if you've got any problems. Don't hesitate to call on me. That's my job, and I'll always be there to help you.' He smiled at them again. 'So first of all, please tell me your names. Best you start.' He pointed at Annabel.

After they had all told him their names, Contractus smiled again. 'Jolly good. Now let's go and explore your new school— and your new home. We are now in the Ferum. Here meetings are held, the meals are served, and it is the main common room.'

They looked around the large room once more.

'Okay, so follow me. We'll come back here later.'

He ushered them out through the glass doors. They went down the corridor and came back into the great foyer through which they had passed on their way to the Ferum. Will looked around. It was spectacular. And stylish. The foyer was a large, round room. Corridors or stairs led from it in all directions, except on one side where there was a set of huge and heavy wooden doors decorated with fine engravings. Scattered throughout the foyer were white benches with gold cushions on them, looking rather comfortable as well as elegant. Set between them were large Christmas trees, heavily decorated with glowing red globes, lots of tiny, glittering lights, tinsel, sugar canes, and all the other things that belonged on a proper Christmas tree. Grand white columns were integrated into the walls. Gold-coloured festoons were chiselled into them and wound their way right to the top. Decorative, bright red and green tapestries hung from the ceiling. An imposing glass dome formed the roof, and sunlight filtered through it, glittering on the golden festoons on the columns. The floor was made out of large, polished, cream-coloured marble tiles fitted together seamlessly.

'This is our great entrance hall.' Contractus looked around admiringly. 'Rather beautiful, I think. Don't worry, this is the only place in Snowfields where there is always Christmas decoration the whole year round. Oh, this and the Plaza in the village, of course. Everywhere else is only decorated at Christmastime.' He pointed to the wooden doors. 'Those are the entrance to our school. Outside lies the rest of Snowfields. Finding your way around the school can be a bit difficult at first but you'll get to know the different passages in time. Now follow me and I'll take you to your rooms.

They climbed several flights of stairs and passed through a confusing number of corridors until they finally reached another large door.

Mr Contractus moved in front of it and mumbled something, and Will thought he heard another voice answer. But he could not see anything, for whatever Mr Contractus was doing was hidden by his body. Will guessed he was opening the door with a key. At any rate he was much too busy looking around to pay proper attention to what the teacher was doing.

The door opened, and they followed Mr Contractus into the room. There were high-backed, upholstered chairs, deeply-cushioned sofas, and tables with chairs around them. A cosy fireplace dominated the room. Colourful tapestries hung here and there from the walls, while the spaces between were either grey stone or brown wood. Will felt quite comfortable in here. The room exuded a sense of homeliness, ideal for relaxing or for sitting together with friends.

Contractus made a sweeping motion with his hands. 'Now we are in the part of the school that will be exclusively yours. This will be your new home. We are standing in your personal common room, where you can spend your free time.'

Then he headed towards a door, and they went into the next room. Will could easily tell that they were now standing in the study: desks of all sizes were scattered everywhere. The chairs had straight backs and only minimal upholstery. The walls were covered with high bookshelves, all filled to the very top. There was even a ladder on wheels to reach the top shelves. This room spoke of hard and sober work, and they left it rather quickly.

Just as they were stepping out through another door and into the corridor behind it, an enormous grandfather clock to their left emitted a loud, deep, and penetrating 'gong'. Will and the others jumped at this sudden sound, and they turned around and went to the clock. It was by far the most impressive grandfather clock Will had ever seen, made out of dark, polished wood, and with heavy, golden weights. The face was richly ornamented and the golden hands stood out clearly. But the most interesting aspect was the sign underneath the face—red letters on a white background. Will read: 'Lunch in five minutes'. He looked at the time. It was twenty-five minutes past twelve.

Mr Contractus laid a hand on the side of the clock. 'Ah, yes, the clock. You'll surely have noticed the sign underneath the face. You see, every time the gong sounds, a sign like this will appear telling you what's up. And, of course, to remind you if you're late, or even in the surely highly unlikely case that you should have forgotten the next lesson. It will notify you at mealtimes, when the lessons start, and so on. It's actually quite useful when you're buried in your studies, as I presume will most often be the case.'

The students' faces fell when he mentioned all the work. But then Will saw that Mr Contractus was winking at them. He waved them onwards. 'Let's go and have lunch then.'

And they followed him back to the Ferum.

Chapter 4

When Will and the others entered the Ferum this time, it was full of people. Contractus led them to the only free table.

'Enjoy your first meal at Snowfields. I'll join my colleagues at the head table. After lunch I'll pick you up again and show you more of the school.' And he walked towards a table at the end of the room where the other teachers were sitting.

Will and the others sat down at the table and waited. All around them the older students were talking. From what he could hear, they were mainly telling each other about their holidays or talking about the new term. Then a man stood up at the teachers' table and tapped a spoon against his glass, waiting for the students to quieten. Will thought he was quite an impressive figure. It took him a while to realise he was in fact quite small, for there was such an air of authority surrounding him, he easily dominated the room. He wore matching dark blue trousers and a shirt. A silver cape hung from his shoulders. He had no beard, and in fact had not much hair at all, only a ring of short, silver strands that surrounded a bald top. When the room fell silent and he had everybody's attention, he cleared his throat.

'Hello again, back at Snowfields, and welcome to our new friends! I'm pleased to see you all here for a new term. I would especially like to welcome all our new students. I am Beltorec, vice-chancellor here at the school. It is my honour to accompany you during the next few years and to provide you with the best possible training for the White Christmas Organisation. And now....' He cleared his throat and, to Will's utter amazement, started to sing:

I hold that in our school
A teacher's word should rule
And that his word is regarded with respect
This is as little as of you we do expect
That is as little as of you we do expect
That of you we do expect!

I believe in joy and fun
And I don't think all must be done
By just telling you to dumbly react
This is as little as from us you can expect
That is as little as from us you can expect
That of us you can expect.

All the teachers had stood up during the song, and bowed at the end of it. Then they sat down again—all except the vice-chancellor, who smiled benignly. He clapped his hands together and said brightly, 'I wish you all a successful new term here at Snowfields! And now we come to one of the most important events of this day—let the feast begin!' Then he bowed deeply and his cape caught the sunlight. It gleamed and rippled like molten silver.

A score of goblins entered the hall, all clad in bright-red garments, wearing golden top hats and each carrying an enormous turkey on a huge, silver platter. The goblins went to each table and put the turkeys down. Then they picked up silver knives and forks, but did not start cutting. Instead they all looked over to the teachers' table expectantly. Two goblins had carried the largest turkey there, and had placed it in front of the vice-chancellor. They handed him a knife and fork, and he smiled with satisfaction, eyeing the turkey. Then he cut into it.

But when he touched the turkey with the knife, it exploded with a loud bang, and a silvery cloud floated from the platter. Where the turkey had been a second before there was now a rabbit, sitting quite calmly and nibbling on a piece of lettuce, and two white doves launched themselves into the air, passed through the silver cloud, and settled on the shoulders of the goblins who had served the turkey. The blast, the flash, the overall surprise, and especially the rabbit and doves left everybody in a stunned silence. Only the goblins seemed not perturbed at all, for they were all doubled over, roaring with laughter. Will was flabbergasted, and not for the first time on this day, as part of his mind noted dryly.

The goblins calmed down again, and the one in front of the vice-chancellor removed the dove from his shoulder, straightened up, and announced gleefully, 'My pleasure, sir vice-chancellor.' Then he bowed deeply, flourishing his top hat. When he straightened up again, he took the hat and dumped it over both of the doves and the rabbit in turn. When he removed it, the animals were gone. By then most of the students had mastered their surprise, and were laughing and clapping their hands. The vice-chancellor, who at first had looked rather appalled, now laughed heartily. Then the whole hall roared with laughter, so much that the glasses were vibrating.

When the laughter finally subsided to a mere giggling here and there, the vice-chancellor cleared his throat once more and looked around the room slightly apologetically. 'Well, I guess this was my own fault really. At the beginning of the last term, I mentioned to the chief goblin that the whole event had been a bit dry, and much too formal. So he seems to have taken the initiative.' He gave the goblin, who was still standing next to him at the table, a sidelong glance and got an irreverent snigger in return. 'And thus he provided us with this amazing spectacle. Thank you ever so much.' And he bowed to the goblin.

The goblin bowed overly deeply in return and, still sniggering, removed the platter. He motioned to another goblin, who brought another turkey and placed it in front of the vice-chancellor. Beltorec then again lifted the knife and fork, shot the goblin a sharp glance, and, looking not quite as sure of himself as last time, managed to cut a piece of the turkey without further incident. Then the rest of the goblins started cutting up the turkeys at the tables, and served them to the students.

It was one of the best meals Will had ever had. In addition to the turkey and all its trimmings there were beef, lamb, and even fish. Then there were croquettes, baked, roast, mashed, boiled, fried potatoes, Yorkshire Pudding, lots of vegetables, and delicious gravy. During the meal there was not much talk at Will's table nor, in fact, in the whole Ferum. Everybody was much too busy enjoying the scrumptious meal. Talk mainly consisted of comments on the tastiness of the food and pointing out special treats to each other.

In between all of this, the red-clad goblins dashed about, offering more helpings or a yet-untried dish. Then finally, when everyone seemed to have eaten their fill—Will certainly had, for he was feeling ready to burst—there was yet another highlight. A worthy conclusion of the meal: the dessert. Or rather the desserts. First the goblins came round and placed generous mounds of Christmas pudding on all the tables. Then they went out again, and the lights dimmed. An expectant hush fell over the hall. When the goblins came back in they were carrying enormous ice-cream cakes ablaze with sparklers. But Will had never seen sparklers like these. They were more like roman candles, and much brighter than usual. And they did not just emit silver sparks, but sparkled in different colours. They even changed their colours while they were burning.

Will gazed at the ice-cream cakes. He had never seen anything like them before, not for real, not even on television. They were formed like massive sailing ships. And they were so delicately made. He could see tiny cannons protruding from the sides, some even with smoke-like foam attached. Then there were the tall sails made out of ice sheets, billowing as if in full wind. The brown hulls were made out of chocolate and rested on waves of blueberry ice cream. The ships were quite unbelievable, and all the students stared at them open-mouthed.

A smaller ice-cream ship was placed on either end of the teachers' table. The head goblin, the one who had done the trick with the turkey, carried the largest ship up. While he passed between the tables, all the students followed him with their eyes, craning their necks, trying to see every detail of the great ship. He placed it in front of the vice chancellor, who smiled appreciatively again, his eyes sparkling.

'I say, you have exceeded yourself this time. This really is a masterpiece!' He looked around the Ferum. 'Well, if any of you happens to like a bit of ice cream, I suggest you get yourselves up here, and my colleagues Mr Worker and Miss Dustfall'—he gave them each a nod—'will deal out the portions, while I will have the sad duty of dividing up this beauty here. But then I'd imagine most of you don't like ice cream anyway, so there will be more left for me.'

This was met by loud protests from all the students, and they rushed up to the teachers' table, forming queues. Will was glad he got a piece of the large ship. It tasted even more delicious than it looked. He savoured every spoonful.

After everybody had finished, the older students started to leave the room, and Mr Contractus came over to Will's table.

'Well, I hope you liked our little feast here. I definitely enjoyed it. It gets even better from year to year.' He looked around their table and rubbed his hands. 'So, ready for your first lesson, are you?' He did not wait for an answer, but continued straightaway, 'Well, you'd better be, because it'll start in five minutes. Come on, I'll show you to your classroom.'

Will and the others got up, looking at each other in surprise. Their first lesson? Right away?

'You'd think they'd let us get settled in a bit first,' Richard grumbled.

Will thought he did have a point there. They followed Mr Contractus, who led them through the school again, marching in front of them like a teacher followed by a bunch of first years—which, as a matter of fact, was exactly what they were. They went out of the Ferum and up some stairs, then passed through several other corridors and went up and down more stairs, until they ended up in front of a solid-looking door. Its frame was neatly decorated with Christmas greens, red ribbons, golden stars, and a garland of small, wrapped presents.

'Here it is,' said Contractus. 'Your main classroom.' He pointed towards the frame and said, 'Don't worry. This will only be here for the week because you are new here. You don't have to endure Christmas decorations the whole year.'

'Why not?' Fredorgius asked.

Contractus laughed. 'If you had Christmas every day, you would really get fed up with it, and it wouldn't be special anymore.' He turned towards the door. In the middle of it was a wide, square area where the wood was completely smooth. Contractus touched it with his hand.

'Ouch,' it said. They all jumped back, the ones in front landing on the toes of those behind them. Will stared at the wood, and for the who-knew-how-many times this day could not believe his ears. Or his eyes for that matter. The wood was moving! Structures were emerging. Contours. And finally there was a face looking at them curiously.

It turned to Contractus. 'One would very much appreciate it if thou wouldst be so kind as to refrain from disturbing my contemplation in this manner,' it grumbled.

Contractus laughed. 'That's one of our door guardians,' he said, pointing a thumb at the face. 'Many doors here have one —some affable, some not.'

The face gave him a withering look, then ignored him and turned to look at Will and the others.

'But pray do tell, are these formidable young humans by chance the new first years, hungry and forever striving in their most noble and restless seeking of knowledge?' The face inspected them. 'It then is my honour to welcome all you most noble ladies, whose charm and beauty will surely cause every single flower on the grounds to wilt in shame, and to greet all you noble lords, whose bravery and unremitting toil in the quest for knowledge will only add to your courteous and noble bearings. My name is Branchhole, your faithful servant. Forever I guard the entrance to thy place of knowledge. Pray tell, kind ladies and noble sirs, thy names of birth, and I will take it as my most noble duty to learn thy titles by heart, so I can greet thee in future in a more seemly fashion.'

The face smiled at them, and Will was sure that if this Branchhole had arms and a hat, he would have flourished it. Will looked more closely at the face: it was not ugly or even unseemly, but it was different from any face he had seen so far. It looked human all right, but there was a certain, well, woody quality about it. Will suddenly realised that the face was looking straight at him expectantly.

'Who art thou, then, noble sir?' it asked.

'Er, Will... Will Burns.'

'Uuuuhhh!' The face shuddered and actually grimaced. Then it coughed and straightened its features. 'Sorry, sorry, forgive me,' Branchhole said. 'But thy words just surprised me. Thou must understand, it is not one of my favourite terms.'

'What? Which word...oh, I see, you mean "burn"... Sorry', Will added quickly as Branchhole shuddered again. 'Just call me Will then.'

'I'd prefer Master Will', Branchhole replied stiffly.

'Oh, sure, whatever you like,' Will replied rather helplessly.

The girl next to him introduced herself, trying to change the subject. 'I'm Annabel—Annabel Winston.'

Branchhole immediately turned to her. 'Oh wonderful, wonderful. What a pleasant and noble name. And well suited to such a noble lady indeed. Let an old, wooden door great thee properly and bid thee a splendid and warm welcome to Snow-fields.' He actually lowered his eyes and turned his face down in greeting.

Annabel turned red.

'Oh, no need to blush...though the colour doth indeed suit thee, my dear lady.' He turned to look at Wesley.

'Hi, I'm Wesley Limerick.' He nervously rubbed his nose and raised a hand.

'Oh, what a pleasure to meet thee, Sir Limerick. An old, honoured and traditional name indeed. Wear it well, and grant it and thyself the honour it deserves. Hail, Sir Limerick.'

He turned to Bianca expectantly. 'And who art thou? A highborn noble lady for sure, if ever I were a judge of superb and shapely exterior.'

'Ha...hallo,' she said shyly, 'Bianca Lane.'

'Oh.' Branchhole's face fell for a moment. But then it brightened up again. 'Wait, there was a Lord Lane...of Manchester, I believe. Oh, no.' He shook his face, which was quite astounding, Will reflected, as he had no neck. 'No, that was Lord Leicester of Manchester, of the high society. No, wait, there was a Lord Chief Justice Lane. Thou wouldst be his granddaughter then?' He peered hopefully at Bianca.

'No...sorry.' She turned pink. 'Really, just Lane.'

'Oh, very well then, Madam Lane, welcome.' Branchhole sounded disappointed, and turned to the next of them.

'Hi, hello, I'm Fredorgius Bagshot.' Freddy beamed at Branchhole, waving frantically.

'Ah, the young duke,' Branchhole said, relieved. 'Splendid, splendid indeed. Welcome, Your Lordship.'

'Er, what duke?' asked Freddy

'What meanest thou, what duke?' Branchhole replied un-believingly. 'Duke Bagshot! As in the works of the noble Benjamin Disraeli!'

'Who?'

Branchhole shook his head in disgust. 'Well, obviously thou dost not know thy family history. Better thou shouldst learn it! But'—he beamed again—'welcome to Snowfields, Duke Bagshot. Mayest thou prosper here.' He turned to the next student.

'Hi, I'm Michelle Summer.'

'Ah, Lord Summer. Hmm...not much of him in the histories. Even less of Viscount Summer. But perhaps a beauty like thee will change that, my Lady Summer. Welcome to thy new palace.' He looked at Richard. 'And who might this fine gentleman be?'

'The name is Loxley—Richard Loxley.'

'Loxley, eh? A descendant of the famous Robin of Loxley. A worthy lord! And then a Richard! Also a great name, promising great deeds. Prove thyself worthy of thine ancestor. Hail and salute, Lord Loxley!' He bowed his head deeply for a long moment. Then he looked at Sabrina inquiringly.

73

'Hello, I'm Sabrina Bluetonic.'

'Yes, I'll have one, thank you.' Branchhole's booming laugher reverberated woodenly from the rest of the door. 'Sorry, sorry. *Haruuump.*' He cleared his throat—*did a face in a door have a throat?* Will asked himself absentmindedly—with a wooden, rasping noise. Then he looked rather uncomfortably at Sabrina. 'Sorry, kind lady. To my great shame, I have to admit I could not resist that pun. So...Bluetonic,' he rumbled. 'An interesting name. Not rooted in history, no, not at all. But thou canst turn it into something to remember. Do thy best. Hail, Lady Bluetonic!'

Stiff as Branchhole was, Will saw he could not resist a small grin when he said the name. *Stiff as a stick, actually,* was Will's amused afterthought.

'And what would thy name be, milord?'

'Spencer Long, Mr Branchhole, sir.'

'Ah, Viscount Long, well-known indeed. Also baronet of the City of Westminster. Most excellent. And Spencer. A lordly name. I'm looking forward to seeing much of thee in the next few years. Hail, Viscount Long!' He turned to the next in their row.

'Hello, I'm Wendy Wildberry.'

'Eh? Wildberry? Never heard of such a dynasty before. Must be a new one. But we have to go with the times, and one can also expect much from a fresh, unspoilt dynasty. Welcome, Lady Wildberry. I wish thee a successful start at Snowfields.'

Will was by then rather disappointed. Branchhole had greeted all of them most extravagantly, and titled them as high lords and ladies—all but himself. Branchhole had just brushed him aside like a nuisance. This hurt Will quite a bit. All the others were something special—and he was less than ordinary. He couldn't really understand why.

When they had all introduced themselves to Branchhole, he bowed his face deeply in a final salute, and the door swung inwards. Contractus started to walk through the door, but then he suddenly stopped and turned back to them. 'Oh, I nearly forgot: there is a similar guardian in the door to your rooms. I didn't want to overwhelm you earlier, so I didn't make a fuss of it then, but I'll introduce you to it later on.' Then he led them into the quite plain classroom. Will looked around. He saw benches, desks, blackboards, and everything else one would expect in an ordinary classroom that was not in a school of Christmas. He was a bit disappointed by this; he had expected something more spectacular.

'Please find yourselves somewhere to sit,' Mr Contractus told them. They sat down, and Will saw he was sitting next to Annabel—well, not quite by accident, he had to admit to himself. Then Mr Contractus told them the basic things they needed to know about their new school and home.

After a break they came back into the room, and Freddy raised his hand. 'Mr Contractus,' he called, 'I've got a question!'

Mr Contractus turned and faced Freddy. 'Yes?'

'I've tried to call home to tell them what I've seen here so far. They won't believe it. I can't really believe it myself, especially the amazing ice-cream ships and...' He didn't draw a breath.

Mr Contractus's smile froze, and his eyes glazed over. Will got the feeling this often happened to people when Freddy was talking to them.

'Oh.' Even Freddy noticed it and caught himself. 'What I wanted to say... I tried to call home with my mobile phone and never got any connection. The phone couldn't find a network. How can this be?'

'Right, there is a simple explanation for it,' said Mr Contractus. 'The whole village has to remain hidden from the normal population. For your mobile you would need antennas, and we would have to set them up in the village. Then the phone companies would have to locate your phone with the antennas and our village would hardly remain hidden. Much to the contrary we have to block the village from any transmissions and antennas from the outside, using electromagnetic and magic screens. Our development department has to work very hard in order to be always at least one step ahead of the latest technology in the world outside.'

'Oh!' Freddy looked crestfallen. 'Then I can't call home?'

Mr Contractus smiled and shook his head. 'No, no, of course you can call home. But you have to use one of the normal phones that are installed throughout the village. You can use these phones to call anywhere inside Snowfields. But if you want to call outside, you'll have to use the operator, who will establish the connection for you. But, and this is important, you can only call your parents. Their numbers have been lodged with the operators. This is for the same reason as I've said before. We have to stay hidden from the normal world, and only your parents may know where you are and what you do. Therefore all outside communication has to be restricted in this way.' He looked around at them apologetically. 'Sorry, but that's the way it has to be.'

Freddy brightened. 'Oh, that's fine. I only wanted to talk to my parents anyway.'

Mr Contractus grinned. 'Okay then.' He looked around the classroom seriously. 'Now we come to something very important. I'll hand out your personal badges that will identify you as members of the White Christmas Organisation. It's essential that you always carry them with you, especially if you go out of the school into the village, so you can always identify yourselves as regular members of our organisation.'

He opened the drawer of his desk and pulled out a small sack. Then he walked through the rows and handed each student a badge. Will took his and looked at it. He saw the familiar logo on it, the same he had already seen on the official papers Conrad had given him not so long ago, when he had first heard about this organisation and the school he was now sitting in. The badge was rather small, round, quite heavy, made out of metal, and with a fine engraving of a large, red Christmas parcel and a garland of holly around it.

Mr Contractus finished handing out the badges and stood in front of them again. 'Now put away your badges safely, and look after them carefully! If you should ever lose them, you must immediately report this to any member of our staff here. Immediately! Don't be afraid, we won't hold you responsible, and there won't be any punishment or personal consequences for you. We just have to make sure there won't be any breaches of our security. This is very important for us all!'

He looked around the classroom to make sure they had all been listening. Then he went on to tell them the main things they needed to know about Snowfields and the school, explained their timetable and subjects, and finally released them from their first lesson. He helped them find their way back to their common room and introduced them to the door guardian there. This one was not as lofty as the one on the door to their classroom, but was quite jovial, and the introduction was rather uneventful—which was fine by Will, for this guardian did not object to his name at all. After they had all been introduced so that they could enter the rooms on their own, Contractus left them to get settled in and to explore their new home.

As it had already got rather late, Will stored his personal belongings in his wardrobe and then just wandered around the quarters with the others, looking here and there. They were having a discussion about whether they should continue exploring other parts of the school when a deep 'gong' from the clock reverberated through the common room. Immediately they went over and looked at it. The sign under its face said, 'Five minutes till supper!' And right on cue, Mr Contractus stepped into the corridor and led them once more to the Ferum.

There Will had another delicious meal—not as spectacular as lunch, but very tasty all the same. After supper Mr Contractus left them to find their way back to their rooms on their own, and with Wesley in the lead they got there without a wrong turn. By then they were all yawning, as it had been a long and eventful day, and so they went straight to bed. Will settled into the soft and comfortable bedding, sighed contentedly, and thought about the wonderful events of the day. Soon he fell asleep.

Chapter 5

Will sat on a sofa in the common room of his quarters, reading the summary Parchmentinus had handed out about the topics they would cover in his class. He looked up as he heard voices coming nearer. Bianca and Wendy entered the room.

'Hi, Will,' Bianca called. 'We're rounding everybody up because we want to go and explore the village. Are you interested?'

'Yes, of course. I already thought of going outside earlier today.'

'Well, then come with us.'

Will put away the paper he had been reading and got up.

'Could you look into your dorm to see if anyone's there who'd like to come too? I wouldn't want to go in there.' Wendy smiled primly.

'Yes, sure.' Will went into his dorm. He found Wesley, who was rummaging through things in his closet.

'Hi, Wesley. Bianca and Wendy are down in the common room and asked if we want to join them exploring the village.'

'Yeah, great idea. I'm coming with you.' He stuffed his things away and followed Will back to the main room.

Bianca and Wendy had found Spencer, Annabel, and Freddy, and they were standing near the door.

'Okay, that's everybody we could find,' said Bianca. 'Michelle and Richard just went outside, but they didn't want to join us.'

'Has anybody got the map they gave us on our arrival?' Will asked.

'Yes, I've got mine here.' Spencer held it up.

'Let's go then.' Bianca led them from the wing.

They went down the corridors and stairs to the entrance hall, through the magnificent door, and then out onto the street in front of the school.

'Let's see,' said Spencer, unfolding his map. 'This is School Lane. And the school is right on the western edge of the village. Where do we want to go? To the Plaza?'

The others nodded their agreement.

'Then we go down there.' Spencer pointed to the east.

As they walked down the street, they went past average-sized, two-storey buildings made out of red brick.

Spencer looked up from his map. 'These are living areas for teachers and other staff. And that'—he pointed to a building just two houses away, opposite the school—'is the students' café, called The Jolly Reindeer.' He studied the map again. 'It says here: "A jolly place to have a cocoa after school with your mates."'

Will looked at the building. It was like the ones next to it, but its front consisted of a row of windows. The door was bright green and decorated with holly. A sign above the door showed a dancing reindeer.

'Look!' Bianca giggled and nudged Annabel. Will looked where she was pointing and saw a sprig of mistletoe hanging right above the door.

'Shall we have a look inside?' asked Wendy.

'Yes, let's see what it's like,' answered Will, and went towards the door. He opened it and passed quickly under the mistletoe, before any of the girls could get the wrong idea. The others followed him.

'Come in, come in! Ther' be drinks an' food for all o' yer in 'ere.'

Will was greeted by a booming voice and looked up. Standing behind the counter was a heavily-built man, with a round face and a huge, round belly. Above a wide, brown beard that covered his upper mouth and lower face, his cheeks were red, and he wore a red, slightly-battered bowler hat. He grinned at Will and the others. 'Please, take a seat whe'ever yer like. Not many customers 'ere at this time o' day. Yer must be some of the new students just arrived, right? Cause I ain't not seen yer a'fore, and'—he touched a finger to his left temple —'I ain't forgetting me customers.'

Bianca nudged Will, who was standing in the front.

'Er, yes,' Will managed. 'Yes, we've just arrived at Snow-fields. We were just having a look around the village and found your café.'

'Good, good! I 'ope I'll be see'n' yer most often from now on. I serve the best cocoa in al' o' Snowfields. I'll prove it! Sit yerselves down and I'll serve yer a round.'

'Oh, thank you very much, sir, but.... Uhm.... We've just arrived in Snowfields and...well, I'm not sure what money you are using here.' Will faltered under the almost affronted look he got from the man behind the counter.

'No need t' worry, no need t' worry at all, me young friends.' The man flashed them a wide grin. 'The first round's on meself. It won't cost yer nothin'. An' by th'way, of course we use the Christmas dime an' dollar in Snowfields. Best yer arsks yer teachers about it. Teachers are there to expl'in.'

'Oh, that's great. Thank you very much, sir.' Will smiled at the man and started to go to a table by the window.

'Stop!'

At the sharp command, Will stopped dead in his tracks and turned round.

'There's one thing yer'll all 'ave t'do 'ere in me café! There's no sir'in' me! Me name's Jolly—just Jolly.'

'Oh, okay Mr J—' Will started to answer, but the big man behind the counter immediately raised a chubby finger.

'Ah?' he said.

'Oh, I mean...okay, Jolly.' Will grinned as Jolly cracked a smile.

''Ave a seat, 'ave a seat.' Jolly waved them towards the table.

Will and the others sat down at the table next to the window.

Immediately Jolly came with a heavy tray. 'There y'are, me young frien's.' He deftly placed a mug of steaming cocoa with a huge mountain of cream topping in front of each of them. Then he put a plate heaped with biscuits in the middle. ''Ere y'are, there y'are. With no chargin' t'day. Dig in! Tha's an order.' He laughed, booming deeply, and was gone again with surprising speed considering his bulk.

The students did not need to be told twice. They started munching the biscuits.

'Mmmmh, these are gooood!' said Freddy, his mouth full and spluttering crumbs on the table. 'Oh, sorry.' He tried to brush them away.

Annabel shook her head in disgust. Will smiled and tried his own biscuit. Freddy was right, though. They tasted really good—almost as good as the ones his mother made at Christmastime.

'Nice place,' said Spencer. 'Don't you think?'

'Yes, indeed,' replied Bianca. 'And the cocoa is really excellent. With real chocolate and not just some tasteless chemical powder.'

They crunched through the biscuits and sipped from their mugs.

Then the door of the café opened and a goblin came inside. Immediately Jolly's behaviour changed completely.

'Get out,' he snarled. 'Get out'f her' quick.'

The goblin looked up in surprise.

Jolly growled at him: 'I ain't servin' folks like you. Not now. Not wi' all the trouble wi' Bluerin tha's goin' on at the moment!'

The goblin hung his head, nodded wearily and walked out again.

Jolly continued to growl something into his beard. Will had noticed this strange exchange and he wanted to mention it to the others. But they were all so absorbed in their cocoa and biscuits that they had not noticed anything. So what should he say to them? He left it, but still thought it was all rather strange. And what the heck was Bluerin? Or did Jolly miss a few syllables?

'Everybody finished?' asked Spencer finally. 'Then we should move on! I want to see the rest of the village.'

'Everythin' all right, was't?' called Jolly from behind his counter as the students started to get up. He sounded bright and friendly again.

'Yes, it was excellent. Thank you very much,' Freddy called back to him. 'I bet I'll become one of your best customers!'

Jolly laughed heartily. 'Tha's fine, me lad. That's how't should be. I'll see yer soon!'

The students said goodbye, and trooped out.

'Well, that was nice,' said Bianca outside. 'Where do we go now?'

Spencer peered at his map. 'That way!' He pointed down the street. 'The next buildings are all living quarters.'

They walked down the street and passed fronts of different sizes and slightly different styles, but all basically built of red brick, if in slightly different hues, and brown, wooden beams. All had lattice windows of different sizes and forms, and some even had coloured lead glass designs, mostly Christmas motifs like green holly or golden stars.

The students went down the street and reached a junction.

'Which way, Spencer?' asked Will.

'Well.' He pointed to the left. 'Down there seem to be mostly production buildings and stores. In the other direction lies the centre with the Plaza.'

'I'd like to have a look at the production buildings. They ought to be interesting,' said Freddy eagerly.

'Well, why not.' Bianca started down the street to the left, and the others followed.

'This street's called Production Road.'

'Funny name for a street,' noted Wendy, 'but easy to remember.'

They went down the street, which was noticeably wider than School Lane, and it looked to be well-travelled. On both sides were, again, red brick buildings, apparently homes to the inhabitants of Snowfields village.

They reached a curve to the right. In front of them loomed the brick front of a huge building, stretching away in the distance along the street. There were enormous steel doors at regular intervals.

'These are production halls,' Spencer noted rather superfluously, as if something this big could be anything else. It looked rather like a factory from the early ages of industrialisation, thought Will, remembering photographs he had seen in his schoolbooks.

'Can we have a look inside?' asked Freddy.

'Hmm,' said Bianca. 'I don't think we should. It seems pretty closed up. And we might get into trouble if we just stumble in there.'

'Oh.' Freddy sounded disappointed. 'But I'd really like to see what's inside.' He squared his shoulders and walked determinedly towards the building.

Annabel rolled her eyes.

'Well, surely one look won't hurt,' Will ventured as he was also pretty eager to see what was inside.

He got a disapproving glance from Annabel. But suddenly she broke into a smile and said, 'All right, let's go then.'

Will and Annabel went after Freddy. The others followed, as they were no less curious. They approached a large window that promised a good view of what was going on inside. But when they were only a few steps in front of it, a huge load of snow dropped right on top of them.

'Ugh!' Freddy exclaimed.

They jumped back, coughing snow and trying to wipe it off their faces and clothes.

'What was that?' Spencer yelled. 'How could the snow just drop on us like that?'

'Well,' replied Bianca, still trying to brush it all off her coat. 'Snow sometimes does slide down off the roof.'

'But we are standing near the face of the building.' Spencer stared up the front of it. 'There's no roof here where the snow can slide off!'

Bianca shrugged her shoulders. 'Don't ask me. It certainly happened!'

Meanwhile Freddy was walking towards the window again, trying to peer inside. Suddenly another load of snow dropped on him.

'Will you look at that!' Spencer said. 'That can't just be a coincidence.'

'Hmm,' said Will. 'Let's try again.' He took a few careful steps towards the window, squinting up as he went. Suddenly all went white and cold, and he was covered in snow again. He jumped back. When he could see again, the others were looking at him in confusion.

Wendy said, 'That can't be simply bad luck. That looks to be on purpose.'

Will had a thought. 'Maybe that's a very sophisticated bur-glar alarm. If you come near the building, you are covered in snow.'

'That makes sense,' said Bianca. 'Well, another of the won-ders of Snowfields. But one I could have done without.'

'We could all have done without it,' grumbled Freddy. 'And I haven't even seen anything inside. That's not fair.'

The others laughed.

'Well,' Bianca said, 'let's go on. I'll bet there are other things to see. Things we're allowed to see.'

They went down the street, along the front of the produc-tion building.

'Look!' Will pointed ahead of them. 'What is *that*?'

They stood in the street and stared: there, high above their heads, clouds moved above the street. But not randomly. Will looked to the right. He could see a—well, a sort of pathway made out of cloud. A few inches above it, small squares of cloud slowly floated along. The pathway started at a door back in the wall of the large production building; at intervals the door would open, and a square of cloud would come floating through it. On the squares were all sorts of products. Will could see dolls, wooden trains, a rocking horse, a television, a bicycle, and lots of other stuff.

The cloud pathway led to the street, where it turned up-wards at a ninety-degree angle and rose high above the stu-dents' heads. Up there it turned again through ninety degrees and led across the street. On the other side, it turned down-wards again, and when it reached the ground it led onwards towards a set of doors in the building on this side of the road.

Will watched the drifting squares of cloud with the products on them.

'That must be a transportation system—you know, like those conveyor belts we travelled on at Cloudy's Transportation Service,' said Annabel finally.

'Yes, looks like it,' answered Will, still staring. 'Fascinating, isn't it?'

Spencer looked at his map. 'On this side are stores. So I guess the finished products are being transported from the production halls to the stores here.'

They went on, passing directly underneath the cloud conveyor belt, still looking up at it, for they had never seen anything like it in their lives. They continued along the street.

'Oh my, these buildings are never-ending!' said Bianca after some time. They were still walking along the fronts of the buildings.

'Reminds me of a car factory,' replied Freddy.

Finally they reached the end of the buildings and a junction.

'Look!' said Freddy. 'There's another one.'

And indeed. Will looked where Freddy was pointing. Across the junction, along the road that ran crosswise to the one they had just walked down, was a long strip of the cloud conveyor belt raised slightly above the ground. The single cloud units moved slowly from right to left. On them there seemed to be all kinds of raw materials. Some carried loads that looked like dirt, others seemed to be carrying ore. Will even saw one unit in the distance that looked as if it were carrying a large glass basin full of water.

The conveyor belt ran along the side of the road and disappeared through large steel doors into another building to their left. The building was indeed immense—and beautiful. It had pristine, white walls, lots of glass windows with golden window frames, red-tiled roofs (at least those parts that were not made out of glass), and many towers and turrets. The students all stared at this magnificent building.

'What on earth is that?' Sabrina was the first to recover her voice.

Spencer consulted his plan. 'That's the Bluerin Production Palace.'

'Bluerin? What's Bluerin?' asked Will, remembering Jolly and the goblin.

'No idea,' said Spencer, 'but it must be something important.' He looked up at the building and added, 'At least judging by this grandeur.'

Freddy had been staring at it open-mouthed. 'Wow. I'd like to have a look at that!' And he started walking purposefully towards the building.

'Oi, Freddy, you sure you want to get covered in snow again?' Bianca called after him.

He stopped. 'Hmm, you're right.' Then he brightened up. 'But this is a totally different building. Surely they're not all protected like that? And I want to see what's going on in there.' He started towards the building again.

The others, equally curious but more cautious, followed slowly, with lots of space between them and Freddy. He was getting near one of the enormous windows of the grand structure. When he was quite close, a huge and very thick wall of holly suddenly sprang up, making him jump backwards in surprise. Strangely, the wall of holly was in front of only him, between him and the window, and only reached a few yards to his left and right. Next to it the others could still see the wall and windows.

Puzzled, Freddy took a few steps backwards, and as suddenly as the wall had appeared, it vanished again. There was no trace left; it looked as if it had never been there at all. Freddy, of course, could not leave it alone, and took a few slow and tentative steps towards the window. And promptly the wall of holly was there again. Will and the others walked carefully over to Freddy. He was touching the holly curiously. Suddenly he jerked back his hand.

'Ow! Dad sftufff really forney,' he said, sucking his thumb.

Will studied the wall. He had never seen holly this thick before. It formed a massive green wall, and he could see only one or two inches into it, then it just turned dark—that was how thick it was. He could also see lots of the nasty, spiky thorns Freddy had discovered.

Will offered: 'Well, at least we didn't get wet with this one.'

'You can talk,'grumbled Freddy.

'It seems to me that all the important buildings are rather well-protected in Snowfields,' added Bianca.

'How stupid,' said Freddy, still eyeing his thumb. 'I never get to see the interesting things.'

'Never mind,' said Annabel. 'I'm sure they'll show us everything in due time.'

'But I want to see it now,' replied Freddy sullenly.

'Well, you can't,' countered Bianca.

Freddy glared at her.

Will didn't want them to start another argument, so he quickly said, 'Let's just move on. There's so much we still have to discover.' He was just turning away from the building when he saw something. 'Look!' he called and the others stopped to see where he was pointing.

'Well, that seems to be Richard and Michelle, doesn't it?' Spencer said.

And indeed, in a partly closed-off yard to the side of the building Will could see Richard and Michelle, talking to a goblin. Strange as this was—for why should they know a goblin at Snowfields well enough to talk to?—even stranger was the fact that the goblin was holding a small box with something blue inside. It was sparkling and gleaming. Will had never seen anything like it. Then suddenly a door in the building banged open and Beltorec, their headmaster, burst out of it, jumping down the steps two at a time. The goblin cringed and Beltorec tore the box from its hands, shouting something incoherent. The goblin fled. Then Beltorec turned towards Richard and Michelle, growled a few words at them, glanced around quickly, and when he saw Will and the others down the road, he roughly seized Michelle and Richard by their arms and dragged them inside the building. The door slammed shut behind him.

Will looked at the others around him.

'What was that about?' he asked.

Freddy shrugged his shoulders: 'Don't know. But they do seem to be in trouble,' he grinned wolfishly.

The others laughed.

Annabel turned around: 'Well, let them be in trouble, fine with me, but I want to see more of the village. Let's move on. Spencer, which way?'

Spencer consulted his map. 'Well, down here is only the Bluerin production. We should go back and follow the cloud conveyor belt. The centre of the village is in that direction.'

They walked down Workers Lane with its small but neat houses, past the harbour and the landing site for raw materials and stopped next to a shabby-looking building.

Spencer consulted his map. 'Security Office,' he said, rather dubiously.

'Well, security doesn't seem to be a big issue here judging from that pathetic place,' said Bianca.

Will said, 'What crimes would you expect here? A stolen wooden train? A pinched doll? If crime were a problem, they surely wouldn't have the school here. I'm a bit more interested in the next building.'

Behind the security office loomed a rather more impressive edifice that had caught Will's interest. It was not nearly as large as the ones they had seen before, but it had brilliant white walls and the now familiar large windows and red roof tiles.

'What's this then?' asked Freddy.

Spencer looked up from his map. 'That's the local headquarters of Cloudy's Transportation Service.'

'Oh, right. There's a sign up there saying "CTS".'

'Also looks quite grand,' said Wendy.

'Of course. Surely they have to be one of the biggest departments here in Snowfields. What with the large amounts of raw material they need and, of course, the delivery of the presents. That alone has to be a huge task to manage, I'd think,' replied Will. 'What's that building on the other side?'

'That's the department for Letters to Father Christmas.'

It was also a rather impressive and tall building. Will thought it looked a bit like a post office, but then, he reflected, it actually was one—at least sort of.

'Hey, Freddy, want to have a look inside?' Bianca nudged him and gave him a thumbs-up.

'No, thank you,' he grumbled. 'Have a look yourself.'

'I did warn you, you know.'

'Knock it off, will you!' He glared at her.

'Why, no reason to get grumpy.'

Freddy turned away from her.

The students passed between the immense buildings until they reached another junction.

'The Plaza is to the right now,' said Spencer.

They turned in the direction he indicated, dwarfed by the department for the Letters to Father Christmas. Then they reached a wide-open space. It was beautifully decorated with Christmas hangings, Christmas trees, lights, and all the other decorations they had already seen in the school. The square was paved with white marble that shone beautifully in the light.

'Well, this is it,' Spencer noted.

Right in the middle was the largest fir tree of all, richly decorated and hung with great red globes, loads of tinsel, red bows, candy, and seemingly millions of lights. On the side of the Plaza to their right was another impressive sight: a remarkable clock tower. It was made out of the ubiquitous red brick, inlaid with slabs of sandstone on the sides, with detailed Christmas motifs chiselled into them. At the top, on each side of the tower was a large clock with a white face. The hands were golden and massive.

The only other sight the Plaza had to offer was an expensive-looking inn, the Golden Sleigh. Following Spencer's lead, they reached another junction. He pointed down the left-hand road. 'Down there are mainly living quarters, also for the goblins and elves. That building over there is for Cloudy's goblins.' He pointed towards a massive complex. Mainly it was an oblong block, but the single living units and levels were staggered. There were no sharp corners, and everything was brightly-coloured.

'Looks a bit like a Hundertwasser building,' said Will.

'Yes,' replied Sabrina, 'but I think it's rather fitting for Cloudy's goblins.'

Will had to agree, thinking about his experience with the goblins on his way to Snowfields.

'I'm sure we can have a look inside that one,' said Freddy, stressing the last words. 'After all there's nothing special to hide or protect in there, is there?'

Sabrina said with a mischievous grin, 'Why don't you have a go at it then? We'll watch.'

Freddy straightened up. 'I will indeed!' And he marched off in the direction of the complex.

The others stayed where they were and looked after him with interest, waiting for whatever might happen this time. Freddy walked up to the entrance, but then he stopped. Will looked closely, but he could see nothing out of the ordinary. Nothing had sprung up in Freddy's path, and the door was not blocked. As far as Will could see, nothing had happened at all.

Sabrina called, 'What is it, Freddy? Why are you stopping? Afraid, eh? Just go on inside!' she teased him.

'I can't!' Freddy called back, sounding frustrated. 'When I got closer to the building, the first step to the door got higher and higher. I'm standing right in front of it now, and it must be at least twelve feet high! I'm coming back,' he said. And he walked away from the building and went to where they were waiting.

'What was that?' asked Sabrina when he reached them. 'From over here we could see nothing happening at all. The building didn't change a bit.'

'When I was right in front of it, the first step of the stairs was at least twelve feet high! I even touched it, and it definitely felt most solid,' Freddy answered. He shook his head. 'Let's get moving. No need to waste more time here,' he said sourly.

The others grinned.

'Which way?' asked Wesley.

Spencer looked at his map. 'I'd say back in that direction, back to the school. Down this road are only living quarters, and I'm not really interested in them. Are you?' he asked the others.

They shook their heads and muttered their agreement.

It was getting late when they got back to the school, stamping their feet and glad to be out of the cold.

'Well,' said Bianca, 'that was a good look around the village.'

Freddy replied with his usual enthusiasm. 'Yes, it looks really great. It will be fun living here and exploring everything. What do we do now?' He stood on the tips of his toes because he was so excited and eager to be off again.

Spencer had been looking at the clock on the wall of the entrance hall. 'Well, I'd say we'd best have a wash or a shower, and then it will be supper-time anyway.'

Freddy looked disappointed. Seeing this, Bianca laughed. 'Hey, Freddy, cheer up. Tomorrow will be another day to explore and learn more about this place. And of course we will be staying here for the next few years. So there should be enough time.'

'Yes, of course you're right. But I'd like to see everything now,' Freddy replied.

The others laughed.

'Oh, come on Freddy, you have at least supper to look forward to,' said Wesley.

Freddy brightened up visibly. 'Oh, yes, that will be great.' The others laughed even harder, and they started walking back to their common room.

Chapter 6

Will sat in the production lesson early on Thursday morning, expecting another boring lecture about the structure and organisation of the production of Christmas presents. Mr Worker taught them exciting aspects like four-shift models for the workers, the organisation of a steady flow of basic materials, and the magnificent details of the configuration of conveyor belts. When Will had heard that he would learn about the production of Christmas presents, he had been most excited. He had expected things like jolly little gnomes working away happily, and presents appearing almost by magic. He had certainly not expected such dry topics.

But this morning he was in for a good surprise. Mr Worker came into the classroom and walked up to his desk. But instead of opening his book, turning to the blackboard, or pulling out some of his ever-feared overhead projector slides, he just stood beside his desk. With a broad smile, he announced: 'Today we are going to do something special. First of all you'll have to put away your books. You won't need them today. Instead I'm going to show you something: the most important thing we have in Snowfields!'

He paused dramatically before continuing. 'I'm sure at least some of you have been wondering where we get all the presents from. One possible answer would be that we produce them just like everything else is produced in the outside world. But that would be a bit difficult. We would need huge factories, machines without number, thousands of specialist workers, enormous amounts of parts, storage room for them, and so on. As you can see, we don't have any of these in

Snowfields. But, as you know, we have very big stores with all kinds of presents in them. And, in a way, we really do produce all these presents here. But we have our own way. The secret— some would say the secret our whole organisation is based on —is Bluerin.' He smiled in satisfaction as he saw the students' puzzled expressions. 'Ever heard of it before you came here? Any idea what it is?'

Almost everyone shook their heads.

'See, that's how secret it is. Bluerin is very fascinating stuff. As you can guess from the name, it is blue. It looks like mist. We keep it in something like a very big fish tank, which is made out of a special kind of glass. This glass was created by our magicians in the development department and doesn't re-act with Bluerin, as nearly everything else does. Including skin. Your skin! So, and this is important, be sure never to touch Bluerin with your bare hands. Use it only with the greatest care, for nobody can tell what will happen if you get some of it on your hands, as it always reacts differently. Don't ask me why.'

Mr Worker held up his hands in defence. 'The magicians tell me it has to do with the way Bluerin is embedded in the structure of time, energy, and matter, as they all are the same, but I don't even understand the basics of what they're trying to tell me. If you want to know, you can ask them yourselves. But you're the ones asking for headaches.' He wandered around the classroom while he talked. Now he went back to his desk, opened it with his key, and removed a small, black box from it.

'Let's get to the interesting part then.'

He opened the box and took out a smaller box made out of glass. Something brilliant blue shimmered in it. But when Will looked at it, it was also a pale blue that he could look right through. And in the next instant it was also the darkest blue he could have imagined. While he looked at it, it changed through all possible hues of blue, and even some that were impossible. Looking at it hurt his eyes in the first moment. But then he was drawn into it. It was the most beautiful colour he had ever seen. The students all stared at it, caught by its beauty.

'This,' Mr Worker said, raising his voice to catch their attention, 'is Bluerin! The stuff dreams are made of. Now, where do we get this fascinating stuff from...? Well...? Anybody?' Finally Sabrina raised her hand tentatively. 'Ah... Well, Miss Bluetonic?'

'You collect it from all around the world... You take stuff like sand, stone, and water and mix them all together.'

'Right you are!' He beamed at her, and she turned red. 'We have specially trained people all around the world looking for the raw materials and sending them here. They look for stone, earth, wood, sand, water, and so on. We even have some people at rubbish tips and destructors. But it's rather more difficult if we use materials from there, for they have to be sorted and broken into their basic components before we can use them—although of course it's much more eco-friendly. Mainly we have our people in remote areas all around the world, where the loss of hundreds of tons of stone or several million litres of water won't really be noticed. So we get all these raw materials sent here, and then our specialists working in the Bluerin Production Palace make sure they're mixed properly in the right amounts, and in the end we get our marvellous Bluerin.'

He handed the small container of Bluerin to one of the students and let it circulate round the class. There were many 'ohs' and 'wows' while the container went round. When it finally reached Will, he looked deeply into the blue mist. It passed quickly through different blue shades, sparkling and shiny. Will nearly lost himself in the colours. Finally he regretfully passed the container on to Freddy, who kept nudging him excitedly, not willing to wait any longer.

When the container got back to Mr Worker, he took the box and looked pointedly at everyone still talking, until all the conversation had died down and he had their full attention. He took out his wand and concentrated on the box in his hand. Then he performed a spell and touched the lid of the glass container with his wand. The top sprang open with a tinkling sound.

'Oh,' Sabrina murmured, and another girl gasped.

Mr Worker glanced around and gave them a quick wink. Then his brow wrinkled, and he concentrated on the open container. He murmured softly, performed a long and complicated spell, and pointed his wand at the Bluerin. It shimmered and wavered. Then, in the blink of an eye, it was gone, and in the glass container there was a small but highly detailed model of their school!

Everyone was amazed. Freddy exclaimed, 'Wow, did you see that?'

Mr Worker grinned and handed the model of the school to Spencer, who was sitting in the front, so the students could have a good look at it. When Will took it from Annabel, he felt it was quite solid and heavy. It was highly detailed as well. He could even make out the windows of his dormitory. It was hard to believe that moments earlier this solid model had been some sort of blue mist. He passed it on to Freddy, who took it eagerly. When the last of them had had a good look at the model, Mr Worker took it back.

He said, 'Okay, that's Bluerin for you. During the next lessons, I'll show you how the transformation of Bluerin into presents works. We'll start in the next lesson by visiting one of the workrooms, where there's a huge Bluerin tank and where the specially trained Bluerinics create the presents. Good day to you.' He walked out of the classroom.

'Wow, that was great!' Freddy exclaimed, and Will had to agree.

*   *   *

Later Will was sitting at a desk in the working area of his quarters. He was reading a rather boring treatise: 'The History of the Underlying Principles of the Overall Structure of the Sorting and Reviewing of Christmas Lists and the Subsequent Allocation of Parcels, i.e. Christmas Presents, Based on Principles Deduced from the Last Two Centuries.' He had already started yawning after he read the title. He had to read it three times before he understood it. But he needed to read the article to complete the homework Parchementinus expected for the following week. Will was nearly nodding off when he heard someone coming near. He looked up: Bianca and Wendy were walking up to him.

'Hi, Will,' Bianca greeted him. 'What are you doing?'

'Oh, sorting through this treatise for Parchementinus' homework.' He tossed the paper on the desk in front of him.

'Oh, that.' Wendy nodded gloomily. 'I haven't had the nerve to start on it yet.'

'I certainly didn't, but there's no help for it. I've got to do it sometime. And the sooner I'm done with it the better,' replied Will.

'There's that,' Wendy admitted.

'Anyhow,' Bianca interjected, 'we want to go to the Jolly Reindeer for a break. Fancy joining us?'

Will looked down at the treatise and compared it to the prospect of a nice, hot cocoa in the Jolly Reindeer. There was not much to decide. He pushed his papers together, stuffed them into his bag, and stood up. 'Yes, of course! Let's go. I can finish this later.'

Bianca and Wendy smiled, turned around, and led the way to the door.

***

Eventually they had their next lesson in production. Mr Worker had been waiting for them in their classroom. And, just as he had promised, after a short introduction he led them over to the production building which Will and the others had already discovered when they had explored the village, at which time they had also discovered one of its—rather un-pleasant—peculiarities while trying to get near to it. This time, though, with Mr Worker in the lead, they had no problems when they approached the building. They were not covered in snow, and no hedge blocked their way, so they reached the door without incident. Mr Worker opened the immense steel door and led them inside. They passed through an entrance area, with a bored-looking desk clerk who belatedly snapped to attention when he saw the teacher, and they went up some stairs until Mr Worker opened another heavy door and led them onto a balcony overlooking a large hall. In the centre was a very big glass container filled with the brilliant-blue mist of Bluerin.

'This is one of our production rooms—one of the most amazing rooms we have in Snowfields,' Mr Worker told the students.

Dozens of small glass tubes, all filled with the swirling and sparkling Bluerin, ran from the glass tank to workbenches all over the room. There they zigzagged up unto the working sur-faces and ended with golden valves. Under the valves were shallow glass basins. At each bench someone clad in royal blue worked, busily forming all kinds of goods out of Bluerin. First they would open the valve and let a bit of Bluerin flow into the basin. Then they would work at it with their wands. And after a while some sort of present would appear. Right beside each bench a small white patch of cloud hovered. Every time one of the workers finished a product, he would place it on top of the cloud, and the cloud would float through the room to a door on the far side as if on invisible rails. Then the door would open, and the cloud would float out of sight.

Above each bench was a beige-gray stone-like pyramid with the vertex pointing down directly at the glass basin. On the sides of the pyramids were complicated engravings—on some of them only one side was covered with a few rough lines, on others all sides were filled completely with very finely-etched symbols.

Will and the others looked around wild-eyed.

'Cor, look at that, look at that—that's amazing!' Fredorgius gabbled as he gaped at the room.

'Look at those lovely tiny clouds', Annabel said. 'They're beautiful, aren't they?'

Then all of the students were babbling simultaneously.

'Look, there! He just conjured up a television. Wow!'

'Blimey! Look at all that Bluerin.'

'I wonder what those pyramids are for.'

'Those clouds can really carry a lot!'

'Look, they're making mobile phones over there.'

'See how fast he's doing those small balls over there?'

'Where do you get all that Bluerin from?'

They all pointed this way and that, all talking at the same time, all wanting to show the others what amazing things they had discovered.

When they had calmed down a bit, Mr Worker called, 'Gather round me, will you? Please, boys, you too. Mr. Bagshot? Mr Bagshot... Finally. Well, I want to explain some of the things you're seeing.'

They gathered around him in a rough semicircle. Though Freddy could not resist throwing a glance back at the room now and then.

'As you can see, and as I've already told you, in this room the presents are being made out of Bluerin. In the centre you see the Bluerin tank. That is, of course, not all the Bluerin we've got in Snowfields. This is just a smaller, temporary storage for the production units. It's fed by a pipeline from the main Bluerin stores, which are in another building, in the Bluerin Production Palace. You can see the small pipelines that lead from the tank to the single workstations.

'Each station is manned by a Bluerinic. They're the trained workers who specialise in the transformation of Bluerin. They have to be able to concentrate strictly on the work at hand, or the pieces they're working on will be flawed. In the last lesson, I demonstrated how Bluerin can be transformed. Most of you would call it magic. But, as you've been told before, our magic here at Snowfields is really only a special form of focussing one's will. To focus the will, you use a wand and utter a word or clause—a magic spell, if you want. And the Bluerin in your wand is the vehicle to transport your will.

'But enough talk for now. Off you go, get down there and have a good look round on your own. You can talk to the Bluerinics and ask them questions. Just don't touch anything without asking first.'

Freddy was the first to bound down the stairs and hurry through the rows of Bluerinics. Will followed more slowly. He stopped at the first workbench. The Bluerinic smiled briefly at him, then concentrated on his work again. Will watched closely as the Bluerinic turned the tap so that some Bluerin flowed into the basin on the bench. The Bluerinic was in deep concentration. He slowly pointed his wand at the Bluerin. Then he did something strange—he turned his head and looked up at a strange pyramid that was hanging upside down from the ceiling with its tip pointing straight down to the work-bench. Then some sort of blue mist started to flow from the tip of the pyramid. The Bluerinic pointed his wand at the mist and guided it down towards the Bluerin in the basin. It started to shimmer even more brightly and suddenly a pocket calculator was lying in the basin, still with a slight blue gleam that faded slowly. The Bluerinic exhaled deeply, took the calculator and looked it over critically. Will had watched all this spellbound. Suddenly the Bluerinic held the calculator right in front of Will.

'Here, for you,' he said to Will.

Will took the calculator carefully and looked at the Bluerinic in amazement. 'Thank you,' he finally managed to say.

The Bluerinic laughed. 'No problem at all,' he said. 'The minute I saw you all entering our production room I switched to making this, because you'll need it for your accountancy lessons.'

Will looked at the calculator, which did not shimmer blue anymore. He looked back at the Bluerinic and said once more: 'Thank you. Er, sir,...can I ask you a question?'

'Of course.'

'This pyramid,' Will pointed upwards. 'What's it for?'

'Oh, that's easy,' the Bluerinic replied. 'The pyramid helps me focus my will to transform the Bluerin. You see, the more complex the product you want to create is, the more you've got to concentrate, and the more willpower you've got to put into the transformation. Nobody would be able to do this the whole day. Even making simple things like wooden building bricks or rubber balls would take way too much concentration and energy.'

Will nodded slowly. 'I see. And what are those engravings on the sides?' he asked.

'Ah,' the Bluerinic said. 'Very sharp of you to notice them. These engravings contain most of the information needed for the fabrication of the products. You see, you can produce anything with Bluerin by the power of your will and with the right spell. But, as I've told you, it needs a lot of concentration and energy to produce even small things. So you can produce even the most complicated things with little energy if the information in the engravings is explicit enough. But the engravings have another use: if you want to turn Bluerin into a complex product like this,' he pointed towards the calculator in Will's hands, 'then you need to picture every detail of the calculator in your mind. Not only the general look of it, but also everything that's inside it. The whole technical process, the complete electronics, every single capillary joint on the circuit board. Nobody would be able to do that. But this information is stored completely in the engravings on the pyramids. So I just have to imagine the product and assemble the general look of it in my mind. Then I channel my will through the pyramid and thus create complex products.'

'So you can make all kinds of products with this pyramid?' Will asked and pointed towards it once more.

'No, unfortunately not,' the Bluerinic replied. 'This pyramid is just for the specific calculator model you are holding in your hands. If I want to produce something else, I've got to change the pyramid like this.' And he reached up, loosened some clamps, and pulled the pyramid out of its mounting. He placed it on a carrier cloud beside him and picked up a different pyramid from the next cloud. He touched the first cloud with his wand and it slowly floated away. Then he fixed the pyramid above his workbench. 'There,' he said to Will. 'Now I can produce another present. You see, the engravings just code the specifics for one special kind of product.'

Will nodded. 'Okay. I understand. But how do you...' Before he could go on, he was interrupted by Mr Worker calling them back.

Will quickly thanked the Bluerinic and hurried back to the teacher.

When they were all gathered round him again, Mr Worker said: 'Well, I hope you all had a good look round. Any questions so far?'

Will felt a movement beside him. Sabrina had put her hand in the air, waving it frantically until Mr Worker finally saw it.

'Miss Bluetonic?'

'Can you produce really everything, every single present here? I find that a bit hard to believe.'

Mr Worker shook his head. 'Alas, no. As the Bluerinics should have told you, the pyramids help us tremendously. But unfortunately we can't produce all the presents we need. We can produce all of the simpler things, or things that are not too new. But we can't produce the newest products like the latest mobile phones or computers.

'Yes, Mr Bagshot?'

Freddy had raised his hand while Mr Worker had been explaining. 'I don't understand that. I was told with the pyramids you could produce everything.'

'Ah, yes. We are indeed able to produce almost anything with the pyramids. But if you think about it, there is one obstacle. Maybe you can figure it out yourselves. Remember I've told you we especially can't produce the newest products.' He looked around. 'Does anyone have an idea what the problem might be?' He waited.

Will thought about it, but he could not come up with a reasonable answer.

'Maybe you don't have enough Bluerinics to do it all,' said Spencer.

'Hmm, not a bad thought, but we're constantly expanding our facilities, and are training new Bluerinics to keep up with the demand. Any other ideas?'

'The Bluerinics are not good enough.' This was muttered by Richard, but loud enough for them all to hear. As had been his intention, Will was sure.

'Ah, no, Mr Loxley. We do try to keep their training up to date, you know. I can personally assure you of that.'

Beside Will, Sabrina had raised her hand again.

'Miss Bluetonic?' Mr Worker said.

'I think because you first need to produce the pyramids, and that takes much time and effort,' she said.

'Excellent.' Mr Worker beamed. 'That's exactly the reason. Very good. Let me explain: when, for example, a new mobile phone is out on the market, we first have to obtain one. Then our magicians take it into their labs. There they have to work out the exact structure and composition of the phone, and transcribe it onto a pyramid. Only then can we produce this article. And this simply takes a lot of effort and also much time. That's the reason we can't produce the really modern things.'

After that the lesson was nearly over, and they went back to the school, where they reached the classroom just in time for the break.

Chapter 7

Early in the morning, Will awoke to the dull 'gongs' of the clock signalling it was time to get up. He rubbed his eyes and glanced around blearily. Of course Freddy was already up and bouncing about.

'Get up, everybody, time for breakfast. Boy, am I hungry,' Freddy called brightly, and was off to the bathroom. Will suppressed a sigh and swung his legs out of bed, looking for his slippers. Then he padded after Freddy into the bathroom.

Will was the first to arrive at their breakfast table—after Freddy, of course, who already had a heaped plate in front of him and was chewing noisily through a croissant. The table overflowed with breakfast. There was bacon still sizzling, scrambled eggs, sausages, tomatoes, baked beans, toast, jam, and all the rest. Will dug in, for he was hungry. The others arrived one by one. There was not much talk, because it was early in the morning and they would rather have enjoyed their beds for some time longer. After breakfast they got up.

'What do we have now?' asked Bianca.

'Our first lesson in magic!' replied Spencer.

'Ooooh,' cried Freddy. 'I could hardly wait for this. Just imagine: us, being able to do real magic!'

They were all getting rather excited at the thought.

'Well, let's go then,' said Will. 'Does anyone know the way?'

'Of course,' said Richard, walking past with Michelle in tow. 'I do know my way around here. So if you'd care to follow me, I'll enlighten you.'

He walked onwards without looking back. Michelle looked back and made a face at the others, then hurried after her idol. Freddy was doing a fairly good pantomime of Richard and of the superior air he radiated, and they all had to laugh. They followed Richard and Michelle at a moderate distance. Finally they reached the classroom and settled down inside. They did not have to wait for long before a small lady, clad in a glittering black robe, swept into the classroom and went to the front.

'Good morning, class. My name is Adora Star Dustfall. Please call me Miss Dustfall.'

'Good morning, Miss Dustfall,' Will and the others chorused, more or less in tune and simultaneously.

'It's nice to meet you all. I'm sure you all know I have the pleasure of teaching you the basics of magic.' Her eyes twinkled. 'It's actually the best subject to teach, because everybody is most eager to learn it.' She looked around the classroom: 'I expect you are no different, are you?'

This was met by a few embarrassed grins. Some students nodded eagerly. Will noticed—rather by chance, because he just happened to look that way—that Richard seemed much more interested and eager than Will had ever seen him be in other subjects. Richard had always acted supremely bored and disinterested. But this seemed to fascinate him. Will smirked. This was probably because real magic was one thing his father —who was, according to Richard, the greatest manager ever in the automobile industry—could not do.

'So, first of all, why do we, and especially you, need magic at all?' Miss Dustfall asked them.

'Because it's cool?' exclaimed Freddy.

They all laughed, and Sabrina nudged Freddy in the side with her elbow. 'Ouch, what was that for?' he asked her, looking surprised. Sabrina just rolled her eyes.

'Ah, yes,' said Miss Dustfall, who was also laughing. 'That may be one reason. Would anybody know a second, maybe more practical reason?'

She looked around, but nobody put their hand up or ventured an opinion. Will could not think of any real reason either; he tended to agree with Freddy that it was rather cool being able to do magic.

'Well,' said Miss Dustfall, 'As you all know, the purpose of the White Christmas Organisation is the production and delivery of Christmas presents for Father Christmas. You may also be aware of the fact that Cloudy's Transportation Service is the main means of delivering the presents. But they cannot do it all, and, most important, sometimes presents go to the wrong places. To correct these errors, you must have the equipment and the ability needed to get into the houses unseen, to get through locked doors, closed windows, or smoky chimneys and move the presents around inside. You need to be able to disappear instantly if somebody threatens to discover you. And of course sometimes presents get damaged on their way under the Christmas trees, so you need to have the means to repair them on the spot.

'There are lots of other areas in our business where magic is essential. Just think about Snowfields: it is right in the middle of Britain, but nobody outside the organisation knows about its existence or has ever been here. Even you never knew about it until you got your letters of invitation. Therefore Snowfields must be protected heavily by magic, so nobody can see it from the outside and nobody can accidentally walk in here. And we have to hide it from modern techniques like radar, satellites, or any other detection devices without giving even the slightest hint of any irregularity in this area. This, of course, needs rather strong and complicated magic, and we will not deal with these issues here in your basic training. But if you should decide later on to work in such a specialised field, then you will study these aspects in great detail.

'In this class we will also deal with the basics of the creation of Bluerin and the magic connected with the exploitation of the raw materials needed for it. Of course the transformation of Bluerin into presents also needs magic. Part of this will have overlapping aspects with what Mr Worker is going to teach you. But in my lesson we will deal mainly with the magical aspects, and he will deal mainly with the physical aspects of Bluerin. So that is roughly what we will be doing in this class.' She looked around. 'Any questions so far?'

Nobody seemed to have any at the moment. Or rather nobody knew which question to ask first—they had so many.

Miss Dustfall went on. 'Now then, magic! It is such a legendary word. In Snowfields it is basically the strong and concentrated will for something to happen, used in combination with Bluerin. You need to concentrate, you need the will, and you need the strength—for the stronger and let us call it *bigger* the magic is, the more strength it will take from you. And you need a device to channel the will. For the latter you will need... this!'

She picked up a bag from her desk and started walking through the rows, stopping at each desk to reach into her bag and hand an object to the student there. Will looked at what she handed him: a very plain, wooden stick, roughly twelve inches long, with no decoration or distinctive features at all. That was it really—just an ordinary wooden stick. He felt a bit disappointed, for he had expected something more...well, more grand, more mystical. But this just looked as plain as any stick you would pick up at random in a forest.

From the murmur that was spreading through the class, he gathered that the others were thinking the same. He looked around. Some waved their sticks a bit, with nothing happening; others just put theirs down on the desks in front of them. He saw that Richard was holding his between two fingers and with rather unveiled distaste, as if he were mightily offended by its mere plainness. After everybody had received a stick, Miss Dustfall walked back to the front of the class.

'I know,' she began, 'that stick does not exactly look like a mighty magical instrument, but it is really all you need. Well, nearly all. Because you have to personalise the wand before it can be of any use to you. You have to infuse it with part of your personality, with part of what makes you yourself. After you have done that, the wand is yours. It has become part of you. It has adapted to you, and only you will be able to use it as a wand. After you have done this, there will be a few marks on the wand to reflect what has been instilled into it.'

She reached into her pocket and pulled out her own wand.

'Look at mine for example. You will see some marks on it. You can pass it around for all to see.' She handed the wand to Wesley, who was sitting in front. 'Don't worry, it's not dangerous.'

The wand was passed through the rows. When it reached Will, he took it carefully and looked closely at it. He saw that there was a fine pattern around its lower third. A mostly lavender-coloured band wound intricately around the wood. In it were small, golden stars and some kind of flowers Will did not recognise. Right at the lower end of the wand was a smaller, unadorned black band. About in the middle of the wand was a red band with small, silver bolts of lightning on it. He passed the wand on to Annabel next to him, thinking about what his own would look like, what kind of aspects of his personality he could put into it.

When everybody had had a good look at Miss Dustfall's wand and it was finally handed back to her, a low murmur spread through the class, as everybody wondered what to put into their wands. Some even speculated what the markings on the teacher's wand could mean.

Miss Dustfall clapped her hands twice to get their attention. 'Very well. Now you have all seen what a personal wand can look like. So, as homework, I want you to sit down and think about yourselves! Think about what is special about you, what makes you unique compared to others. This can be attitudes, feelings, even things like flowers, animals, food, or whatever you have got a particular emotional attachment to. Just think carefully about it. Everything you believe is intrinsic to your personality might be useful.

'In two days we will talk about what you have thought of, and then we will infuse your wands with the characteristics you have chosen, thus making the wands unique so you and only you can use them. You will have no other lessons today, tomorrow, or the day after, so you will have enough time to think about this. And please!' She raised her finger high in the air. 'Really use the time for this. It is imperative for the utilisation of your wand that you do this right!'

Then she started handing out small pieces of paper. 'On these you will find the time when you will come to me on the day after tomorrow, and then we will personalise your wands.'

She handed Will a piece of paper, and he looked at it: 9:30 a.m., it read. He was pleased. He could sleep longer and still have the larger part of the day for himself—maybe he could even try out his wand.

'What's your time?' he asked Annabel.

'Two thirty in the afternoon,' she answered, then read his paper. 'I'm not as lucky as you are.'

'Oh, well, you'll have the whole morning off. That's not so bad either.'

'Very well then,' said Miss Dustfall after she had returned to the front of the class. 'You have all got your times, and, I want to stress this once again, please really do think about this carefully! It is in your own interest. It is crucial for the functioning of your wand to get this right. The better it mirrors your personality, the better it will work and the easier it will be for you! I will see you in two days.' With this she ended the lesson.

Will and the others packed their belongings, especially their new wands, and started leaving the classroom. Bianca walked next to Will and Annabel along the corridor.

'Wow,' she said, 'our own wands! Do you have any idea what you're going to put into it?'

'No,' said Annabel. 'I'll really have to think about that. It's not something I've ever really thought about before. I'm not that self-centred.'

Will suddenly laughed.

Annabel and Bianca looked at him curiously. 'What did I say?' asked Annabel.

'Well,' said Will, still laughing, 'Richard should have no problem with that!'

'Why would you think.... Oh,' said Bianca, then she also had to laugh.

'No, definitely not as self-centred as he is,' Bianca agreed. '"What makes you special?" is such an awkward question. I think I'll call my parents and ask them what they think. After all they know me best.'

'Good idea actually, I think I'll call my parents too,' said Will. They reached a smaller hall. 'I'm going to the library to think about this. See you later.'

'Yes, good luck,' Annabel answered. She and Bianca went off in the direction of the common room.

Will went into the library, which was rather empty at that time of the day, and looked for a quiet corner. As he passed by the shelves, he thought surely there had to be books about wands in there. Perhaps they could help him, give him some suggestions that would be useful. He looked in the index, and indeed there were some books on the subject. He went to the shelves and took the three books that looked most promising. Then he sat down by a window and started to thumb through the pages.

There was something: 'Personalizing the Wand' was the heading of one chapter. He started to read. 'Most important when personalizing the wand is to extract a most accurate impression of the personality and infuse this into the wand. Such it is warranted that the wand works with its most efficiency, providing the maximum of output with the least input.' Will turned the page and was dismayed. That was it. On the next page was a new chapter dealing with other aspects of wands. That had not been helpful at all. He looked through the other books, but there was nothing more specific in either of them. Only variants on what he had just read in the first book and what Miss Dustfall had told them.

He sighed and put the books away. Instead he took out a piece of paper and tried to make a list of attributes he could think of that might be useful. He noted down some that seemed to describe him. After he had tried for about two hours, he started to get hungry. He looked at the clock on the wall of the library: lunchtime. He looked back at his list. There were several characteristics he thought were special for him. But it was still a rather short list—too short, he felt. There had to be more to him than this! He gave another sigh and packed up his things. Best to get some lunch and then try again. He left the library and went towards the Ferum, towards lunch.

***

The day of decision arrived. Will sat at the breakfast table still thinking about what he should choose to go into his wand. The other students were also quite preoccupied, and there was not much talking during breakfast, except that occasionally someone would ask someone else whether this or that would be a good characteristic to put into the wand.

Will noted Richard was indeed the most relaxed of them all. He sat leisurely at breakfast—of course as far away from the others as possible—and idly chatted with Michelle, who on the other hand looked as tense and preoccupied as the rest of them. Her answers appeared to be rather monosyllabic. Richard seemed to be having no problems defining his personality. Will decided he could think of a long list of characteristics which made up Richard's personality and distinguished him from the others. He had to grin. They were probably a bit different from the ones Richard was thinking about, as Will thought mainly of things like selfishness, ruthlessness, and rudeness, just to mention a few.

Finally breakfast was over, and Will decided to get some fresh air before he had to meet Miss Dustfall. He went through the entrance hall and to the back of the school. There he went out onto the lawn and farther into the gardens. He strolled along the well-kept gravel pathways between the lush, green plants. He was still thinking about things that seemed to be part of his personality and that distinguished him from others, but he was not able to pin down specific, single characteristics.

'This is useless,' he said aloud, though there was nobody around to hear him. 'I can't just point out three details or so and that's it, that's what makes me special. It's the combination of lots of different small facets that make the whole of me! This is rubbish.' He continued along the path. 'That's what I'll tell Miss Dustfall!' He decided to return to the school building. On his way back he ran into Annabel.

'Hi, Annabel, how are you doing?'

'Not good,' she replied, shaking her head. 'I can't think of just a few catchwords that make up my personality.' She looked at him interestedly. 'How about you?'

Will snorted. 'I couldn't either. But I decided I can't just squeeze my personality into a few distinctive features and that's it. I'm more than that. That's what I'm going to tell her, and then I'll see what she says.'

'Hmm, I guess you could try that. I'll still think about it a bit. Good luck.' She quickly looked around and then, to Will's surprise, took his hand and squeezed it. Then she quickly brushed past him and was gone. Will looked at his hand, shook his head, and started back towards the school. He looked at the large clock on the wall and saw it was time to go to the classroom. When he got there, he sat down outside, as there was still someone in there before him. After five minutes the door opened and Spencer came out. He looked slightly be-mused, and carried his wand in front of him, looking at it intently.

'Spencer!' Will called, and got up.

'Oh, hi Will,' Spencer replied, finally looking up from his wand.

'How was it?' Will asked.

'Oh, great. It was really rather easy. Look.' He held up his wand for Will to see.

Will looked closely at it. Near the end was a green band with a smaller yellow band woven around it. Farther up the wand was another yellow band with tiny blue spots.

'It looks great,' Will said slightly dubiously, for he had no idea about the meaning of the bands.

'Yes, I think it's beautiful. And it's definitely me!' He looked at Will. 'Good luck to you. It's really not so bad.' And he walked away, still admiring his wand.

Will faced the open door, took a deep breath, and went inside.

The classroom was rather darker than during the previous lesson because there were thin shades in front of the windows. The desks and chairs had been moved to the sides, and in the middle of the room was a table with a velvet cloth and two comfortable chairs. On the table were several candles, filling the area around them with a sphere of warm, subdued light. Miss Dustfall was just placing two teacups on the table.

She turned round when she heard Will's approach. 'Good morning, Will. Welcome. I hope you are well this morning.' She smiled.

'Yes, thank you. I'm a bit nervous, though,' Will replied.

She nodded. 'There's no need for that, you'll see. Please, sit down.'

She put a teapot on the table. 'Would you like some tea?'

'Oh, yes, please.'

Miss Dustfall poured a cup of tea and placed it in front of Will.

'There you are.' She smiled. 'Shall we begin?'

Will nodded.

'Then please take out your wand-to-be and place it on the table right between us.'

Will reached into his pocket and pulled out the wand-to-be, which was just a wooden stick so far, and placed it on the table, right in the middle.

'Right then.' Miss Dustfall looked gravely at Will. 'Have you thought about your personality and what makes it unique?'

'Well, yes, I did. But I wasn't able to come up with just a few catchwords that describe my personality and distinguish me from all the others.'

As Miss Dustfall did not protest immediately, he hurried to get the rest out before she could stop and reprimand him. 'I believe it's a combination of lots of different small facets that make the whole of me, that form my personality and make it actually distinguishable from others.'

Will stopped, fearing he would surely be told off now for being defiant. But Miss Dustfall just smiled.

'Very good, Will,' she said. 'Really excellent. That was exactly what I wanted you to think about. Only very few students reach this conclusion on their own—and you did! Excellent indeed.'

Will was stunned. This was not at all what he had expected. He had been sure she would tell him off. Instead she praised him. Most amazing.

'The secret of personalizing a wand is to infuse it with your personality. Not with a few parts of it—as you have so brilliantly realised yourself—but with all of your personality.'

Will thought about this. 'But then the task you set us was totally useless, wasn't it?' he asked, feeling a bit wound up.

Miss Dustfall laughed. 'Oh no, not at all. You needed to think about your personality rather thoroughly so you conceive it completely. That's what the task I set you was for. Only when you have thought about your personality in all its depth and about what distinguishes you from all the others can you personalise your wand and get the most power out of it.'

She sat up straight. 'Now, let's get on with it.'

Will inched forwards on his chair and focussed his concentration on Miss Dustfall.

'No need to worry,' she said. 'You don't have to do much, and it will be easy. I'll do the transfer. You only need to relax and concentrate on your personality, on what you have thought about the last two days, what makes you special. Now then, Will, the tea I gave you will help you to relax and to focus.'

Before he could protest, she held up her hand. 'Don't worry,' she said quickly, 'it's nothing illegal or harmful.' She smiled. 'Now you just have to concentrate. Concentrate on yourself, on your being—your essence. That's all you have to do. I'll do the rest. I'll transform your awareness, your perception of yourself into your wand. I'll use my wand to achieve this. You may feel a light tingling and a slight warmth. Don't be afraid.'

'Okay, I'm ready—I think,' said Will, taking a deep breath.

'Good.' Miss Dustfall smiled. 'Just close your eyes and relax. Raise your hand when you feel ready.'

Will nodded and closed his eyes, trying to breathe slowly and evenly. He tried to concentrate on himself, on his core. He gathered his innermost feelings, his ambitions, his fears, his dreams. He thought about his being, his inner self. Then suddenly it all became one! It was a clear, distinctive, and complete picture of himself. He raised his hand, feeling...well, just himself, actually. Indeed, more himself than he had ever felt before.

'I'll start the transfer now,' said Miss Dustfall softly.

Will was still completely relaxed. He did not feel afraid, not even nervous, not anymore. At first he felt nothing at all. Then, slowly, a very faint tingling sensation started up his arms. It reached his chest and washed over the rest of his body. This was followed by a slight warmth. It was not unpleasant; rather it emphasised his current relaxed mood. Then the feeling faded away slowly.

'Open your eyes.' Miss Dustfall's voice seemed far away, and Will slowly rose to the surface of reality again and opened his eyes. He blinked.

Miss Dustfall was smiling at him. 'We've finished. It went very well. You've done very well!'

Will looked down at the table, at his wand.

'Go on, pick it up,' Miss Dustfall urged him.

Will reached for the wand and picked it up. He looked closely at it. It was beautiful. It looked exactly like he had felt. There was a small, blue and silver band right near the top, then a light-red band spiralling from the middle to near the end. There were little, golden stars in the red band, and a thin, green band was woven around it. Near the end were four short, blue lines, each with a star at the top, and they were connected by a golden garland. He had no idea what these markings meant, but altogether it felt like him.

Miss Dustfall smiled at him. 'Good, Will. Tomorrow in my lesson I'll begin teaching you how to use it. Goodbye.'

'Goodbye,' replied Will. 'And thank you very much.'

She smiled again. 'My pleasure.'

Will left the classroom and went back to the common room, where he met the others who already had their wands. They spent the rest of the day comparing their wands and admiring them.

On the next morning, right after breakfast, Will hurried back into the classroom. The desks and chairs were back where they had been before. This time he was really excited, for this was not another boring lesson with Dr. Parchmentinus, who would read endlessly from some manual in his stodgy way that could put Will to sleep in minutes. This was it! Finally! His first lesson in which he would learn how to do magic. The first lesson in which he would use the wand he had received the previous day.

Admittedly, he had tried to use it right after he had got it, as soon as he had found a quiet corner where he would be undisturbed. He had tried to wave it around in an impressive and mystical way. He had tried saying spells like 'hocus pocus' and impressive Latin words, but nothing had happened. He had to admit that all he had been doing was standing in a dark corner, waving around a wooden stick, and overall looking rather stupid. He had been a bit relieved when he had caught several of his classmates all over the school waving around their wands, also to no effect, and also looking rather stupid.

But today they would be told how to do it. And Will was not the only one who was so excited. All around him his classmates buzzed; Freddy was easily the worst of them by far. Will looked over to Freddy when he heard his excited babbling and saw he was so excited his red face actually seemed to be glowing. He looked like a bonfire, and a rather nervous one at that. Will grinned. He reached into his bag, took out his wand, and placed it carefully on his desk in front of him. The door opened, and Miss Dustfall walked gracefully into the classroom. The noise died down.

'Good morning.' She smiled at them. 'I know you are all excited about this. Today will be your introductory lesson in the use of your personal wands.'

Will saw excited smiles all around, and smiled broadly himself.

'I am sure none of you have tried your wand yet.' Miss Dustfall raised her eyebrows and looked around the class. As soon as her gaze fell on one of them, they looked away rather embarrassed. Will was rather surprised to see that even Sabrina looked away.

The stern expression melted away from Miss Dustfall's face, and she smiled. 'No need to worry. I am positive you have all tried and...nothing happened. Nothing at all, no brilliant sparks shooting out of the wands, no princes or treasure chests appearing? No? Of course I know all this. Hard as it may be to believe, even I was young once, and I was a student at this school. And right after I received my wand, I immediately tried doing magic, feeling like a witch. But of course nothing happened. I was so disappointed.'

They all laughed. Everybody was listening intently to what Miss Dustfall was saying.

She continued: 'First of all you have to remember why you have been given wands. We do not intend to turn you into wizards and witches who run free in the world to spell all and everything. You are going to work for the White Christmas Organisation. You are going to help in the production and distribution of presents. That is where you are supposed to use your wands, where you are to do magic. I am sure a few of you will even have tried some magic that would be related to these uses, but still nothing happened. There is a simple reason for this: the wands have to be charged before they can be used. And how do you charge them? Any ideas?'

She looked around the classroom, and Will was surprised that even Sabrina could not offer an answer.

'With Bluerin, of course,' Miss Dustfall provided the answer herself. 'The wands need to be charged with Bluerin to work. But this is not all. Apart from that you will have to learn spells and the corresponding gestures with the wands to do any magic.' She smiled a bit apologetically. 'I am sorry, but there is a lot of learning and hard work waiting for you before you can wield magic proficiently.' There were a few groans throughout the class, the loudest coming, of course, from Freddy.

'I said the wands have to be charged with Bluerin to work, so how is that done? We have got special containers here in Snowfields that hold Bluerin, at which you can charge your wands. Yes, Fredorgius, you have a question?' she said to Freddy, who was waving his hand enthusiastically in the air.

'Yes, Miss. Where are these containers?' he asked.

Miss Dustfall laughed. 'Now don't get your hopes up too high! Although the containers are spread throughout Snow-fields, they are well-guarded to prevent any theft or misuse. There's no way you will just walk out of here at the end of the lesson, find the nearest container, fill up your wand with Bluerin, and start waving it around.'

There were quite a few disappointed faces throughout the class, and Will even heard a quiet, disappointed 'oh' from Freddy. He had to admit he was also quite disappointed as he learned how complicated this was going to be. This was not at all the easy, waving-your-wand-around-and-conjuring-up-wonder-after-wonder he had imagined when he was told he would get a wand to do magic. This sounded like a compli-cated, technical procedure they would only be able to apply under close supervision. That did not sound very promising. Almost absently, Will noticed that Richard, for one, looked rather annoyed by this and leaned over to Michelle, whispering a comment to her. Michelle seemed to be similarly annoyed, and responded with a grim nod.

Then Miss Dustfall went on: 'Well then, let's get right into it. Please take out your wands and lay them on the tables right in front of you.'

There was a rush and a clutter all around Will, and then everybody had their wands lying in front of them.

'I want you to pick up your wands and hold them in your right hands—if you are left-handed then please use your left hand. Ready? Now then, please pay close attention to what I am going to show you. We will start with the first basic move-ments. Every complicated spell is made up of basic movements arranged in complicated patterns. Watch!'

She picked up her wand, which looked rather old and used now that they compared it to their shiny new ones, from the desk beside her. She held it up for them all to see and lowered it again. Then she moved the wand round in a perfect circle in front of her.

'Now, that did not look too complicated, did it?' She received a few low calls of 'no' from the class.

'I am sure you all believe I just waved around the wand in a simple circle.'

Some of the class, including Will, were nodding.

'But,' Miss Dustfall continued, 'what you have seen is far from easy or simple. Let me explain. First of all the circle has to be perfectly round. Secondly it has to have depth, meaning it is formed a bit like a cone, a wider circle at the far end of the wand and a smaller circle at the near end. And finally it has to be a complete circle, with the starting and ending points in the same place. When you do not draw it far enough, you will not get a complete circle. When you draw it too far, you overreach and already begin with the next element.

'Now, why all this detail? Why make it so complicated? It might not seem to matter much when, for example, you overreach when drawing the circle. But imagine you are performing a complicated spell where the circle is followed by another element. Then, by overreaching, you would already start an element you do not need, and when you then start on the correct element the circle will not be connected in the correct way, and the spell will not work. Do you understand?'

She looked around the classroom, mainly into questioning faces. 'Well, I admit that sounded rather complicated. In short: just learn it correctly right from the beginning, then you will not have problems later on. And, just to motivate you even more, always remember that most of you will already need these skills next Christmas, when your task will be to help with the delivery of the presents.'

This sounded great to Will, and he vowed to himself that he would be really diligent in his studies for this subject.

'Now then,' Miss Dustfall continued, 'let's get down to work. I will demonstrate it once more and then you will try it. Do not worry if you make mistakes or do not get it right in the beginning, for your wands are not loaded with Bluerin yet, so no harm will be done. Only if you wave your wands around too wildly you might rap somebody over the head or stab each other in the eyes.'

She lifted her wand again so they could all see it, and slowly drew a perfect circle in the air in front of her, wide on the far end and tighter on the near end, forming a perfect cone.

'Now it is your turn,' she said. 'First we will do it together. Hold your wands in front of you and make sure there is enough room on your right and left sides so you do not interfere with your neighbours. Everybody ready? On the count of three: one...two...three!'

Will held his wand in front of him, and as Miss Dustfall said 'three', he tried to imitate the perfect circle she had drawn in the air. And then he had to admit she was right—it looked and sounded quite easy, but was actually quite hard when he tried it. He realised his attempt was rather like some sort of ellipsoid than a smooth, round circle, and the starting and ending points did not meet at all.

Miss Dustfall looked around the class at the students' rather feeble tries. 'I think you now see it is not so easy at all, and a lot of practising and training is required before you can achieve anything with your wands. But do not worry, I will help and train you. It is really a bit like dancing: first you have to know the moves and then it is practise, practise, practise. Some of you have a talent for it and will learn easier and faster, and some have not. But at the end of this term, every one of you will at least be able to perform the basic spells. And there are some tricks to make it easier. I will show you the first one right now: Yellowrin! Anyone heard of it before?'

Nobody in the class raised their hand, and a few, including Will, shook their heads silently.

'It is a very useful substance. We can use it to charge the wands, just like with Bluerin, and when you wave the wand Yellowrin will leave a trace in the air so you can follow the path of your wand and see the figure you have created. Then we can analyse the pathway and see what is good and what can be improved. The advantage of Yellowrin is it just marks the pathway and does nothing else—no magic will be done and nothing can go wrong.'

She went over to the side of the classroom, where something covered by a grey cloth stood against the wall. Will had noticed it right away when he had entered the classroom, but had not thought much about it. Miss Dustfall removed the cover, and Will could see a small box made out of glass with a bright-yellow substance inside. On the front of the box and pointing towards the desks was some sort of device that looked a bit like a round window.

Miss Dustfall pointed at the box. 'This is the kind of box I told you about earlier in the lesson, in which Bluerin can be stored to charge wands. But instead of Bluerin, Yellowrin is stored in here. You can charge your wands with it, and we can continue practising, but then we can track the exact pathways of your wands. Charging your wands is really quite simple: all you have got to do is insert your wands tip first into the charging device on the front of the box and wait a moment. The wands will be charged automatically. You do not have to worry about anything. There is nothing that can go wrong. The device is designed with valves so it cannot leak, and you cannot overcharge your wands. The only thing you have to be careful of is that you do not remove your wands too quickly. Then they will not be charged fully. Watch closely!'

And she took her wand and demonstrated the process.

'When you look closely at the thicker end of your wand, where you are holding it, you will see something that looks like a small, dark window.'

'On your wands this area will be dark,' Miss Dustfall went on to explain. 'When you look here at my wand, you will see that this area is bright yellow.' She pointed at her own wand.

'That is an indicator that shows the level of charge in your wand. As my wand is currently fully charged with Yellowrin, the indicator is yellow. When the wand is charged with Bluerin, then it will turn blue. Now I will show you the use of Yellowrin. Please watch closely.'

She lifted her wand, and again she slowly drew the circle figure that was really more like a cone. Only this time, when she started to move her wand through the air, Yellowrin came out of the tip, leaving a small trail of yellow that marked the pathway of the wand. When she finished the circle, a fine, yellow, perfectly round circle glittered brightly in front of her. She lowered her wand.

'You see? It will be visible for a minute our two, then it will fade away. Now, I want you all to try the circle figure again, but this time with Yellowrin. So please charge your wands. Orderly and row by row, please.'

She stood next to the Yellowrin tank and helped them charge their wands. Will waited for his turn and then followed Annabel eagerly to the tank. There he carefully put his wand tip-first into the device on the front. He could see the indicator on his wand turn yellow as it quickly filled up. Then the whole oblong of the indicator window was completely yellow, and after a nod from Miss Dustfall he pulled out his wand and returned to his seat. After everyone had finished charging their wands, Miss Dustfall went back to the front of the classroom and held up hers again.

'Now we will repeat the circle, but this time your wand will leave a trace of Yellowrin in the air, so you will be able to see what you are doing and we can then look for improvements. On three: one...two...three.'

Will again draw a circle in the air and watched in amazement as a trace of Yellowrin appeared. After he had finished the circle he could not resist the urge to touch the Yellowrin hanging right in front of him. His finger passed right through the fine yellow line without any resistance. He could not feel a thing as he moved his finger several times back and forth through it. The line was not even smeared, but just glittered undisturbed in the air.

Then he looked at the circle itself and had to admit it was far from perfect: it was rather wobbly, it was not round at all, and at one point there was even a right dogleg in it. It bore no comparison to Miss Dustfall's example. Will looked around the classroom at the circles his classmates had drawn. Then he felt better—much better—for he saw lots of misshapen figures. Only Sabrina had, of course, done exceedingly well, and a perfectly round yellow circle was hanging in the air in front of her.

Miss Dustfall wandered through the rows, looking critically at the odd circles shimmering in front of the students. Here and there she merely nodded, but more often she pointed out mistakes. As she reached Sabrina she nodded, smiled at her, and said, 'Well done! That is what it should look like. Good.'

Then she looked at Will's result, while he stood sheepishly behind it. Of course she pointed out the prominent dogleg, but Will did not get the impression that he had failed totally. And, when he looked around the classroom again, he had to admit his result seemed to be one of the better ones. By then the Yellowrin was beginning to fade away, and Miss Dustfall was back beside her desk in front of the class.

'I quite like what I have seen so far. You did well for the first try. As you can see, the Yellowrin will fade away quickly. It will disappear completely and leave no residue. Let us try once more.'

And they drew another set of yellow circles in the air.

'You can judge your performances yourselves: just see if the circle is evenly round, and that the starting and ending points match, without any gap in between.' Miss Dustfall glanced at the clock on the wall of the classroom. 'As homework you can practise the circle on your own. When you run out of Yellowrin, try drawing the circle without it, for that is the goal. Then recharge the wand with Yellowrin and check again to see how much progress you have made and how much of a feeling you have developed for drawing the circle. You can recharge your wands as often as you like—there is a tank in the entrance hall that is always full. That is all for now. I will see you tomorrow.'

Right on cue the clock marked the end of the lesson. Will and the others reluctantly put away their wands, stood up, and left the classroom.

After that Will sat through another boring hour of Letters to Father Christmas, in which he mostly thought about the thrilling first experience with his Yellowrin-charged wand. He decided to practise in the afternoon, for this was something really exciting and something he definitely would not learn at an ordinary school. He could not help feeling elated again. He would become a real wizard, conjuring up real magic—something he had only read about in fairy tales or fantasy books.

After he had survived Mr Parchmentinus' lecture, Will went to the Ferum for lunch. He got himself some meat, gravy, potatoes, and vegetables and carried his tray over to his customary table, which was deserted so far. But he was soon joined by Sabrina and Wendy.

Sabrina put down her tray next to Will's. 'That was a great lesson, wasn't it?'

Will looked at her most seriously and replied, ripping off quite a good imitation of Mr Parchmentinus' dry and wheezy droning, 'Yhes, hindeed, my good ghirl, Lehtters to Fahther Christmas was absolutely fhas-cih-nah-tin.'

Sabrina made a face and punched him in the ribs—hard.

'Ouch!'

'You deserved that, you git!' she told him. 'You know very well I meant Miss Dustfall's lesson.'

Wendy was laughing hard.

'Oh, did you?' said Will innocently. Then, as he saw that Sabrina was striking out again, added quickly, 'Okay, okay. Yes, of course, it was really great. After all that's what we came here for, to learn about such things as magic and spells, and not to have some manual read to us.'

They started to eat. Sabrina had the same as Will. After a few bites he looked at Wendy's plate. She was rather listlessly poking her fork into the homogeneously brown mass on it.

'Just what are you eating there?' he asked her.

She looked up unhappily. 'I thought I'd give the vegetarian menu a try. Supposedly it's carrots and tofu, but nobody told me it was mash like this.'

'It looks really revolting,' Sabrina said.

Wendy nodded sadly. 'And it doesn't taste any better.'

She took a few more hesitant bites, then she suddenly put down her fork.

'Why don't you get something else?' asked Will.

'No, that's it for me. I'm not hungry anymore. I'll go over and see what's for dessert.' She returned shortly after with a huge bowl of chocolate pudding, looking far happier than before.

Will looked at Sabrina meaningfully, 'Ah, yes, not hungry anymore.'

She nodded and said, 'No, of course not! For girls chocolate pudding has nothing to do with hunger. It's one of the bare basics of survival. Just like lip gloss.'

Wendy smiled sheepishly. Will looked back and forth between them both, and finally shook his head.

'Girls...' he muttered under his breath.

Sabrina and Wendy laughed, and Wendy attacked her pudding much more vigorously than she had her lunch. Will thought again about his wand and the Yellowrin.

'Look,' he said after a while, 'we don't have any lessons this afternoon, so I thought I'd practise some more with the wand and the Yellowrin. Would you like to join me? I think it'll be more fun if we do this together, and we could correct each other's mistakes. What do you think?'

Sabrina nodded. 'I'd thought about practising too, and you're right, it would be more fun doing it together. How about you?' She looked over at Wendy, who by then was halfway through her enormous pudding.

Wendy made a face. 'I'd love to join you, but unfortunately I've got choir practise right after lunch.'

Will had by now cleared his plate and stood up to get himself some chocolate pudding.

'Shall I bring you some, too?' he asked Sabrina. She looked up, surprised.

'Why, yes please.'

Will went over to the cooks and fetched two helpings.

'Thank you,' Sabrina said as he put hers down in front of her.

They both dug in greedily.

'Mmm, that's delicious,' moaned Sabrina.

Will had to agree. Desserts were always the best part of lunch there—even more so than at home. Finally they finished and agreed to meet up later in the common room, when Wendy was through with choir practise.

Will got up, left the Ferum, and went to the library. He found himself a quiet table out of the way where he could sit on his own, and gathered the books he would need to write a paper for Mr Worker. Then he got down to work. At a quarter past two, he had finally finished. He thought a moment, then decided to head back to his room. He returned the books and stepped out of the library into the corridor outside. As he walked along it, he passed a rarely-used side passage that was rather darker than the main corridors. He glanced down it briefly. Then he suddenly stopped. He had seen something glimmer yellow down there. He took a step backwards so he could have a proper look. Then he had to grin broadly at what saw at the far end: Freddy in deep concentration, waving his wand around, drawing wobbly circles of Yellowrin in the air.

Will laughed quietly as he went on towards their common room. Sabrina, Wendy, and he were certainly not the only ones who were eager to train with their wands. Shaking his head he went on his way. When he arrived in the common room it was empty. Will looked at the large clock standing on an ornamental table next to the wall. It was just after half past two, so there still was time. He looked at the clock more closely. It was really wonderful—he always enjoyed looking at it. The face was white with scarlet numbers, and the hands were golden with a thin layer of glistening, artificial snow covering part of them. Below the clock face was a beautiful and very detailed landscape. The face rested on a white mountaintop. At its foot was snow-covered countryside and small cottages with tiny windows from which soft, golden light illuminated the whole scene. There was a lane running from behind the mountain range, past the cottages all the way through the countryside and disappearing again behind the mountain range on the other side.

At every half and every full hour, accompanied by the chiming of a silvery bell, a small sleigh drawn by four very detailed reindeer came forwards from behind the mountain range, glided slowly along the lane, and disappeared again behind the mountains. On the sleigh was a jolly Father Christmas with all the presents—brightly-wrapped parcels in red, green, and blue—piled high in the back of the sleigh. And, as Will had discovered when he had tried to touch it, the clock was protected by a spell that prevented anyone from coming close to it. But he immensely enjoyed watching it.

He finally turned away and sat down in one of the comfortable chairs that were scattered throughout the room, and waited for the girls. He did not have to wait for long, because almost as soon as he had settled down, Sabrina came bounding down the stairs from the girls' bedroom, and nearly simultaneously Wendy walked in from the corridor.

'Wow, that's timing,' said Will in greeting. Sabrina and Wendy grinned at each other.

'You'll never guess what I've seen,' continued Will. 'When I left the library, I glanced down the corridor to the side—you know, the small one, the one that doesn't really lead anywhere —and I saw Freddy there, rather far down into it, and guess what?' He looked at the two girls rather dramatically. 'He was practising with his wand!'

'Oh, yes,' replied Sabrina, 'when I walked back here, I also saw a couple of students from our class practising.'

133

'Oh,' replied Will.

Wendy nodded. 'I saw some too. On the way here, I took a shortcut that's hardly used by anybody, and I accidentally came across Richard and Michelle as they were trying out their wands down there.' She grinned. 'They were quite annoyed about that.'

Will laughed. 'I'm sure they were.'

Sabrina laughed as well. Then she asked, 'So, where do we go then?'

'I thought we could go over to the closed-off inner courtyard near the classroom where we have choir,' said Wendy. 'It's not used in the afternoon, and it's well out of the way and secluded, so I don't think anyone will disturb us there.'

Sabrina nodded. 'That's a good idea.'

Will jumped up from the seat. 'Let's go then. Do you have your wands?'

When he went past the sideboard, he picked up a bottle of juice and took it with him.

Sabrina looked at him quizzically.

'If we stay there long, we might get thirsty,' he told her.

'Good thinking,' she replied.

And the three of them left their common room and headed towards the courtyard.

***

That evening, when they were having supper in the Ferum, Freddy suddenly asked Richard, 'Why is it you're always so disgruntled? Don't you like it here?' Only Freddy could be so straightforward and innocent to ask Richard this direct if rather obvious question.

Will looked up. That was a question he had been asking himself too. Richard turned to look at Freddy. Will thought he could see a slight flicker of emotion on his face, as if he were startled by Freddy's direct question.

'I don't think that's any of your business,' he finally told Freddy.

'Well, but I do. After all, we are all here together.'

'Yes, most unfortunately,' Richard replied.

'Well?' Freddy was not one for backing down.

'Okay, okay,' Richard said, sounding rather annoyed. 'If you really have to know: my father is a top manager for a large motorcar company. He knows what real management and efficient production have to look like. I've always looked closely at his work and tried to learn all I could from him. And I can tell you for sure, if he were in charge here, everybody would be dancing to a quite different tune. No more of this oh-so-merry, bloody Christmas rubbish, but taut guidance and efficient production—that would be the focus. He would show them. I will show them!'

By then he was quite red in the face, and he was nearly screaming. Will and the others stared at him. He looked back, nodded curtly as if satisfied with himself, got up, and left the room. The others stared after him, quite stunned. Only Michelle moved and hurried after Richard.

Chapter 8

Finally the day's lesson in accounting was over. It had seemed to last forever. Mr Ancy had bored them all with his tedious explanations of double-entry bookkeeping, lingering endlessly on how each entry in one account had to be matched by an entry in its according account. He went on and on about how everything had to be double-checked so all accounts were balanced. They then had toiled on the exercise he had set them, which had not been too bad, but they had spent ages looking for the mistake, as the accounts naturally were not balanced in the end. And, to 'keep their spirits up', Mr Ancy had given them homework: a long list of items they had to enter and balance in one week's time.

That would take ages, Will thought gloomily as he walked back to his room. He had best get a start on it right away, as he would surely have to trace some mistakes when balancing the accounts.

Will took a shortcut he had found only recently—a rarely-used corridor that was sparsely lit, matching his gloomy thoughts about accountancy. He was speculating about whether he could get Sabrina to help him a bit. Sabrina seemed to be born for accounting, as she matched the accounts with ease and they always balanced out perfectly. Suddenly he stumbled over a loose tile and fell hard against the wall. He swore under his breath and fingered his arm, where he could already feel a lump. Then he looked down. He saw the loose tile, but his eyes were immediately drawn to something else. He peered closely. In the joint between the tiles, right at the skirting board and partly under it, he saw a faint, blue glint that seemed vaguely familiar—it was a shade he would never forget. It was Bluerin.

He squatted down, tugged at the edge that protruded from under the skirting board, and pulled it out: a small, thin, and rectangular piece of paper. He gaped at it. It looked like a twenty-pound banknote. Well, at least nearly like one, for there was the faint, blue glimmer, and the outlines of the printings were blurred. But he could see well enough that it was meant to be a banknote.

He held it in his hand and wondered what to do. He could stick it back where he had found it. But he could also take it with him. Probably he should show it to somebody—but to whom? Sabrina? Well, what could she do about it? She would only tell him to get rid of it, to hand it over to a teacher immediately.

Suddenly he heard a noise. Someone else was coming down the corridor. He quickly pushed the note deep into his pocket.

'Will.' The voice held suppressed contempt.

Will groaned inwardly. 'Ah, hello Richard.'

The other student stopped. 'Everything all right, Will? You look a bit flustered.'

Will was hoping fervently that Richard had not seen what he had been doing. He smiled nervously. 'No... Yes! Sorry. I just stumbled on this loose tile here and kind of hit my head.'

'Oh, nothing serious I hope,' Richard said in false sympathy.

'No... No, just a bruise, really. I'm fine.'

'Okay, if you say so.' Richard looked at him suspiciously.

'Well, I'll just go on to my room and have a break. Bye, Richard.' Will hurried away. He felt Richard's stare boring into his back right until he turned the next corner.

'Stupid! So stupid,' Will reprimanded himself. 'You couldn't have acted more suspiciously than that.' And why did it have to be Richard who caught him there?

He hastened back to his room. When he got there, he was still angry with himself. He then remembered his other problem: where should he hide the note? He gazed around the common room. Then he heard voices from the corridor. Searching desperately, he saw the rug at his feet, quickly lifted the corner of it, and shoved the note underneath.

The door opened just as Will straightened up. 'Hi, Will, what are you doing here?' It was Freddy, followed by Wendy. 'Oh, hi, Freddy, Wendy,' Will floundered. 'I, er, I was just going to...to look at the timetable, you know, to see...what lessons we've got tomorrow.' He started to move over to the wall where the timetable was hanging.

'Oh, good idea. Let's have a look.' Freddy went over to the timetable too. Will saw out of the corner of his eye that Wendy was looking at the floor, at the rug, as if she had seen him hiding the note. Sweat started to form on his forehead.

'You know,' said Wendy, still eyeing the rug, 'I really like this carpet. It has nice colours.'

Will sagged visibly and sighed, feeling highly relieved. 'Yes, I think it's really nice, too.'

'Hmm, first lesson tomorrow is Handling of Letters to Father Christmas. Great! I could just continue sleeping through that one.' Freddy was looking at the timetable and had not taken any notice of the exchange between Wendy and Will—but then he often did not take much notice of what was happening around him.

'Yeah, right,' replied Will. 'Well, I guess I'll take a shower before dinner. See you there.'

'Yeah, see you,' said Freddy.

Will nodded to him and Wendy and went towards the boys' bathroom. Inside he went over to the shelf where all the shower gels where stacked. When Will had gone into the bathroom the first time on the day of his arrival, he had been positively amazed. It was easily the grandest bathroom he had ever seen. The walls and floor were white marble, and there were separate niches with sunken bathtubs and shower stalls. The taps were covered in gold. There were shelves filled with fluffy towels, endless bottles of shower gel, soap in different colours and scents, bubble bars, and bath pearls for the tubs. He selected a bottle of one of his favourite shower gels—rather sweet and pink, so he would only use it when nobody else was around—then undressed and went into a shower stall.

As the warm water poured over him, he started to relax and could think more clearly about the latest events. He had certainly found something serious. Something made out of Bluerin, out of that strictly-guarded and highly-secured basic material, and then something that looked like a banknote? That could only mean forgery! He turned the tap so that more hot water flowed over him, and savoured the feeling. He wondered who in Snowfields would commit something as unthinkable as forgery—and using Bluerin to carry it out! Well, he thought, Richard was someone he could easily imagine doing the unbelievable, like selling his grandma for a pound.

Will enjoyed the sweet smell of the gel as he applied it liberally. But Richard could not have done something like that alone, now could he? How could he even have got access to the Bluerin? Let alone being able to create something like pound notes. Especially after Will had seen him floundering around when they were practising how to form simple square blocks out of it during production lessons. No, he must have had help. Like from the goblins working in production, or maybe a Bluerinic, or, Will realised with a jolt, perhaps even a teacher.

He needed to tell someone, that was certain. But whom? When even a teacher could be involved? The only possible person he could tell was Beltorec. He would go and see him the next day, right after lessons.

***

'I'm sorry to disturb you, sir, but this young man is most persistent—says he needs to see you immediately. He says it has something to do with problems among the students, but he won't be any more specific.' She shot Will a dark look. 'But he really insists, sir.'

'That's all right, Mrs Script. I appreciate the effort.' The vice chancellor waved for Will to come into his office and to take the chair in front of his desk. Will sat down.

'Want anything, Will? Tea? Lemonade? Water? Hmm?'

'No, no... Thank you, sir,' Will said. He looked at Mrs Script.

'Thank you, that will be all for the moment, Mrs Script.' The vice chancellor looked at her pointedly. She shot Will another glance, turned on her heel, and marched out.

'You know, you really made her cross there.' The vice chancellor chuckled. 'Like every secretary in the world, our dear Mrs Script can't stand the thought that something is going on she doesn't know about. I'd step around her for a while if you don't want her nagging all the time,' he said with a wink. 'Now then.' He looked closely at Will. 'What do you have to tell me so urgently?'

'Well, sir, two days ago I found this in a corridor.'

He pulled out the blue banknote and laid it on the desk. The vice chancellor gravely looked down at it. Then he picked it up, turned it round, felt the paper, and put it down on the table again, right between the two of them. He looked up at Will.

'Well, it looks like a banknote, but a forged one. Where did you get this?'

'I found it in a rarely-used corridor, a shortcut in the eastern wing I use to get to the lessons there. I think the colour looks very much like Bluerin. Could it be that someone is using Bluerin to forge money?'

The vice chancellor turned it round in his hands again. 'Hmm.' He stroked his beard. 'Look, Will, there are tales about a student of Snowfields a long, long time ago. He was said to have been experimenting, trying to turn Bluerin into gold coins. But he was caught and strictly banned from any contact with Bluerin. It seemed he never succeeded. However, years after he left school, a few strange gold coins turned up that were minted rather poorly, and some said they had a faint, blue sheen. I saw one once, and I think they were right—the coinage is poor, and the gold looks oddly bluish instead of the more reddish hue you'd expect with real gold.'

He sighed. 'It was never ascertained or even seriously pursued whether these were fake coins, whether they were made of Bluerin, or if this student had anything to do with it.... There were more important issues during that time. Nevertheless this student became rather influential and quite rich at that specific time. Not many people nowadays know this story or would draw such conclusions, but I always thought it was all rather too coincidental.' He gave another sigh. 'It would be very disturbing if something like this were to happen again. It would affect not only our world but also the outside world, especially if it involves something like banknotes that have real value there, whereas here they are mere pieces of paper.'

He paused and looked at Will. Then he got up and walked around the office, deep in thought. Will waited, thinking about what Beltorec had told him.

'You know, Will,' Beltorec said, and Will jumped, for Beltorec was suddenly standing directly behind his chair. 'I've reached a decision.' He paused. 'I believe you are old enough, and from what I know from your teachers, you are the right person for this.' He sat down behind his desk again and looked gravely at Will. 'Actually, for some months now, such notes as you have brought me have been turning up here and there in Snowfields. I've seen five of them so far—well, really six now.' His eyes went back to the note. 'This is greatly worrying me, as well as the other directors here at Snowfields. We've discussed it several times, and we believe we must act now.' He looked even more soberly at Will. 'This has to stay between you and me! Not a word to another student, you hear?'

Will nodded. 'Yes, sir, of course. I'll talk to no one.'

Beltorec gave a short laugh. 'Actually there are a few people you *have* to talk to about this. You see, Will, we reached the conclusion that we should form a special group to investigate and deal with this problem. I'll call a meeting. The others have to know about this.' He stopped, looking across the room without actually seeing anything.

Will waited. Finally he asked, 'Yes, sir?'

Beltorec looked at Will, coming out of his thoughts. 'Hmm? Oh, I'll take you to the meeting. You'll help us with this investigation. You can try to find hints among your fellow students, as we fear there might be some students involved.'

Will stared. 'Me?'

'Yes, you of course. You found the note and know nearly as much about this mess as we do. So you'll be a perfect member of our group.' He fixed Will with a chilly glare. 'Remember, don't talk to anyone about this! You're to talk about anything remotely connected to this only with members of the group.'

Will nodded. 'Of course, sir. I will and won't.'

Beltorec nodded. 'Fine then, come to my office at seven o'clock on Wednesday evening. Mrs Script will have left by then, and I'll take you to the meeting.' He got up. 'I'll see you then. And thank you for telling me, and not anyone else. You haven't so far, have you?' He looked intently at Will again.

'No, sir,' Will said, 'I came straight to you.'

Beltorec smiled. 'That's good. Well then, I'll see you on Wednesday.'

Will jumped to his feet. 'Okay, sir, I'll be here at seven. Thank you.' He hurried to the door and let himself out.

'Well? Have you said everything that was so important?' Mrs Script looked at Will over the rim of her glasses, which perched perilously on the tip of her nose.

'Uh, yes, thank you.' Will raced past her.

'You know, you can't just storm in here like this. No you can't, young man. Really!' she called after him as he dashed through the door, nearly slamming it behind him before he had to tell her what his meeting with the vice chancellor had been about.

Chapter 9

It was near the end of the lesson when Mr Contractus said, 'All right, that's it for today. But I still have something important to tell you, so listen up all of you. Starting tomorrow you'll have lessons in a new subject. It'll be one of the most important ones you'll have here. We call it Fieldworks. In this subject we'll teach you how to apply all the others things you're learning when you are out in the field helping with the proper delivery of the presents.'

He definitely had the full attention of Will and the rest of the class. This was something different from boring Letters to Father Christmas!

'And I advise you,' Mr Contractus continued, 'to work hard and do your best now, for you'll all be deployed in the field as soon as this year's Christmas!' This announcement received a few exclamations of surprise from the class.

'Of course you'll be accompanied by a member of the staff, but you'll need to know what you're doing. In Fieldworks you'll receive a few more theoretical instructions, but the main part will consist of practical exercises. For this we have a special area where you'll train in a realistic environment. That's also the reason this was your last lesson today, and why you have the rest of the day off!'

He waited patiently for the noise from the class to die down. When he was sure they were listening again, he continued: 'This is because you'll need training outfits for this work, so please go to the clothing department today, all of you'—he looked around the classroom sternly—'so they can do the fittings. They are open until five this afternoon. That's it for now. I'll see you tomorrow.' He stood up from his desk and walked out of the classroom while Will and the others packed their things, talking to each other animatedly about the exciting new lessons they were going to have.

'Shall we go to the fitting together?' Will asked Annabel.

'Yes, we can,' she answered and led the way from the classroom. They had passed through the door and were walking down the corridor when Will heard someone call his name from behind.

He turned round and saw Freddy hurrying up to them.

'Hi, Freddy.'

'Are you on your way to the clothing department? Can I join you?'

'Of course you can,' replied Will, then he looked at Annabel.

She nodded. 'Certainly. Let's go then.'

Freddy hurried off in front. When they had gone down several corridors he stopped so suddenly Will ran straight into him, and Annabel ran into Will.

'Ouch!'

'Ow!'

'Sorry.'

'Sorry.'

'What the...' said Will. 'Why did you just stop like that?'

'Er, sorry,' Freddy turned around and looked at them rather embarrassed: 'Er, do you remember the way to the clothing department?'

Annabel laughed. 'Oh dear. Just follow me.' And she led the way confidently, with Will and Freddy trotting after her.

When they reached the clothing department, they were the only ones there. Therefore, as soon as they opened the door, they were ushered in by Scissorius, the fitting goblin.

'Come in, come on in, my young friends,' he greeted them, bowing deeply and then beaming at them. 'You are here because you need outfits for your fieldwork lessons, yes?'

'Yes, that's right,' replied Annabel.

Scissorius beamed at her again: 'Excellent, Miss Winston, most excellent. We'll begin with the lady, right gentlemen?' He looked pointedly at Freddy and Will.

'Er, sure, sure,' said Will, somewhat taken by surprise.

'Charming, just charming,' said Scissorius, turning back to Annabel and leading her through the room. They went past rows of school clothing hanging in armoires next to the walls, past a large counter with a glass cover, under which were small accessories, and went into a separate part of the room that was divided off by a wide and thick red curtain with golden borders. Scissorius held it open for Annabel and ushered her in.

He turned to Will and Freddy: 'Gentlemen, this will take but a moment. Please have a seat on the sofa and help yourselves to some lemonade and biscuits.' He graciously waved a hand at the sofa and followed Annabel behind the curtain.

Will called a belated 'thank you' after him, then looked at Freddy, who just looked back, shrugged his shoulders, went over to the sofa, and plopped down on it. Will sat down beside him and looked around. It was pretty much as he remembered it from his first visit when he had just arrived at Snowfields and had been led through the school and then into this room to get his school outfit.

Freddy was already happily crunching biscuits, so Will also helped himself to one and drank some lemonade while he wondered what to expect. He did not have to wait long before Annabel came back carrying a large bag. She looked a bit dubiously at it as she walked towards the sofa.

'Right, gentlemen,' said Scissorius, stepping from behind the curtain. 'Who's next?'

Will and Freddy looked at each other, but Will said to Freddy, 'Go on then.'

'Right,' said Freddy, then jumped to his feet and quickly walked over to Scissorius, who held the curtain aside for him.

'Well?' Will asked Annabel.

'Well!' she replied and grinned cheekily. She prodded the bag.

'What did you get? Don't stretch it out like that.'

Annabel looked at her bag. 'Okay. He gave me a training outfit. It's made out of some sort of dark, elastic material. Very comfortable and very warm, even as thin as it is. You'll see.

'Okay,' replied Will. 'I'll just wait and see what I get.'

Soon the curtain opened again, and Freddy came out with a bag similar to the one Annabel had received.

'Wow,' Freddy said, visibly excited. 'I feel like Superman in this stuff.'

Even Scissorius had to smile at this enthusiastic outburst. He waved Will forward. Will got up quickly and followed him behind the curtain.

'Hello Will, welcome back,' Scissorius said to Will's surprise, for he had not told him his name again, and he had only been there once before.

'Hello,' he replied. There was a pause. 'Er, I'm here for the training outfit.'

'Yes, yes, of course.' Scissorius smiled faintly. 'You'll find an outfit in your size, based on the clothing you've already got from here, on the hanger over there. Please try it on.'

Will turned round and found a complete outfit with shirt, top, and trousers hanging there. The shirt was grey, had a fine, mesh-like structure, and was made out of some sort of modern, breathable fabric. Then there was the top; it was black with some dark-grey areas, smooth and silky to the touch, but also warm and light. The trousers were made out of the same material and colour, mostly black with patches of dark grey.

'Please,' Scissorius repeated from behind him, 'try them on.'

Will took off all his clothes except his underwear and put on the shirt, the top, and the trousers. As he had thought, they were very light to wear, very comfortable, and quite warm. Scissorius walked around him, mumbling under his breath, and pulled a bit here and there at the clothing until he was satisfied.

'Excellent,' he finally said. 'A perfect fit. What do you think, young man?'

Will moved his arms and legs, then took a few steps: 'Er, yes. It fits very well, thank you.'

'You're welcome. Then please take the clothes off again.'

Will removed them and put his ordinary school clothes back on.

'Now we only need the shoes,' Scissorius announced.

Will waited.

'Don't dawdle. The shoes are right behind you,' Scissorius told him.

Will turned around. Under the hanger with the new outfit was a pair of trainers, also in black and dark grey, matching the clothes. He quickly removed the shoes he was wearing and put the trainers on. They also fitted perfectly. He took a few steps. The trainers were very light and comfortable, but offered a firm hold.

'Well?' Scissorius raised one eyebrow and looked at Will.

'Great!' he exclaimed. 'Thank you very much.'

Scissorius gave a gratified smile. 'You're welcome, you're welcome. That's my job. Now please remove the trainers again.'

149

Will took off the trainers and handed them to Scissorius. He had produced a large bag from somewhere, put the clothes into it with quick, practised movements, added the trainers, and handed the pack over to Will.

'There you are, sir. Enjoy the training. This way, please.' And he stepped up to the curtain and held it open for Will.

'Thank you,' replied Will. 'I'm sure I will.'

Scissorius smiled faintly. 'Goodbye, sir.'

Will stepped back into the main room again, where Annabel and Freddy looked up. When they saw that he was ready, they emptied their glasses and got up from the sofa.

'Well?' Annabel asked and raised her eyebrows. 'What do you think?' She grinned at Will.

Will had to laugh. 'The outfit is great, it's comfortable. And Freddy's right, you almost feel like Superman, or, given the colours, rather like Batman. I'm just curious about what the training will be like. I'd expect it to be rather hard and strenuous, given these outfits.'

'Yes, that's what I'm afraid of too.'

The three of them walked out of the clothing department, bags in hand, and headed back to their rooms.

***

Will was excited. Today they would have their first lesson with Ethan Stunt, their teacher for the practical training, for Fieldworks. Will got up quickly, washed, and dressed. The others were up too, and in various stages of getting ready.

Will went down into the common room. There he met Sabrina and Spencer. The three of them went together to the Ferum for breakfast. While they were eating, they talked animatedly about the coming lesson. As Will looked around, he noticed that even Richard looked rather excited, not nearly as cool and noninvolved or bored as was normally the case.

After they had finished, Will went to the classroom together with Annabel and Freddy. They had been told to bring their new training outfits and to meet Mr Stunt in the classroom where they normally had lessons with Miss Dustfall. About a third of the class was already inside. Will looked at the clock on the wall and saw they were ten minutes early. He looked around and waited. Soon the complete class was sitting there, talking excitedly, all with the bags containing their training outfits lying on the tables in front of them, or on the floor beside their chairs.

Finally Mr Stunt walked briskly into the classroom. He wore a training outfit just like the ones they had received the previous day. Will had to admit that the outfit looked great on him. The tight-fitting, shiny, black material enhanced his wiry figure.

'Good morning, class.' He looked around. 'My name is Ethan Stunt. I'll be your instructor for Fieldworks. I see you all received your training outfits. Except....' He walked towards the back of the classroom and stopped in front of Richard's desk. 'Mr Loxley here. Where is your outfit, mister?'

Richard looked up, mildly surprised. 'Well, I'm sorry sir,' he replied easily, 'I didn't think we'd need it right away. I thought we'd first get a bit of an introduction this morning. I have it in my room of course.'

'Ah,' said Stunt, and walked back towards the front of the class. Richard looked after him, his eyes narrowing. Will did not know what to think. Had Mr Stunt approved of this or not?

Stunt continued: 'Indeed, today I'll give you a bit of an outline and some background on what we'll be doing during the next few weeks.' He pulled his wand from his suit's snug hip holster. Then he waved it quite casually, making a complicated gesture, and pointed it towards the bare wall to the left of the blackboard. Will could see a faint shimmer of Bluerin, and then a detailed map appeared on the wall.

'This'—Stunt gestured towards the wall—'is a detailed map of our training area. What we are going to do in my lessons is put everything my colleagues have been teaching you to practical use. As you can see on the map, we have different buildings, streets, and special areas within the grounds where we'll train the proper delivery of the presents and confront you with the different obstacles you may encounter.'

While he was saying this, he pointed his wand here and there on the map, and a beam of Yellowrin came forth to highlight the different sections. Will was impressed: Stunt had a wand that could be filled with Bluerin and Yellowrin at the same time. He had not even known such wands existed.

Stunt continued to explain the training grounds. There were the lifelike buildings and dwellings, streets, and gardens, and even a special training area with thick, protective screens and sand hills where they were going to practise the spells using Bluerin, without any danger to the surroundings. He showed them the changing areas and the adjoining room where they could gather for theoretical lessons. Then he taught them a spell they would need to enter the training area.

'Okay,' said Stunt, 'it'll all become much clearer when you see it for real. Therefore today's lesson in here is finished. I've told you all I can for now. You've got half an hour, then we'll meet in the briefing room next to the training area. All in your training outfits, please. Dismissed.'

Will and the others got up. He took his bag with his training outfit, and turned to Annabel next to him. 'What are you going to do in the meantime?'

'Not a lot, I guess. Half an hour isn't much time, especially if we have to go to the training area and get changed. It would be best if we went there directly.'

'Yeah, you're probably right,' Will had to admit. 'Let's go then.'

Will and Annabel went through the school towards the training area. They had never been in that part of the building before. Finally they reached a corridor that ended in a huge, double-winged door that was as wide as the corridor. It was easy to see that something special was behind it: a fine, red line ran around the frame of the door, and above it was a large sign: 'DANGER—Training Area'. The letters were slowly flashing in a dull, red light.

Will looked at Annabel and grinned a bit nervously. 'Looks rather impressive, doesn't it?'

'Yes,' replied Annabel. 'It doesn't look very inviting. I wouldn't even think about going in there if we hadn't explicitly been told to.' She stood in front of the door and pointed her wand at it. Then she performed the spell Mr Stunt had taught them. It was not a complicated one, but Stunt had told them it was necessary to prevent illegitimate access. The red line around the frame disappeared and was replaced by a blue one. And the warning sign was also replaced. It now had blue letters and read 'Access Cleared'. Then a face appeared in the rectangle of smooth wood in the middle of the door.

'Halt! Who goes there? Declare yourselves!' the face sharply demanded of them."

'Er, Annabel Winston and Will Burns,' Will answered quickly.

The face eyed them up and down. Finally it nodded curtly.

'Good. Sir, madam, I was told to grant you access. Please come through.'

The doors swung open, and Will and Annabel walked through. Behind them the doors closed automatically. They were now standing in a short corridor that again ended in a large, double-winged door, also with a sign on it: 'NO ENTRY —Service Entrance'. In the middle of the door was a solid bronze lock. Will and Annabel looked around. To the left was an ordinary door with a sign—'Boys'; to their right was a door with another sign: 'Girls'.

Will said, 'Those must be the changing rooms. Best we go in there and get changed then. First one out waits on the other side?'

'Yes,' Annabel agreed, and walked over towards the girls' changing room.

Will went over to the door of the changing room for the boys. He tried to open it, but it was locked—it would not open. He looked around. Then he noticed the rectangular area of smooth wood in the middle of the door, and carefully touched it. Promptly a wooden face started to emerge.

'Yes, please?' it said to Will.

'Er, I'm Will Burns. I've got Fieldworks training in here. I'd like to go in, please,' said Will.

The face eyed him up and down. 'Yes, I've been advised about your lesson. And obviously you are a boy—therefore you may enter. Welcome, Mr Burns.'

The face disappeared, and the door swung open. Will went inside. There was nobody else in there. On his left and on his right were rows of lockers along the walls. In front of him were two doors, the left marked 'Shower Room', the other 'Training Area'. He changed into his new black-and-grey training outfit and put his other clothes into the locker he had selected. He closed and sealed it by swiping his wand across the locking interface, just as Mr Stunt had taught them. There was a large mirror hanging on the wall. He could not help but admire himself in this smart outfit. Then he left the room through the door leading to the training area.

He stood in another corridor. There was no other door, so he walked down, round a corner, and past what looked like the other side of the huge service entrance, until he reached an intersection. To his right was a similar corridor that presumably led towards the girls' room; to his left was a wider corridor extending from the service entrance that ended in a large door with a sign: 'Training Area'. He was still looking up and down when a door at the end of the corridor to his right opened and Annabel came through, looking around tentatively. Will stared: she looked amazing in the training outfit. She saw Will and started to walk towards him. When she reached him, she noticed that he was staring at her.

'What is it?' She demanded of him. 'What are you staring at?'

'What? Oh...sorry. You look great in this outfit.' He looked away quickly.

'In this?' she asked incredulously and looked down at herself.

'Never mind,' said Will, feeling his face getting warmer.

Annabel looked at him critically. 'Okay.'

'Let's go over to the briefing room,' said Will quickly, trying to change the subject.

They went down the corridor towards the entrance to the training area, and then through the door directly in front and to the left of it, with the sign 'Briefing Room'. They were not the first—Wendy and Sabrina were already sitting there talking quietly to each other. Will could not help noticing that the two girls also looked fantastic in their black-and-grey training outfits.

'Hello,' he greeted them as he walked towards the seat next to Sabrina.

They had stopped talking and were both looking at him rather directly. Sabrina giggled slightly and replied, 'Hi there, Will.'

He felt that he was turning red again and quickly turned away, pretending he was looking around the room. Annabel sat down next to him. Soon the whole class was there. Then Stunt walked into the room and stood in front of them.

'Hello, class,' he said, and looked around. 'Good, you've all found your way in here. As you know, I'm here to train you for the tasks you'll have to cope with in the field. First, I'll give you a brief introduction to the training area. Then we'll have a tour around it and I'll show you the main areas.' He pointed his wand towards the wall next to the blackboard and performed a spell, and the map of the training area appeared again.

'If you'll look at this map again, please.' He quickly showed them the locations of the different areas once more. Finally Stunt finished his explanations. 'I'm going to show you the training area now. When you are here for training as a class, you can be sure no one else is in here unless I tell you otherwise. If for any reason you should come here at any other time, you have to be very careful when you enter the training area. Make sure you know who else is in here and what they are doing. Otherwise you might get hit by an ill-aimed spell. But you can come in only with the authorization of a teacher anyway, otherwise you'd be stopped by the door guardians. Follow me inside then.'

And he led them from the room. In front of the door to the training area, he stopped and tapped impatiently several times on the smooth rectangle until a face appeared. It looked rather annoyed.

'What the—' it started to say, but then it saw Stunt. 'Oh...you.'

'Yes, me. Hurry up, open the door!' Stunt said shortly, looking disdainfully down at the face. The door swung open immediately, and Stunt walked briskly through it. Then he stopped inside the training area, and Will and the others gathered around him.

Stunt smiled grimly. 'As you have seen, the guardian is not the brightest or fastest, but he won't let anyone inside without clearance. Anyhow'—he pointed to his left—'over there is the basic training stand. We'll go there first,' he said, leading the way.

Will saw that they were walking towards some wooden walls that were staggered so they formed a shielded entrance. The students went inside and passed between the wooden walls. Will could see a large, open area with several piles of sand. A few worn targets and mock presents were lying around in between. The walls far at the back were heavily padded.

'As you can see,' Stunt said, 'we are now in the basic training stand. Here we can safely practise spells without doing any damage because they can be aimed at the sand—it dampens their effects. The targets and mock presents are for training your aiming skills. The walls are specially shielded so the effects of the spells won't leave this area. Any questions? No? Then we'll move on.'

They went out through the opening between the staggered walls again. Stunt took them over to an area where a living room had been erected. But it had only one wall; the other sides were open. Otherwise it looked like a real-life living room. There was a fireplace built into the wall. Will saw that there were even stockings pinned to the mantelpiece. In one corner stood a decorated Christmas tree. There were a sofa and some armchairs, a dining area with a table and chairs, cupboards and sideboards, vases and typical decorative items standing around. There even were dummies of parents sitting on the sofa and of two kids standing near the Christmas tree and the fireplace.

Stunt waited until they had all gathered around him, then he pointed towards the living room that was not really a room. 'This is the place you are going to spend most of your time. As you can see it's completely decorated as your normal living room, with dummies for people. But—I'm sure you did notice—there are no walls! Now why is that?' He did not wait for an answer, but answered the question himself: 'This way everybody can watch what happens inside, so we can all comment on your actions and discuss the methods. Here you will train the delivery and placing of the presents in a lifelike setting. Questions?'

Nobody asked anything. They were all still looking around the room. Then Stunt led them onwards. Now they were standing in a street in front of a row of buildings. But—although the fronts looked very realistic and were as high as they would have been on ordinary houses—Will saw that they were in fact just the façades with a bit of roof, chimneys, and gutters. There were no real houses. Behind the façades was just the wall of the training area.

'Now here we are in Training Lane,' Stunt told them, and pointed towards the fronts of the buildings. 'As you can see these are real fronts, and they have fully functional windows, doors, and chimneys. But there is nothing behind them. This is because here you will concentrate on practising how to get into a house.'

They went down the street, and Will could see all sorts of structures—or at least the fronts: small ones, large ones, houses with very steep or very flat roofs, wide and small chimneys.... There were even a bungalow and a full-sized mansion. Finally they reached the last of the house fronts, and Stunt stopped once more.

'Now you have seen the main parts of the training area. There are several smaller parts, but they are for training for special tasks, and you won't need those at the moment. For now your training will be in the parts you've seen, so you will be able to help in the delivery of the presents next Christmas. I advise you to take this training very seriously, because all you can learn in this protected area will help you outside in the real world. And here you can make mistakes. Out there—you can't!'

And with this rather bleak statement, he led them back to the briefing room where he had picked them up. There he spent the next half an hour explaining more about the basics and the rules of the training area until he ended the lesson and sent them off.

Will stood next to Freddy in the changing room.

'This is amazing,' Freddy exclaimed. 'We'll have great fun training in there. And it all looks so real!'

Will grinned. He could always rely on Freddy's excitement about new things at Snowfields. 'Yes,' he said. 'What they have built in there is rather impressive. But I'm afraid it'll mean a lot of work for us.'

Freddy's face fell a bit. 'Oh, yes, you're probably right.' Then he looked up again, beaming. 'But it'll be much better than the lessons we had in the muggy old gym of the school I went to. And better than Miss Horseshoe anyway, always blowing her stupid whistle and jumping around in her pink shell suit.' He shuddered in disgust, and Will had to laugh as he imagined his former games teacher jumping up and down in a pink suit.

Chapter 10

Will had sneaked out of the common room and was on his way to his first meeting with the secret investigation group. He was quite excited. He felt a bit like James Bond on a secret mission as he hurried down the corridors, trying to be as inconspicuous as possible. Beltorec had said Will should join him in his office in the evening, long after Mrs Script would have left, and they would go to the meeting together.

Will reached the vice chancellor's office without encountering anybody; he had glimpsed merely one or two students in the distance, and hoped they had not seen him. The door to Beltorec's office was closed. Will turned the handle, but the door would not open! What should he do? He could knock, but he would have to make a real noise for Beltorec to hear it in his inner office and then others might hear it, too.

Just as he was thinking about this, a face was forming on the door's surface, on the rectangle where the wood was smooth. It was quite a solemn face that looked at Will, reminding him of an old headmaster.

'And what do you believe you are doing here?' it asked sternly.

'Er, I... I've got an appointment with the vice chancellor, sir. He... He's waiting for me!' Will stammered.

'Is that so?' the face drawled. 'And you would know the password then, a green student like you?' It raised its eyebrows. 'I would think not.'

'Dick Deadeye,' Will said promptly.

The expression on the face turned to extreme surprise. 'Oh!' It settled into a friendlier if still reserved expression. 'I must apologise, sir. Nice to meet you. My name is Crown. Please come in. The vice chancellor is still here.' And the door swung open silently.

'Thank you.' Will resisted the urge to bow at Crown's regal voice and manner. 'Ah, my name is Will... Will Burns.'

'Nice to meet you, Mr Burns,' Crown replied.

Will entered the empty secretariat. He was nearing the opposite door when he heard a voice from inside calling, 'Please come in, Will!'

He turned the handle and entered the office of the vice chancellor.

'Hello, Will, good to see you.' Beltorec smiled at him. 'And right on time.'

'Good evening, sir.'

'Well, you know what this is going to be about, and I don't have anything new to tell you, so we can leave right away and go to the meeting. We'll see the others there.' He closed a file, put it in a small briefcase, and got up. 'Let's go, then.'

Will went out, followed by Beltorec. He noticed that all the lights in the office went out when the vice chancellor walked through the door.

They left the outer office.

'Good evening, Crown,' said Beltorec.

'Good evening, sir! I will be awaiting your arrival tomorrow. I wish you a pleasant evening.'

'Thanks, Crown, same to you.'

Beltorec led Will down the corridor, but not in the direction of the entrance hall. Instead he turned the other way. Will had not been there before. When they had turned round several corners, Will noticed that the corridors became less and less decorated and did not look as if they were often used by anyone. He and the vice chancellor went on, and the intervals between the lamps grew longer and longer, so the corridor turned rather gloomy. All the time Beltorec did not say a word to Will, but led him quietly down passages Will had not even known existed.

Finally they went through a door, mostly hidden in a shadowy corner so Will would have walked right past it with no idea it was there. After they had passed through, they went down a flight of stairs, also barely lit. They went down other gloomy corridors and ill-lit stairs. The walls there were made out of cold and bare grey stone blocks. Will noticed that the air had become rather clammy and that the walls had a faint, green sheen.

'Any idea where we are?' Beltorec finally asked.

'Well, sir, I'd say we are underground,' replied Will.

'Yes, that's right. We are indeed walking under the streets and buildings of the village now.'

Will dared to ask, 'Where are we headed?'

'To an abandoned building where we can meet without being obvious about it. And it is rather conveniently connected to the school building by these tunnels. It isn't much farther.'

They went on and finally reached another well-hidden door. Beltorec took out a silvery, old-looking key and unlocked the four locks on the door.

'Well-guarded,' he said laconically.

'Indeed,' Will replied politely, not knowing what else to say.

They went through, and Beltorec scrupulously fastened all four locks again.

'Won't the others have to go through here too?' Will asked.

'No. They come from elsewhere. The building has several unobtrusive entrances.'

They went up several stairs and passed through dusty, bare corridors. Will wondered what their destination would look like and who he would meet there. Finally they reached a part of the building that was not quite so bare, and that was better lit. Beltorec finally stopped in front of a nondescript-looking door and knocked on it in a complicated pattern. The door opened.

'Follow me,' Beltorec said to Will.

Will followed Beltorec inside. The door closed behind him on its own. Will looked back quickly, but there was no one there.

'Good evening,' Beltorec said. 'I see we are the last ones to arrive, but I had to bring Will with me.'

'Who's he?'

Will looked up and saw a goblin in a dark coat eyeing him suspiciously across the table.

'He's one of my students. He only started this term, but he'll prove rather useful, as you will see.'

'I'm sure we will,' the goblin replied slowly.

'Be polite, Caretrus. Best let me do the introductions first,' Beltorec said. 'This is Will Burns, new at my school. And he discovered something rather important. That's why I called for this meeting tonight.' He put a hand on Will's shoulder. 'Will, these are the other directors here in Snowfields. Over there on the right is Mr Factorius. As the name implies, the director of production.'

A small man in a pinstripe suit nodded politely at Will.

'On his right is Lektrarissima, chief goblin of our local branch of Cloudy's Transportation Service.'

'Nice to meet you, Will.' The she-goblin beamed at him. 'Your obedient valet.'

Will grinned nervously, but felt like groaning when he heard that phrase again.

'Next to her is Mr Blues, responsible for obtaining, generating, and distributing the Bluerin used in Snowfields.'

164

Mr Blues was of normal height and average figure, clad in a blue, well-fitting boiler suit.

'Hello, Will.'

'Next is Mr Securitas, chief of the security service at Snow-fields, inasmuch as it exists.'

'Greetings.' A rather plump and casually-dressed man nodded to Will.

'And that is Caretrus, who has already greeted you in his most direct way. He's chief of the caretaker goblins in Snow-fields. He joined us because he and his goblins get around everywhere here, and if anything is afoot they are the ones who'll most likely know it. You see, nobody takes note of care-takers.'

'That's a fact!' Caretrus gave Will a brisk nod. 'And thank you very much, sir, for phrasing it so sensitively.'

Beltorec pointedly ignored this. 'So, let's get started. Will, you sit here.' He pointed to a stool on his right. Then he sat down next to Will and cleared his throat. 'As you all know, we have gathered here this evening because of the rather disturb-ing indications that Bluerin is being misused at Snowfields.'

The others around the table nodded gravely.

'I'm introducing Will to our group tonight for two reasons. Firstly because he can be useful as an informant among the students at the school. As I told you before, there are rather strong indications that students are involved in this affair. And secondly Will came to me the other day and gave me... this!'

He took out the Bluerin note and laid it in the middle of the table for all to see. There were several astonished exclama-tions. Blues picked up the note, felt it between his fingers, held it up against the light, and rubbed on it with his fingernail.

'Well, now this really *is* rather disturbing,' he said. 'This is by far the best-made note I've seen.'

Caretrus nodded curtly. 'Indeed!' He looked at Will. 'The question is, how did *he* come by it?'

Will cringed.

Beltorec came to his rescue. 'He told me he found it in the school. Isn't that right, Will?'

'Er, yes sir. I wanted to take a shortcut after a lesson, and I went down this corridor I had only discovered a few days earlier. It's hardly used, and so it isn't in good repair. I stumbled on the edge of a loose tile and fell. Then I saw the note there, more than half of it stuck under the skirting board.'

Beltorec sighed. 'Well, I think you'll all agree that this is serious, and we need to decide what to do next. Let's start up the table.'

The others nodded, except Will, who did not understand this. Start up the table? To do what?

The others removed everything that was lying on the table. Factorius took the note and eyed it closely. Then Beltorec took out his wand, pointed it at the table, and performed a spell. The tabletop started to shimmer blue as a faint stream of Bluerin flowed to it from Beltorec's wand. Will stared, unbelieving. The whole top of the table, which just a moment before had been smoothly finished, bare wood, had turned into an LCD-like monitor. Amazing as this was, Will could nevertheless see the symbols he knew from his own computer there, as well as other strange symbols he had never seen before, and he had no idea what they meant.

'Well then,' Beltorec continued, and put his wand away. To Will's further amazement Beltorec started touching several of the symbols on the screen with his fingers. It was certainly the largest touchscreen Will had ever seen—except maybe in some science-fiction films.

'That's incredible,' he exclaimed, not able to stop himself.

Beltorec smiled. 'Good, isn't it? It's one of the best achievements of our development department.'

Beltorec continued tapping the surface and moved around some of the symbols, and started some programs. Finally he started one that filled the whole screen. Will could see what looked like a map of the whole village of Snowfields. It completely covered the surface of the table.

Seeing Will's confusion, Lektrissima told him, 'You see, our development department invented this computer and implemented a system that can trace all personnel inside of Snowfields. Of course its use is highly restricted, and luckily we have only had to use it a few times in the past.'

Beltorec was still busily tapping on symbols, and a virtual keyboard appeared under his fingers. He looked up at the others around the table and said, 'Well, we can see all of Snowfields and everything that is currently happening. Any ideas where we should start looking?'

Factorius stroked his beard. 'As for me, I'd start looking either at the production sites or at the Bluerin stores. I think illegal access to Bluerin would most likely be there, if you can call it "likely" anyway.'

Blues cleared his throat. 'I would not think so! Such access to Bluerin would be more likely at the production sites, but certainly not in the stores. I've got strict admission protocols in place so that only the most-trusted and most-essential personnel are allowed near the Bluerin stores. And they would never be alone near it anyway. Admission is only allowed in groups of three. And there have been no reports of any forced intrusions or breaches of protocol.'

Factorius rolled his eyes. 'Yes, yes, of course we all know your strict admission protocols and what have you. I only wanted to say that at production sites or in the stores, Bluerin is most concentrated and, therefore, these would be the places where an attempt to withdraw it would probably be most successful and the least noticed.'

'But it would surely be noticed in *my* stores, thank you very much!' Bluerin replied.

Beltorec held up his hands. 'Gentlemen, please! Let's just gather ideas and then we can rule them out, for whatever reasons there may be.'

Lektrissima looked thoughtful. 'It would also be quite appropriate to think about less likely places to obtain Bluerin. If there are places where Bluerin is stocked but seldom used, a loss of it might not be noticed immediately, or it might be assumed that the records weren't up to date and the Bluerin was taken out a long time ago. Places like the school or the laboratories of the development department.'

'Hmm, good thought, actually,' Beltorec replied. 'In what other places would lesser amounts of Bluerin be stored that could be taken without anybody noticing?'

Securitas answered, 'Well, apart from the school and the development departments, there would not be any Bluerin elsewhere except in the stores and on the production sites. Maybe a bit in the magic department. But that's about it. Bluerin would not be used anywhere else.'

Lektrissima interrupted him. 'Excuse me, Securitas, but that is not quite correct. You are forgetting the emergency stores. You know, the small containers all over Snowfields if you need Bluerin in a hurry to recharge your wand.'

Securitas looked at her darkly, but then he conceded, 'Yes, of course you are right. But as you might recall, these are well-guarded, and I would not think that such a small amount as is stored in there for emergencies would be of any interest for a large-scale fraud.'

Lektrissima said soothingly, 'Yes, I agree, but I do not think we should dismiss these containers altogether.'

'So,' Beltorec summarised. 'The Bluerin has to come from one of these places: the development departments, the school, the production sites, the stores, or the magic department. And the emergency containers would not be of paramount interest. Which would be the most likely?'

'You can certainly rule out my stores!' Blues announced. This time even Caretrus rolled his eyes.

'Would you know anywhere else where Bluerin is used?' Beltorec asked Caretrus, ignoring Blues.

He thought for a moment. 'No, not really.'

Beltorec nodded and typed in a few commands on the table-top. Blue spots appeared throughout the village. Everyone looked at the map.

'These are places where Bluerin can be found,' Beltorec explained.

'Hmm,' said Securitas. 'We've just mentioned all of those, as far as I can see. Even the emergency containers are shown, I might note,' he added after a rather pointed pause.

'Of course, you would not see any Bluerin that is covered in lead, you know?' interjected Factorius.

'Yes, that's true!' Beltorec's brow furrowed. 'And it's more than likely that the forgers would cover their Bluerin and keep it well-hidden.' He looked at the map for a moment, thinking. 'We don't seem to be making much progress here. What else can we do?'

Factorius replied. 'I think for now we should all look into the uses of Bluerin in our own departments, and see if we can find any discrepancies before our next meeting—yes, even you, Blues, please, just to rule it out properly,' he added immediately as Blues started to protest once more. 'And Lektrissima could look for clues that notes have already been taken out of Snowfields.'

She nodded.

'Caretrus could talk to his goblins and ask them to look out for any unusual activities or traces of the forgery process—maybe some clippings or leftovers from failed attempts. Our newest member, Will, could try to find any other notes in the school, as quite a few of the ones we've already acquired were found in or near the school, so someone in there seems to be involved rather directly. Blues and I should check our departments for any irregularities in the flow of Bluerin. Yes, I know,' he added quickly, as Blues was immediately starting to protest yet again, 'there would not be any irregularities in your stores, but please check it anyway, will you?'

Blues grunted. 'Beltorec should also have a rather close look at things in his school, for the same reasons we are involving Will. And Securitas should check with the development and magic departments to see if there have been any irregularities there, and to have a look at their usage of Bluerin.'

Securitas nodded. 'As cryptic and mysterious as they always act, there's quite a good chance that even they themselves don't know who is doing what with Bluerin and where exactly it would be stored.'

The others laughed at this, and Will got the feeling that the magic department was not held in very high regard by the others—especially since there was nobody from that department in this group.

Beltorec looked around the table. 'Thank you, Factorius. I think that about covers it for the moment. Any more suggestions?' Nobody had anything to add. 'No? Then that's all for this evening. We will meet again next week. Hopefully someone will have discovered something useful by then. Good night to you all.'

They got up from the table. Will stood next to Beltorec as the others started to leave the room. Beltorec pointed his wand at the table again. The map darkened and vanished, the computer screen disappeared, and Will was looking at an ordinary brown and smooth tabletop again. There was nothing that indicated it was in fact a large computer display. He looked at Beltorec.

'Well, Will, let's go back. Time to get you off to bed.' And he led Will out of the room.

After Will had gone through the door, the light dimmed behind him and the door closed on its own. They walked back through the corridors and up the stairs until Will finally recognised the corridor outside Beltorec's office.

'Just come inside with me for a minute, will you?' Beltorec said to Will.

'Good evening, sir! And to you, Mr Burns. Still here so late at night?' They were greeted by the ever-attentive Crown.

'Yes, some meeting we had to go to, you know how it is.'

'Oh yes, sir, indeed. I do hope this was a productive one.'

'Yes, quite,' replied Beltorec shortly as he went through the door and into his office. Will followed him inside.

'I sometimes wonder who's nosier, Mrs Script or Crown.' Beltorec scoffed. 'Well, that's it for tonight. Just one more thing: if you need to talk to me at any time during the following week, just tell Crown the code 'British tar', and he will inform me without getting Mrs Script involved. That's all. Good night to you.'

'Thank you. Good night, sir.' Will left the office.

'Good night, Mr Burns,' Crown said gravely as Will went through the door.

'Good night, Crown,' Will replied absently, as he was thinking about all the things he had seen and heard this evening. He went back to his room quickly, longing for his bed after such an eventful day.

Chapter 11

It was at the end of the lesson when Contractus said, 'I hope you're all preparing for next week.' He looked around the classroom. Will and the others looked at each other: what about next week? Were there going to be some tests or what?

Freddy was the first to ask: 'Er, sorry, sir, but just what is next week?'

'Why, summer holidays of course!' Contractus replied innocently.

'Summer holidays?' Freddy asked, looking startled.

'Of course.' Contractus laughed. 'Did you think you'd get no holidays? Of course you do! You'll have six weeks off to visit home and see your families again.'

The whole class was in uproar. Everyone babbled excitedly. Will thought this was really great news. He had been so absorbed in his studies he had never even thought about something like summer holidays. But he missed his parents and his sister very much, and he was thrilled to learn that he would see them again the next week.

The noise died down a bit, and Wendy could be heard asking above it: 'Mr Contractus? How are we going to get back home?'

The class went quiet. This was an interesting question.

'With Cloudy's Transportation Service of course. You'll take a lantern pick-up here and be transferred via the cloud stations to lanterns next to your homes. Fast and easy. No messing about with planes, airports, check-in times, and all the rest that makes travelling in the outside world so bothersome.'

***

Finally the last week was over, and it was the first day of the summer holidays. The previous evening the students had had a roaring party in their common room, so Will had slept late that morning to recover. Now he was standing underneath the lantern nearest to the school, and performed the necessary spell.

In the next instant he was standing on the now-familiar cloud platform of Cloudy's Transportation Service. After being guided through the facility and passing through several transfer stations, he stood underneath the street lantern next to his parents' house. Home again! His eyes turned moist, and he suddenly realised he had missed it far more than he had been aware of. He quickly walked towards the house and before he could even use his key, the door opened, and his mother caught him in a tight embrace.

'Oh, Will! It's so good to see you again finally. I've missed you!' she said when she finally released him.

'It's good to see you too,' Will replied.

'Come in, come in.' His mother nearly dragged him inside.

Once he was standing in the hallway, he heard a shriek: 'Will!' And his sister threw herself into his arms. He held her, feeling slightly embarrassed, but at the same time enjoying seeing her again. Suddenly Lucy realised what she was doing and quickly released Will, saying, 'Er, hi, Will. Good to see you again.'

Will decided to let it go and just grinned. He could always use it against her later on if necessary.

They went into the living room, where they sat down, and Will told them all about his experiences at Snowfields. He told them about the lessons, the spells, and the training. They in turn told him about everything that had happened at home and

174

at his old school. Later his father joined them after he had finished work, and Will repeated his most important experiences.

Will spent a nice, relaxed holiday with his family and met some old friends. But he only saw them a few times because it was quite exhausting for him, as he always had to keep quiet about Snowfields and what he was doing there, and he constantly needed to keep up the story about the boarding school he was now going to. Luckily he had been trained for this during the last week at Snowfields: he and the other students had all made up convincing stories about the school they where supposed to be going to, and the lessons they had there. They even went exhaustively through all the minor details, like what their dorms were like, what the weather was like, what the nearest town was, and so forth. Will had felt like he was an undercover agent taking on a new identity, but now he was glad they had been so thorough with this, as it had prepared him for all the questions and spared him quite a few awkward pauses and contradictions when talking about what he was doing.

Nonetheless it was quite a strain to keep up the pretence all the time, and so he did not meet his friends often. And, of course, as he was now living somewhere completely different and leading a different life, he did not have much in common with them anymore. So he was just as happy to stay at home and enjoy the company of his family and, of course, simply relax after the hard work at Snowfields.

***

Even though the holidays had seemed so long at the beginning, the time was finally over and Will once again left the house with his suitcase in hand, accompanied by his parents, and went down towards the street lantern. After a final wave, he performed the spell and was once more on the cloud platform of the regional base of Cloudy's Transportation Service. The trip to Snowfields was short and uneventful, although this time there was no sleigh ride into the village—he just appeared underneath the street lantern right outside the main entrance of the school. Once inside he met Sabrina and Wendy, who were just signing back in after the holiday. Together they went towards their rooms, telling each other about what they had been doing.

***

Will was standing in an office of the headquarters of Cloudy's Transportation Service. This week he was there for hands-on training. He was to learn all about the internal structure, the distribution network and how they were delivering the presents and transporting the personnel. He had already learned that here at the headquarters were mainly offices from which everything was coordinated. At the edge of the village were the large facilities where the basic materials were delivered and distributed to the Bluerin production facilities. One of the goblins acted as his tutor and was showing him around.

Will asked him, 'What I really don't understand is your slogan, this "We deliver a'f—"'

'*Shhh.*' Lektriorer, a transportation goblin, clamped his hand over Will's mouth. 'We don't say that one anymore!'

Will tried to free himself from Lektriorer's tight grip. 'Why's that?' he asked. 'It might sound a bit odd, but—'

Lektriorer sighed. 'Look, if you really must know, Cloudy's Transportation Service had this slogan you mentioned.' His voice dropped to a whisper. '"We deliver a'fore you've posted it" and it led to some...ah, complications. We've had a case where a customer wanted to send a parcel to his nephew, but he was a bit forgetful, so he set off on his way here, but forgot the parcel at home. When he got here, he wondered what it was he wanted here at all, turned round, and forgot the parcel completely. But on the same day his nephew received the parcel. The parcel that was never posted, and the same parcel that was still at home, where our customer had forgotten it.' He looked at Will in obvious discomfort. 'And in another case, we had an artist who wanted to send a painting. But unfortunately he packed an empty canvas and sent it off. But, true to our motto, the intent was there for the customer to receive the finished painting. So the canvas was filled with the actual painting that hadn't ever been painted.'

Will tried to follow this logic. 'But if it wasn't painted at all, how could it have been on the canvas?'

Lektriorer grinned. 'We've had meetings about this. And we installed committees to look into it. They finally reached the conclusion that as we would deliver before it was posted— true to our slogan—we could also deliver what hadn't been made yet. It was assumed that the actual deed would be done sometime in the future, so in the end it would all sort itself out. The artist would still fill the canvas, and Mr Forgetful would eventually remember and post the parcel. And don't look at me like that. That's what they told me.'

Still trying to follow this logic, Will's brain shut down and went AWOL.

'At that point we decided it would be an immensely smart thing to change our slogan to "We deliver after you posted it".'

Will blinked. 'That's, er, not much of a slogan, is it?'

Lektriorer grimaced. 'I know, I know, it's not quite the pick of the bunch, but we had to come up with something quickly, before we had any more, ah, let's say incidents. At least with this slogan, we won't have any deliveries ghosting around somewhere or delivering themselves. At least that's what I hope,' he added, looking a bit wild around the eyes.

Will shook his head. He was getting a headache trying to think about parcels posting and delivering themselves, containing what was believed to be in them without actually ever being packed. Or posted. Or whatever.

He remembered that while he was here he should look for any signs of the forgers as well as any suspicious products or supplies of Bluerin.

Lektriorer's voice roused him from his thoughts. 'If that's all for the moment, I'll take you to our canteen for lunch, and afterwards we'll go to the facilities where we receive the basic materials.'

That was fine by Will for he thought he might find some clues about the forgers' access to Bluerin there. Perhaps they were getting their Bluerin right at the immediate source.

After an uneventful and bland meal in the canteen, Lektriorer picked him up again and they walked to the edge of the village, to Cloudy's large facilities. After they had passed through the entrance gate Will stopped dead in his tracks—and stared. The area was extensive. Lektriorer grinned and then led Will into the complex. They went down a broad path next to the cloud conveyor belt on which huge containers were moving slowly. Finally they reached the back of the expansive grounds. Here were wide landing areas with large transportation sleighs coming and going continuously. As soon as a sleigh had landed a goblin hurried up to it and transferred the contents to an empty container standing nearby. Then, with another spell, the goblin would send the container, which was resting on a small patch of cloud, onto the conveyor belt and it would slowly make its way into the village.

Will and Lektriorer spent the rest of the afternoon walking through the facilities and Will tried to keep his eyes open for any clues as to where the forgers might obtain their Bluerin. But he did not see anything of use at all. In the end it was obvious that these facilities only handled the basic materials and he had not seen any sign of Bluerin—with the exception of the ubiquitous small storage containers the goblins used to recharge their wands, of course. In the end Lektriorer left Will outside the entrance gate and Will made his way back to the school just in time for dinner.

***

Will was sitting in another completely boring accounting lesson. First there had been a very dry monologue about the importance of double-entry bookkeeping; then they had been given a long list of transactions to enter and, of course, when Will did the double check at the end, it did not break even. He could not suppress a sigh, and started over once more. Then he suddenly felt a lot better as he noted that even Sabrina beside him had not been able do it right on her first go. He smiled secretly, being careful that she could not see it.

Finally the lesson ended with the most welcome chiming of the clock on the wall, and Will had even been able to work out his mistakes, so he now only had to write it down in a tidy way on a new accounts sheet as homework instead of having to do all the entries again, as most of the class had to. Only Sabrina had, of course, been able to finish the complete task by the end of the lesson.

***

On Friday Will was surprised when Mr Worker took them once again into the production building so they could watch the work of the Blueronics. This was a perfect opportunity for him to look for clues as to where the forgers might have got their Bluerin from. He looked around intently, taking in all the Blueronics at the worktables as they turned Bluerin into presents. He did not see anything out of the ordinary, so he turned his attention to the flow of the Bluerin, to see whether there was a way to steal it from this room.

He looked at the tank of Bluerin that stood right in the middle of the room. The Bluerin shimmered bright blue. But, except for the tubes that led to the worktables, Will could not see any way to get the substance out of the tank. He looked down intently, following the tubes. There were no interruptions as they wound their way through the room until they reached the first branch, where a much smaller pipe went off towards a workbench, and there on the bench was the only opening, a tap fixed to the end of the pipe. This was the only place the Blueronic could get the Bluerin—he or anyone else who got access to the table.

Will looked around carefully but there seemed to be no possible outlets except the taps and Mr Worker had told them that each of these was locked by the personal fingerprint of the Blueronic who worked at the table, and no other person would be able to open it. So Will reasoned that this could not be the place where the Bluerin for the forgery was acquired, unless of course a Blueronic was an accomplice. But that was something Will did not want to consider at the moment. Right now he rather thought the forgers had to get their Bluerin from somewhere else. He thought he should mention this at the next meeting of the task force.

He turned his attention back to the others, who were just watching the Blueronics in awe as they turned Bluerin into presents. He noted that Richard was standing off to one side and looked rather bored, regarding the others almost disdainfully.

***

After the last lesson of the day, Will was passing along the corridor. He was deep in thought about the last lesson and the new moves with the wand they had learned. They were important moves for the spells they would need for their tasks with the delivery of the presents.

As he walked down the corridor, he saw another student coming round a corner ahead of him. Will was so preoccupied he would not even have noticed the other student if he had not visibly started when he saw Will. He looked up and realised it was Richard, who was by then passing him without a word or any other hint that he recognised or even saw Will. He looked back after Richard, thinking it had almost looked as if he had caught him doing something he did not want others to see.

Will went on round the corner and passed a place where a narrow corridor branched off to the left. It was darker than the one he was walking down, for there were no windows, only a few lamps lit. He walked onwards then he suddenly stopped as he realised what he had just seen. There had been a goblin down the corridor and he had seen the typical, distinctive glimmer of Bluerin! The goblin had seemed to be carrying a glass box full of the stuff.

Will turned round immediately and tried to follow the goblin, who by now was nowhere in sight. Will broke into a run, going farther and farther down the corridor. He saw a junction up ahead and raced towards it. He could still see no sign of the goblin or the Bluerin. Then he reached the intersection and even as he was still wondering which way to go, he crashed straight into a figure that just at that moment was coming from the corridor to the right.

'Oooof!'

'Ouch!'

Will stumbled away from the figure he had run into, and the momentum made him hit the wall. Then he managed to catch himself, stood up, and turned round to see whom he had collided with.

He started. It was Beltorec!

'Sir, sir,' he stammered. 'I'm really sorry, sir! I didn't see you!'

Beltorec turned on him. 'What the... Who... Will! What on earth are you doing, young man? You can't race around here, running people into the ground like that! What were you thinking?'

'Sorry sir. I'm very sorry, sir,' Will stammered on.

'Well? I'm still waiting. What were you doing?' Beltorec asked sternly.

'Well, sir.' Sweat was forming on Will's brow, and not just from running. 'You see, sir, I went past the entry of that corridor.' He pointed. 'And as I glanced down it, I thought I saw a goblin carrying a glass box with Bluerin.' Beltorec looked at him in disbelief. 'Then I turned round to have a proper look. I thought I could see the goblin way down the corridor, so I started to run. But then I lost sight of him completely, so I ran even faster. That's when I ran into you, sir. Sorry about that, sir.'

Beltorec did not look pleased. 'I find that tale very hard to believe. What should a goblin do with that much Bluerin? And carrying it around like that? And doing so just here? Right in the middle of the school? Sorry, Mr Burns, that doesn't sound likely at all.' Beltorec looked down at Will in contempt.

'But sir, didn't you perchance see the goblin? He must have passed here just before you.'

'No. I didn't see anybody down here—at least not until you crashed into me like a maniac.'

Will could not understand why Beltorec would not believe him. The vice chancellor knew him. They were together in the task force examining the Bluerin fraud!

He tried once more: 'But sir, if you look at it in the light of this...*project* we are working on, especially as I also saw Richard coming out of the corridor and I'm sure he'd met the goblin—'

'Will. Will!' Beltorec raised his voice. 'Stop! Stop it!' He lowered his voice to a whisper. 'We don't talk about this in public! And stop trying to excuse your behaviour with this wild tale. Go, Will.' He sighed. 'Just go and get out of my sight! And I'll forget about all this.'

'But sir,' repeated Will plaintively. He could not believe this! However, Beltorec was not listening to him anymore; he just turned around and walked away without even looking at Will, who was left standing alone in the corridor. He was stunned. Why would Beltorec react like this? Why did he not believe Will, did not even listen to anything Will was saying? Will did not understand it. Well, nothing he could do about it now. He looked down the other corridors that were branching off, but of course he did not see anything at all—no hint of where the goblin or the Bluerin had gone. He shook his head and went back the way he had come, walking thoughtfully to his room.

Later on in the evening, Will was lying in his bed, still thinking about his encounter with Beltorec. It still did not make any sense—none at all. The only possible reason he could think of for Beltorec's strange behaviour was the unlikely chance that Beltorec wanted to cover for the goblin. But how would that make any sense? No, it had to be something else. Perhaps Beltorec was just angry at Will. But why? Will was not getting anywhere with this, and he finally drifted off into a restless sleep.

***

Will was sitting in another incredibly boring lesson about the Handling of Letters to Father Christmas. He supposed the subject was important enough, and it might even have been interesting, but the way Mr Parchmentinus taught it, it definitely was not. Will was beginning to nod off, then he awoke with a start.

Unfortunately Parchmentinus noticed this. 'Yes, Will? You want to add something?'

'Er, no sir... Sorry, sir.'

'What was it then? Hmm?'

'Er, just an itch, sir,' Will floundered.

'Oh, all right then. Ah...where was I?' Parchmentinus scratched his head. 'Perhaps you can help me, Will. What did I just tell you?'

'Ah, sir.... You were telling us about the handling of the letters to Father Christmas, sir.'

Parchmentinus shot him a disdainful look. 'That's a remarkably poor answer.' He snorted. 'The subject is called the Handling of Letters to Father Christmas, as you might recall. Try to listen a bit for a change, Will, it might even help improve your marks.'

'Yes, sir. Certainly, sir.'

'Now then, class...' Parchmentinus continued with his tedious monologue.

Will sank back on his chair in relief to be finally off the hook.

***

Late in the evening Will was sitting once again with the other members of the task force in the secret meeting room in the abandoned building. He listened intently to the others' reports, but there was not really anything new.

Finally Beltorec turned to him. 'Will? Do you have anything you can report?'

Will shook his head. 'No, sir, not really anything new, just a thought I've had.'

Beltorec nodded encouragingly. 'Yes?'

'Well, when we were recently observing how the presents were produced, I was thinking about how the forgers might get the Bluerin. But I've reached the conclusion that there's no possible way to get the Bluerin out of the production building. The only place with access to the Bluerin is the taps on the working desks, and I've been told each tap is coded to the Blueronic working at that desk.'

The others around the table nodded in agreement.

'Er, so I'd guess the forgers can't get the Bluerin there,' Will continued. 'Do we actually have any idea at all where they're getting the Bluerin from?'

Nobody said anything. Will looked nervously at Beltorec.

'Sir, there was one thing. Remember I told you about the goblin and...'

'Yes, yes,' Beltorec snapped. 'That was easily cleared up. Now, it appears we still don't even know where the Bluerin is coming from.' He sighed. 'We need to do better. So far we have next to nothing except hunches, rumours, and a few forged notes. Let's hope we've got more to work with at our next meeting. Please keep your eyes and ears open.' With that the meeting was ended, and Will headed back to the school building through the underground tunnel, feeling rather frustrated.

***

Will was sweating. He stood in the middle of the model living room in the training area. Stunt and the rest of the class watched him from outside the room. Will could especially feel Stunt's stern look on him.

He had got into the room without any problem. Then he had managed to gather the scattered presents and was now preparing the spell to transfer them to their correct positions under the Christmas tree. As he released the spell, the presents shimmered blue and disappeared. Instantly they reappeared underneath the Christmas tree in an orderly stack. Will, who had been holding his breath, relaxed and wiped away the perspiration that had gathered on his brow. He thought he had done quite well. He turned around and walked through the nonexistent wall and towards Mr Stunt. There was an unreadable look on Stunt's face as he glanced briefly at Will, although Will could see his lips curl in a tight, somewhat ironic smile. Then Stunt turned towards the class.

'Okay, you've all seen Mr Burns's performance. What's your judgement?'

At first nobody said anything, but then several of Will's classmates raised their hands. Will groaned inwardly when he saw Sabrina's hand shoot into the air, and even Annabel raised her hand, which could only mean he had made some serious mistake.

Stunt pointed towards Wesley. 'Yes, Mr Limerick?'

'I think he did quite well, sir. The presents are all stacked neatly in the right place.'

Will was relieved to hear this. So perhaps he had not made such a big mistake after all. But then he saw that Sabrina's arm was still straight in the air, although she was straining to stop herself from waving it—which was hard for her, Will suspected.

Stunt gave Wesley another tight smile, nodded once, and said, 'Yes, the presents are okay. But what was the problem? The big problem?'

Will froze. *Big problem?* he thought. What had he missed? He could not think of any major mistake. And Stunt had said the presents were okay. So what else could he have done wrong? He saw that only Sabrina still had her hand in the air. He could barely refrain from groaning loudly: now she was even waving it, eager to point out his mistake.

Mr Stunt looked at her. 'Okay then, Miss Bluetonic, please enlighten us.'

'Yes, sir,' she replied, completely missing Stunt's irony. 'He forgot to perform the covering spell before entering the room.' She smiled, pleased with herself, until she caught Will's expression, then she quickly looked down. When Will turned to Mr Stunt, out of the corner of his eye he saw that Richard was smirking.

Mr Stunt looked back at Will. 'Yes indeed, Mr Burns, that would have been quite a good performance if you had remembered to use the covering spell.' He frowned at the entire class. 'First thing you do before you enter a house or any area where somebody might see you, like a garden or some street, the very first thing you do is to cover yourself and anyone with you with the covering spell.' Then he very nearly smiled at Will. 'But otherwise, Mr Burns, it was a really good performance. The relocation of the presents was excellent.'

He continued with the lesson. 'Okay then, next is Mr Limerick, please.'

Will stepped back towards the rest of the class, glad to have finished. He could have kicked himself for having forgotten the covering spell. But, well, the rest of it had not been too bad. He relaxed and watched Wesley struggle through the exercise.

After everybody had been through the exercise, some doing quite well while others were not so good, they gathered in the briefing room. Mr Stunt summarised their performance, especially pointing out the main mistakes. Then he dismissed them and sent them off to lunch.

Chapter 12

Finally the great day arrived! Will woke up with a start, fearing he had slept late. He looked at his alarm clock and groaned: four o'clock in the morning! Still plenty of time before he had to get up. He turned over, trying to go back to sleep despite his excitement. At some stage he must have drifted off again, because he woke to the chiming of the big clock in the hall. Will heard the others stir in the dormitory.

'Get up, everybody!' Freddy called. 'Today's Christmas Eve. At last! The great day! We've got so much to do. We've got to go to the Plaza. I don't want to miss a single thing.'

And he bounded out of the dorm into the bathroom. Will grinned involuntarily. He could always rely on Freddy's energy and excitement. But today even Will was quite excited. Freddy was right: it was Christmas Eve, the most important day of the year for Snowfields and the White Christmas Organisation. The day everyone had been working for the whole year—and they were going to be part of it!

Will got up and followed Freddy to the bathroom, though a bit less energetically. He looked out of the window as he passed. It was rather dim outside, but, as he had been told, that was only to be expected. After all, Cloudy's Transportation Service had to move in a lot of their cloud platforms so they could distribute all the presents. And as the platforms were in the clouds, the sky was filled with them.

When he opened the door to the bathroom, he was instantly hit by Freddy's good-natured chatter.

'Good morning, Will, and what a glorious morning it is. It's so exciting, ain't it? The great day is finally here, and we've all got to help with the delivery of the presents. Oh, I do so hope that everything will go smoothly and that all the children get the right presents, all the things they've put in their letters to Father Christmas, and that we manage it all by tomorrow morning before the children get up, and not be late, but that's what the Christmas Clock in the Plaza is for, isn't it, so that everything can be done in time, which, of course, wouldn't be possible in normal time, and.... Blub.... Splutter.... I'd have to.... Blub....'

The rest of the sentence—for it all had been one single sentence, as the part of Will's brain that had not shut down out of self-preservation noted—was drowned out, as Freddy stuck his head under the running water to wash his face, which of course did not keep him from going on talking. This was fine by Will, who was already breathless again—something that happened regularly when he listened to Freddy. He laughed.

'Yes, Freddy, you're right. I'm rather excited too, and can't wait to get started,' he said when Freddy emerged from under the water. 'I hope I'll be chosen to help on a sleigh.'

'Yeah,' answered Freddy, positively aglow with excitement. 'I hope that too. That would be soooo wonderful, that's actually the best job you can get, flying around on a sleigh, visiting the festively-decorated homes, distributing the presents and placing them in the stockings and under the Christmas trees....'

'Okay, okay.' Will held up his hand. 'Let's get ready quickly.' As he went into one of the stalls for a quick shower, he could hear Freddy's chatter pour over his next victim.

Although Will enjoyed the hot water and the Christmas shower gel he had chosen—it smelled of fir trees, of baked apples and marzipan—he washed quickly, as he longed to go to the Plaza and for it all to begin. He towelled himself dry, dressed in his red Christmas working robe and got down to the

Ferum for breakfast. Bianca, Annabel and Spencer were already sitting there. Will joined them at their table and helped himself to rolls and jam.

'Are you ready for the great day?' asked Annabel and grinned.

'You bet! Finally it's here.' Will grinned as well. 'I was already assaulted by Freddy's excitement in the bathroom.' The others at the table laughed, as they were quite able to imagine what he meant.

'Well, it *is* the great day. And I bet even you are excited. Go on, admit it!' Annabel nettled him.

'Okay. Yes, I *am* excited too.'

They were joined by the rest of their class, and wolfed down their breakfast as fast as they could.

'Well,' Spencer said, 'everybody ready? Then we should get down to the Plaza so we can find a good spot in the front. I want to see everything and not just other folks' backs.'

'Yes, yes!' cried Freddy, who had been bouncing on his seat already, barely able to wait for the others to finish. 'Let's go!' He sprang up like a tightly coiled spring that was suddenly released.

They all got up and hurried out of the Ferum, through the entrance hall, and down School Lane in the direction of the Plaza. The whole village was richly decorated. Christmas trees were everywhere, with thousands of tiny lamps, great red, silver, or golden globes, sugar canes, and tinsel. Garlands of fir were strung across the streets along with twinkling lights and intricate red bows.

Bianca marvelled at their surroundings. 'Look, it's so beautiful!'

They went past the street to the main production sites. For the first time ever, Will saw no activity there—none at all. No one was working there on this special day. There were no

191

lights on in the buildings; even the constant gleam of Bluerin was absent. Just one or two of Caretrus's goblins were sweeping the storage areas, wearing special Christmas outfits.

The students continued over the bridge and down the street until they turned left towards the Plaza. Everyone in the village was gathering there around the great Christmas clock tower. Quite a few of the inhabitants of Snowfields were already there: teachers, goblins, students, Blueronics, magicians, and other creatures that lived and worked in Snowfields. A grandstand had been erected next to the clock tower for the top personnel, like the directors of the different departments, the vice chancellor, and the teachers.

Will and the others arrived quite early, so they found a place rather close to the stand and the tower. Of course Richard shouldered his way right to the front with Michelle in tow as usual. Will could see the teachers and directors on the grandstand. Beltorec sat right at the front. Lektrarissima, Blues, Factorius, and Securitas sat next to him, all in their best outfits. The Plaza was getting fuller and fuller as the other workers and inhabitants of Snowfields arrived. Finally the clock struck nine and chimed a merry Christmas tune. Beltorec got up, stepped out onto a small platform in front of the grandstand, and held up his hands, asking for silence. The crowd obeyed him immediately.

Then Beltorec started to speak: 'Dear colleagues, dear workers, goblins, helpers, students, and everybody else. The great day is here once again. The day of days, the one we've been working for all year long.' He made a dramatic pause. An expectant silence hung over the Plaza. Then Beltorec roared: 'It's Christmas Eve!'

A huge cheer went up from the crowd, and Will and the others joined in.

Beltorec smiled. 'As you know I'm not one for long speeches. Therefore...let's get cracking! But before we start, I've got a special guest for you.'

Will stood on the tips of his toes, trying to see above those in front of him, trying to see who this special guest might be.

'Magicuras, if you would, please.' Beltorec nodded towards the head of the magicians standing in front of the clock tower.

Magicuras nodded, turned towards the tower, and started to form intricate patterns in the air in front of him with his wand while chanting softly. A mist formed in the sky above the clock tower. It grew in size and finally settled into the form of a huge rectangle hovering in the sky. Then the middle of it turned luminescent, so it looked like a huge, silver screen. And on it an image was forming, getting clearer and clearer.

Will held his breath. He could not believe it. The image was...Father Christmas himself!

'Ho, ho, ho! Merry Christmas, everybody!' Father Christmas smiled warmly as he looked over the crowd gathered in the Plaza. 'My best season's greetings to all of you. You have all done a wonderful job during the last year. So let's bring it to completion and then have a great party tomorrow! Ho, ho, ho!' He slowly looked around again, as if he could see the whole Plaza. Will had the feeling that Father Christmas was peering at him directly. He felt so warm and comfortable inside.

'And now,' Father Christmas went on, turning more serious, 'I hereby invoke for this place the beginning of Christmastime! Let...the time...slow!' He gestured, and brilliant fireworks exploded from the clock tower. A deep chime rolled over the Plaza. On all four sides of the tower the clock faces started to glow with a bright, inner light. The hands shone golden, and the second hand just stopped as if frozen in place. Will and the others looked wide-eyed at the clocks. They were not moving anymore. The hands stood still. Christmastime had started! Even Freddy only managed an astonished, 'Oh!'

'Now then,' said the image of Father Christmas, 'I wish you all a merry Christmas! Ho, ho, ho!'

The screen dimmed and faded away slowly. A huge wave of applause swelled up all around the Plaza, and everyone cheered excitedly. Will found himself jumping up and down, hollering along beside Freddy, who was, of course, the loudest by far. Beltorec stood on the platform again, and waved his hands until the turmoil finally died down.

'Very good. Christmas has started! Now please, all of you go to your assigned positions and posts so we can start the distribution. To the great success of our ventures!'

'To great success!' was repeated all around the Plaza. The crowd broke up, and everybody hurried off. Will found Annabel in the throng.

'We should hurry back to the school! Where are the others?' he asked her.

'Yes, lead on, I'll follow. Freddy is over there, and I can't see the others anymore. Except Richard and Michelle—they just elbowed their way past me. Anyway we're supposed to be assigned our tasks in the entrance hall, so I don't think we've got to wait for the others.'

Will carefully pushed through the crowd in the direction of the school. Annabel followed so closely behind him that she bumped into him when he had to stop or move around somebody. He briefly thought that the members of the forging group had probably also been right there on the Plaza. But of course he had no way of detecting them. He thrust these thoughts from his mind. It was neither the time nor the place for them—it was Christmas Eve! And nothing else mattered. He would be busy enough as it was without trying to play detective.

194

Will and Annabel hurried down School Lane and went into the school building. Several desks had been set up inside the entrance hall. Above them were signs denoting the different classes. Will and Annabel went over to theirs. Miss Dustfall stood behind the desk and nodded at them in greeting.

'Miss Winston, Mr Burns. Merry Christmas to you both.'

'Merry Christmas,' they replied simultaneously.

Miss Dustfall smiled. 'Let's see then.' She looked at the lists in front of her. 'Ah, here it is.' She looked up at them again. 'You are allocated together. You will go with Mr Contractus on a sleigh to deal with wrongly distributed parcels. Good luck, and enjoy yourselves.'

'Wow, great!' Will gripped Annabel's arm in excitement and beamed at her. 'We're on a sleigh together!'

She grinned back. 'Yeah, that's fantastic. We're going to ride on a sleigh again.'

Miss Dustfall laughed as she saw their excitement. 'Off you go then. Go to the lawn at the back of the school. Mr Contractus will be there. If he isn't then just wait by the sleigh. He will find you there.'

Will and Annabel went along the corridor to the back of the school. On their way they went past Richard and Michelle, who had obviously been assigned together, but were quite as obviously not happy at all with their allocation.

'Hey, Richie, Annabel an' me are going with Contractus. We're on a sleigh to deal with stray parcels,' Will told them brightly.

'Yeah, great,' Richard replied caustically. 'We're to oversee the distribution on one of Cloudy's platforms.' He turned around abruptly. 'Come, Michelle, let's get away from these gloating fools.'

'Have fun,' Will called after them.

'That wasn't nice,' said Annabel. Then she giggled. 'But they deserved it.'

They hurried on towards the lawn at the back of the school, their red Christmas robes flowing behind them. On the platform just outside, they stumbled to a sudden halt. And stared. The lawn was full of sleighs. All of them were brightly and festively decorated with red ribbons, ties, golden and silver bells, and fir garlands. Four proud reindeer were hitched in front of each sleigh. They were also outfitted most festively with shiny, brown tack with silver bells and red ribbons. Even their antlers were polished and almost gleaming with an inner light.

Students and teachers scurried across the lawn, loading sleighs and getting ready to leave. Will and Annabel watched, spellbound, as a sleigh took off just a few feet away from them.

'Can you see Contractus anywhere?' Annabel asked after the sleigh had gone.

'Hmm.' Will scanned the area. 'No, there's too much bustle out there.'

'What now?'

'Well, Miss Dustfall said to wait by the sleigh. Contractus will find us there.'

'Yes, he will indeed,' said a deep voice right behind them, making them jump.

'Hello, Annabel. Hi Will,' said Contractus as they turned around. 'Sorry I'm late, but I had to pick up our flight plan on the way here, and there were quite a few others there who wanted the same. However, I'm here now, and'—he rubbed his hands together—'I'm happy that I have the pleasure of working with you two today.' He grinned. 'I have to admit that even I, even after all these years I've been here, get excited on Christmas Eve. After all, this is what we work for all year long! So let's get started. We've been allocated one of the toughest areas. There'll be loads of work waiting for us already. Follow me!'

And he led them onto the lawn, finding his way around the parked sleighs and through the chaos of students and teachers hurrying everywhere. Will and Annabel hurried after him, trying not to bump into other people. Contractus led them to one of the beautifully-decorated sleighs. He helped them up onto the rear seat and then jumped up onto the driver's seat. He shook the reins, and the reindeer took a few quick steps forwards. Will and Annabel gripped the railings beside their seat tightly. Then the sleigh smoothly lifted off the ground. It quickly gained height, and Contractus flew a wide circle, passing over the school and then over the village of Snowfields. The sleigh glided through the air easily, so Will loosened his grip on the railing. But then he had expected that Contractus would be a good pilot.

He looked over the side of the sleigh and saw the school and the village getting tinier and tinier as they spiralled up-wards. Suddenly Will felt a jolt, and an urgent-maintenance sleigh from Cloudy's overtook them at high speed. It went by so closely their sleigh was hit by the slipstream.

'Oi,' Contractus shouted after it. 'Watch it!'

But it was already far ahead of them, heading as fast as it could to wherever the problem was.

Rising higher and higher, he guided the sleigh in a helix so they were soon as high as the mountains surrounding the vil-lage. Above the mountains was a huge circle of clouds. Con-tractus flew the sleigh along the face of the clouds until they reached a wide tunnel that led through them. It did not take long to fly through, and they passed two other sleighs that were flying back towards Snowfields. The other drivers waved at them cheerfully. Soon they had cleared the tunnel, and Will could see the snow-covered countryside far below.

'Where are we going?' he asked.

'In front of you is a small screen, the grey rectangle. If you tap on it, you'll see a map,' replied Contractus.

Will looked in front of him, at the back of Contractus's seat. There was a grey, smooth, and rectangular surface there. When he tapped a finger on it, it lit up, and he saw a map just like on a tablet computer. The map showed a part of the country. He could see lakes, rivers, hills, villages, and towns. Part of it was enclosed by a red line.

'Can you see it?' asked Contractus, looking back over his shoulder.

'Yes, I can see it. The area inside the red border is ours?'

'That's right.'

'It looks rather small,' said Will dubiously.

Contractus laughed. 'Remember what I've told you before! That sector is the worst, for there are so many areas in there where Cloudy's coverage is just terrible. We'll have enough to do for sure. Well, hold on, it will take us a while to reach the sector!'

They flew high above the snow-covered countryside. Will enjoyed the flight greatly, taking in all the sights. He enjoyed the cool air on his face and, he realised with a start, also the company of Annabel sitting so close beside him. He sneaked a stealthy look at her from time to time, and—to his relief—she also seemed to enjoy being close to him, though he turned slightly red at this thought. He decided he'd better concentrate on the countryside again.

Finally Will felt that they were losing altitude. Suddenly there was a chime, and the screen in front of him lit up. In the corner of the map, a small, red square had appeared and was flashing.

'Oh, great,' said Contractus, who had heard the chime as well. 'The first call, and we're not even there yet. Will, if you'd please have a look at the message?'

'Sure. Er, how do I look at it?'

'Just press on the red square, and the message will pop up.'

'Okay.'

Will pressed a finger onto the red square in the corner of the screen. Promptly a window opened on top of the map.

'It says here: "Job 01, Area F8, Code blue-3. Please confirm." That's all,' Will told Contractus. Annabel had been reading the message as well and nodded.

'Okay,' replied Contractus. 'I assume you recall what a "blue-3" is?'

'Sure,' said Annabel. 'A failed delivery, but quite near the target, in a perimeter of five to ten yards around it.'

Will nodded as he recalled the lectures that had so bored him in the autumn, but now he could see how important they had been.

'Good!' replied Contractus. 'That's correct. A blue-3 should mean little trouble for us, as it's so close to the target. So let's go there. If you'd please confirm the job, Will? Just press the confirmation button.'

Will pressed the button marked 'confirmation'. The window closed, and a red, flashing dot appeared on the map. On the side of the screen, a small window opened in which Will could still see the job description.

'You should now see a flashing dot on the screen. That's our goal,' said Contractus.

'Yes, we can see it,' replied Will.

'Okay, then let's go,' said Contractus, and steered the sleigh into a tight turn to the left. 'I guess it'll take us ten minutes to get there,' he told Will and Annabel after a glance at his own screen.

They flew on over the snow-covered landscape. Will could see them nearing their goal as the blue dot on the screen, representing their sleigh, was getting close to the red flashing dot. Contractus angled the sleigh gently downwards. He turned slightly round to Will and Annabel.

'Okay, you two. I'll activate full screens and security measures for now, as it's still broad daylight and there's no sense in letting Father Christmas appear at this time of the day. His domain is the night. So the two of you will also need full coverage.'

'Sure,' replied Annabel, and pulled out her wand. She turned to Will. 'Do you want me to cover you?'

Will grinned. 'Please. You're much better at this than I am.'

Annabel grinned too. 'Oooh, you finally recognise that, do you?'

She pointed her wand at Will and performed the complicated pattern of the cover spell. She looked at Will critically, then nodded to herself in satisfaction. She pointed the wand at herself and repeated the spell. Then she frowned.

'You know, it always seems harder to spell yourself than to spell others. Somehow it's easier to make the movements with the wand when you're pointing it at somebody else. It's rather different, like the wrong way round, or like doing it in front of a mirror, when you have to point it at yourself.'

Will saw Contractus nod absently to himself as Annabel said this, as he was concentrating on lowering the sleigh and reducing the speed. Then Will saw Contractus take out his own wand, point it at the sleigh and the reindeer, and perform the necessary spells to hide them all from visibility or other forms of detection. Even any sounds they might have made would be covered from ordinary people—ordinary like Will had been not even a year earlier, he reflected wistfully. But only for a moment. Then he looked back at the screen and saw that they had nearly reached their destination, for the red and blue dots were almost overlapping. Contractus flew lower and lower until they were just above the houses. Finally he circled above a certain house, and Will saw on the display that they had reached their goal.

'Can you see—' began Contractus, but just then Annabel called: 'There! Over there, next to the tree.' And she pointed to a jumbled heap lying in the snow beside a large beech tree.

Contractus looked where Annabel was pointing, then he nodded and grinned.

'Right you are. That mess looks like the misplaced items.'

He turned the sleigh round and headed straight towards the untidy mound. As they got closer, Will could see it was indeed a pile of presents wrapped in bright and colourful wrapping paper. Contractus stopped the sleigh right beside them.

'Now, I know you've trained for this thoroughly, but this is your first time in the field, so I'll do this the first time and you can watch once more how the situation is handled.' He grinned. 'Don't worry, the next job will be yours. Just stay on the sleigh for now.'

He jumped off and went to the pile of presents. He looked at them critically. Will could see that some snow had already settled onto them. Contractus took out his wand and pointed it at the packages. When he performed the spell, the snow vanished, revealing undisturbed parcels that looked as if they had just left the stores at Snowfields. Contractus looked pleased. Then he began to walk around them while holding his wand close to the ground, pointing straight downwards, drawing a fine line of Bluerin in the snow and completing the circle when he reached the starting point. He looked over to Annabel and Will, to make sure they were watching him. Then he turned back to the presents, raised his wand and pointed it straight at them. He swung his wand in the complicated pattern of the final transfer spell—the spell which Will remembered all too well from the summer, as it had taken him ages to learn it. The pile started to glow, then it shimmered and seemed to shrink, and then it was gone. Contractus swung his wand a last time at the impression left in the snow. And where just a moment earlier a huge pile of presents had been lying, there now was just an unbroken and untouched layer of snow that looked exactly like the snow around it—just as if there had never been anything lying there at all.

Annabel nudged Will, grinned mischievously, and started to clap her hands. Will suppressed a laugh and joined her. Contractus looked at them in surprise, but only for a second; then he recovered and ripped off a gracious, majestic bow, twirling his wand through the air like a cowboy would do with his colt. Annabel and Will laughed. Contractus grinned, walked back to the sleigh, and climbed onto his seat again.

'Okay then, that was one of the easy ones! You'll do the next one. Are there any new assignments yet, Will?'

Will looked quickly at the display, feeling slightly guilty that he had not checked already, but then he thought that Contractus had told them to watch him closely—and not the screen. But there was no new red square waiting.

'No, Mr Contractus, there isn't one yet.'

'Okay. We still have to confirm the completion of the first job. You can still see it in the window at the side of the screen, right?'

'Yes.'

'Just tap on that window.'

'I've done that.'

'Now the window is larger again, and in the centre of the screen.'

'Yes.'

'Good. To confirm that the job is done, just tap on the button "job done".'

Will pressed the button. The window with the job description turned from red to blue, and a 'done' mark appeared in front of the description, together with the current time.

'Now you can close that window. Press on the small red circle in the top right corner.'

Will did just that. The blue window vanished.

'Okay,' Contractus said, and shook the reins. The reindeer started into a trot, and soon the sleigh lifted from the ground. Contractus guided them upwards again.

'We'll go back a way, more into the centre of our area, so we can respond more quickly to the next call,' he said back over his shoulder to Will and Annabel.

They had only been in the air for a minute or two when Will heard the chime again. He immediately looked back at the screen. Once again a small, flashing red square had appeared in the corner of the map. Will pressed his finger onto it, and the description window opened up.

'What does it say, Will?' asked Contractus from his front seat.

'It says "Job 02, Area A3, Code green-1. Please confirm",' Will replied.

'Ah, it would have been too easy if it were nearby, now wouldn't it,' Contractus mumbled, more to himself than to Will and Annabel. 'Go ahead then and confirm it, Will.'

'Done, sir.'

Contractus shook the reins once more, and the reindeer made a wide curve towards the north-west. Will followed their course on the screen, where the blue dot represented their current position and the red one showed their goal.

'What kind of job is this?' asked Contractus. 'I'm sure you can tell me, Annabel.'

While Will was trying to remember, Annabel answered seemingly without having to think about it at all. 'A green-1 is a minor misplacement in the correct room, for example the presents might be in the corner opposite the tree.'

'Right you are, well done!'

They passed over the snow-covered houses, dazzling in the bright sunlight. Will traced their path on the screen, trying to get a feel for the distances. He thought the area to which they had been assigned was in fact rather large, especially as Contractus had said this was one of the areas with the most work. But then he did not really mind, for this was what he had worked for all year long. He grinned.

'What are you grinning about?' asked Annabel, looking sideways at him.

'Oh, I'm just enjoying this—the fact that we're finally helping with the delivery of the presents. Aren't you?' he asked back.

'Sure. But remember,' she added, 'we'll have to deal with this one on our own.'

'Well,' replied Will, 'that's what we have been training for, isn't it? And'—he grinned mischievously—'I'm sure you'll manage it perfectly!'

'Oh now, none of that! We'll do this together!' Annabel replied firmly.

'Sure.' Will grinned. 'You'll do, and I'll make sure you're doing it right.'

Annabel poked him in the ribs—hard.

'Ooof! That was a joke,' Will said.

'It better have been!' snapped Annabel, but she grinned all the same.

Contractus finally guided the sleigh towards the ground. He took out his wand and spelled the sleigh, the reindeer and himself again, making them invisible. Annabel followed his lead and pointed her wand at Will and then at herself, hiding them both. Contractus took the sleigh farther down and constantly corrected its course as directed by the map on the screen in front of him. Finally he reached the front of the house that was their goal. The sleigh touched down on the snow-covered lawn with hardly a bump, and came to a halt.

Contractus turned around to Annabel and Will. 'Now it's your turn! It should really be no problem for you. As you said before, you've been preparing for this moment during the last months. I'll accompany you for now. But I'll stay in the background—you'll do the job! Of course, if you should run into problems you can't cope with or other difficulties, I'll help you. Don't worry, you'll just do fine.' He smiled at them encouragingly. 'Let's go for it!'

'Yes!' Annabel exclaimed, and punched the air. Will looked at her in surprise.

'Well, let's go,' she said to him pertly. 'What are you waiting for?' She grinned at him brightly.

'But...you...' Will did not know what to say.

Annabel grinned at him even more brightly. 'Yes? Was there something?' she asked him sweetly.

Will sighed. 'Nothing.' *Girls*, he thought, and refrained from shaking his head as this would certainly do him no good. He slid down from the bench and stood beside the sleigh. 'Let's go.'

'Of course. I was only waiting for you,' Annabel replied loftily and stepped down from the sleigh gracefully. They walked towards the house with Contractus following closely. Annabel stopped after a few yards.

'Door? Window? Chimney? How do we get in? What do you think?' she asked Will, not pertly or teasingly anymore, but all business.

'Hmm,' Will said. 'I think we should just use the door. It's the easiest way, and we are covered anyway. And as it's broad daylight, we're not supposed to be seen or to act like Father Christmas at the moment, so there's no need to use the chimney.'

'Yes,' said Annabel, 'I'm thinking the same.'

Behind them Contractus nodded.

'Okay then,' said Will. 'You want to do the spells? You're better at them than I am.'

Annabel smiled, this time just pleased. 'Of course. Are you ready? Let's go on in then.'

She walked towards the front door of the house, stopped in front of it and raised her wand. Will stood at her side and waited. Just at that moment, a cat came round the far corner of the house and froze as it saw them.

Saw? Will thought. But they were covered by the spell! He looked closely at the cat and had the feeling that it looked right back at him. Alarmed, Will looked back at Contractus and said, 'I don't think the spells are working. It looks as if the cat can see us!'

Contractus replied, 'Yes, as a matter of fact, cats can see straight through our hiding spells. Nobody knows why, that's just how it is. But it really is nothing to worry about. Normally they just leave us alone. And if not, well, we have spells to deal with them. You'll learn them in time.'

'Is it just cats, or can other animals see us as well?' asked Will.

'No,' replied Contractus. 'Somehow it's only cats. And snow leopards—but it's not too likely you'll run into one in this area,' he added dryly.

Meanwhile the cat had taken a good look at them, decided they were not interesting at all, and gone on its way. They turned their attention back to the door. Annabel gestured with her wand and spelled the door with the secrecy spell they had learned for this. It effectively hid them from sight when entering the house by projecting the image of a closed door while they opened it and went through. The only thing that could happen was if anybody was standing close to the door, they might feel a draft from the air that passed through. But that should not have been a serious problem.

Annabel finished the spell, and to their eyes the door began to glow faintly blue around the frame. Contractus looked at it for a moment, then nodded with satisfaction and smiled at Annabel.

'Well done! Let's go inside.'

So Will stepped forwards and opened the door gingerly. There was nobody to be seen. The others followed him, and then they were standing in a dimly lit hallway with traditional Christmas decorations.

'And where do we go now?' asked Annabel. 'Should we just try every door and hope one is the living-room?'

Contractus chuckled and reached into his pocket. 'No, no. That would be rather tedious, and would also rather increase the risk of discovery or mistakes. We've got these mobile screens on which our position and the goal are marked. They're just like the screens on the sleigh. See?'

He held up the device he had taken out of his pocket, and showed it to them. And indeed it was a mobile version of the screen they had used on the sleigh. It showed a floor plan of the building they were standing in—not with many details, but Will could make out the walls, the doors, and a staircase, though no furniture or windows. Again there were the blue and red dots for their orientation on the screen.

From the visible contours Will drew the conclusion that the blue dot, which represented their position, indeed showed them standing in the hallway, for the outline on the screen had the same oblong proportions. The flashing red dot seemed to be in the room on their left. And right enough, as Will looked up he could see a door to his left. He pointed at it and looked at Mr Contractus.

'So we have to go in there,' Will whispered.

Beside him Annabel nodded, for she had also been studying the image on the screen.

'Yes, but you don't have to whisper. With the spells we can't be heard,' replied Contractus. 'If you perform the spell, then we can go in there.'

Annabel did not need to be told twice. She quickly drew her wand, pointed it at the door, and again performed the spell that would cover the opening of the door. When the frame began to glow faintly blue, Mr Contractus nodded approvingly, opened the door cautiously, and went into the room that lay behind it. Luckily there was nobody in there. It would not have mattered anyway, for they were covered by the hiding spell, but Will was still relieved that they did not encounter anyone, because he was nervous enough as it was, being on his first field deployment. And doing the job unseen while other people were moving around in their own home was something he was not looking forward to.

The living room was neat and orderly. Nothing was lying around, and it was nicely prepared with Christmas decorations. And, of course, there was a large Christmas tree standing in one corner, colourfully but not gaudily decorated. Will liked it. But he was there to do a job and not to enjoy himself. He looked around the room and saw the pile of presents that were scattered in one corner. Contractus and Annabel were already standing in front of them, surveying the mess. Will joined them and saw roughly a dozen presents all jumbled together.

Mr Contractus cleared his throat. 'Well, you've got two options now. You can either just carry the presents over to the tree, or you could use the spells you've learned for this.'

'I think we should just carry the presents over there. That will be much easier and quicker than using the spells,' replied Will. He saw that Annabel was nodding her agreement beside him.

'Good. That's what I'd do. Just remember that when you pick the presents up, they will disappear behind your covering spell. But there's nobody here who'd see them disappear and then reappear again, so you can do it this way. There's no need to waste time and energy with the spells. You'll need them soon enough anyway.'

And he just bent down, picked up two presents, carried them over to the Christmas tree, and placed them underneath. Will and Annabel quickly followed his example, and after a few passes to and fro, all the presents were lying underneath the tree. Mr Contractus rearranged the presents with a few quick and precise movements that told of years of practise. Then he nodded, satisfied.

'Okay, well done. We've finished here. Let's get back to the sleigh.' And he led them out of the living room, carefully checking that the spell was still covering the door before he opened it. They passed through the hallway and reached the sleigh without incident. They climbed up and settled into their seats.

Mr Contractus turned back to Will and Annabel. 'Well done, you two. I'm quite pleased. It was just as I would have done it. Now all that's left to do is close the job in the distribution system.' He turned back round and looked at his screen. 'Oh, I see we've got two new jobs waiting already.'

This time Annabel leaned forwards and operated the screen. She closed the current job and opened the next one.

'"Job 03, Area B3, Code yellow-2",' she read aloud.

'Good. That's not far from here. Off we go.'

And they took off again.

Contractus turned partly round to them again and said, 'As you know a yellow-2 is a bit more challenging, so I'll handle it, especially since we already have another job waiting and have to hurry. But you can help, of course.'

'Okay,' replied Will and Annabel in unison, and Will certainly did not mind. He was happy just to watch and learn how to handle the different jobs. Because, he realised, even if they had trained and practised at school, being out there and doing the job for real was quite a bit different.

Soon they had reached their destination and Will could see the problem. Just as the code implied, the presents were all scattered around at the far back of the garden of the house. One was even up a tree; another one was stuck in the branches of a bush. Contractus hurriedly performed the cover spell on the sleigh and on himself, then jumped down from the sleigh as soon as it had slid to a stop. He hurried over to the scattered parcels, closely followed by Will and Annabel, covered once more by Annabel's spell.

When they reached the presents, Contractus took out his wand, swept it around in a wide circle to include all the packages, and performed the rather complicated spell that would relocate them to the inside of the house, directly underneath the Christmas tree. Will was impressed by the ease and grace with which Contractus performed the spell. Annabel—and Sabrina of course—could probably have matched it, but Will could still well remember his first tries with the spells in the training area at school. He certainly had not managed to relocate the presents, but had ended up with them scattered even more about the place than when he had started.

Meanwhile the presents had disappeared, and there was no trace of them left in the snow. Contractus looked pleased, and led Will and Annabel over to the house. There he waved his wand again in the pattern of a complicated spell that Will did not know, and part of the wall in front of them turned transparent, so they were looking directly at the Christmas tree inside the living room and could see that the presents were arranged neatly underneath it.

'Wow,' Annabel said. 'That's a fabulous spell. I'd like to learn that one!'

Contractus smiled. 'Yes, it can be very helpful indeed. But it's quite complicated, and unfortunately has much potential for misuse, so I'm afraid it will be some time before you'll learn it.'

'Oh.' Annabel looked rather disappointed.

'Let's go back. We're done here, and we already have the next job waiting.'

Will was the first to climb back onto the sleigh. He quickly closed the current job and opened the next one.

'The next job is in Area F7, and again a blue-3,' he told the others.

'Okay, let's go,' said Contractus, and shook the reins. They took off and rose into the air again. Soon they had reached their next destination. This job was similar to their first one, and they encountered no problems. After they had finished, there was no new job waiting for them.

'Good. A break is most welcome,' said Contractus. He flew them back into the centre of their area. He landed the sleigh on a small, remote hill where they could rest without the risk of being seen. They rested for perhaps fifteen minutes, and Will and Annabel used part of the time for an impromptu snowball fight that left them both panting and slightly wet. Then Contractus called them back to the sleigh.

'Hurry up. We've got an urgent red-5! We've got to leave immediately.'

Will and Annabel ran back to the sleigh and quickly climbed up onto their seat. Contractus took off as soon as they were settled.

Will looked at Annabel. 'Red means someone has discovered the presents that have been delivered to the wrong location. But what does five mean?'

'The same as with the other codes: the wrong location is another building within five hundred to a thousand yards of the intended destination.'

'Oh, I know that, but I thought it had a different meaning with a code red.'

'No, it hasn't. You thought wrong there,' Annabel replied snootily.

Will let it pass. They were flying over the countryside at high speed, and Contractus still urged the reindeer to go faster. Then he took the sleigh downwards so rapidly Will could feel his stomach protesting. Soon they had landed on the lawn in front of the house that was marked with the red dot on the screen. Contractus hastily performed the covering spells on himself, the sleigh, and the reindeer, and covered Will and Annabel far faster than they would have been able to.

Contractus jumped down from the sleigh as soon as it touched the ground, with Will and Annabel right at his heels, and jogged over to the house, pulling his wand out while running. He stopped right in front of the main entrance and quickly spelled it. He glanced at his hand-held screen, then quickly opened the door and walked inside with Will and Annabel close behind. Contractus passed through the hall and went up the stairs. At the top he glanced at his screen again, then backed up against a wall as a door opened and a boy about the age of twelve came out. The boy went past Contractus and then Will and Annabel, who had pressed themselves against another door, without taking any notice of them, and skipped down the stairs. When he was gone, Will took a deep breath, realising he had been holding it while the boy had walked past them.

But the spell had worked! There was no indication that the boy had noticed anything unusual at all. Will felt quite relieved now that he had experienced this for the first time. There was quite a difference between being told that the spell worked and actually seeing it work so well.

Contractus directed a short spell at his hand-held screen, glanced at it again, then waved his wand at the door of the room from which the boy had come and performed the secrecy spell on it. Then he opened it, motioned for Annabel and Will to follow him, and went in. When Will entered he could see it was the typical room of a teenager, with lots of posters stuck on the walls, clothes lying around everywhere, magazines scattered around—all in all the usual mess of a growing boy. He had to think briefly about his own bedroom at home; he felt slightly guilty, but quickly decided his had not been too bad—and he certainly had never made such a mess, had he?

But then Annabel quietly said, 'There.' And she pointed towards a corner in which several presents had been discarded.

Contractus checked his screen again and said, 'There should be seven presents there.' He stepped over to the heap, picked up a parcel, and handed it to Annabel. Then he picked up the next one and also passed it back. 'One, two, three... seven. Good, they're all here. The boy must have found them outside and brought them home.' He turned back to Annabel and Will. 'Okay, we're finished here. Let's take them to the house next door, where they belong.'

'Er, Mr Contractus?' asked Will. 'Wouldn't it be faster and easier to move them there with a spell?'

'Hmm,' replied Contractus. 'You might be right. It definitely would be faster. Okay then, put the parcels down here
on the floor.' Annabel and Will placed the presents where he
had pointed. Contractus pulled out his wand again, waved it at
the parcels, and performed the transfer spell. They shimmered
blue for a brief moment, then they were gone. Contractus
aimed his wand at his screen again, performed a brief spell,
and nodded in satisfaction.

'All good, all done. They are exactly where they belong.
Let's get out of here,' he told Annabel and Will, and led them
from the room. 'On our way out, we still have to spell the boy
and modify his memory so he doesn't remember the presents.
Otherwise it would be very awkward, and he would be wondering what happened here.'

'Sure,' Will replied.

They walked down the stairs. Then Contractus checked his
screen and pointed at another door, performing the hiding
spell once again. He went inside the room. Annabel and Will
followed, and Will saw they were in the kitchen of the house.
There was the boy they had seen upstairs, standing by the
open fridge and rummaging through its contents. Mr Contractus looked at Annabel and Will, then raised his wand, pointed
it at the boy, and waved it in the complicated pattern that Will
rec-ognised as the mind-modifying spell. The spell had been
demonstrated to them, but they had not been taught how to
perform it yet.

The boy froze for a second, looked around in disorien-
tation, then shook his head and started rummaging in the
fridge again. Contractus nodded, winked at Will and Annabel,
and led them out of the kitchen, through the hall, out through
the main entrance, and back to the sleigh.

When they were climbing up into the sleigh, Will finally
asked the question he had wanted to ask for some time: 'Mr

Contractus? Inside the house you spelled your hand-held screen several times. What did you do to it?'

'Oh, nothing special. I checked what people were in the house and where they were located. The other time I ascertained that the presents were in the right place. And then I used a spell to find the boy. You know, this hand-held is really a great tool if you know how to use it.' He grinned at them. 'And you can look forward to it. You two will receive your personal screens next year at school, and then you'll start learning all the tricks and spells.'

Will was stunned. 'Oh, that's fantastic!'

Even Annabel looked amazed.

Contractus laughed. 'Yes, it'll be great, you'll see. I can't even imagine anymore how we were able to manage without them. Well, I see we don't have a new job waiting at the moment, so we'd best go back to a more central position,' said Contractus, and gathered the reins in his hands.

Then suddenly a loud and piercing whistling noise made Will and Annabel jump.

'Oh no,' groaned Contractus, 'what now?' He let go of the reins and touched his screen. Thankfully the piercing noise ended. Will and Annabel also looked at their screen. A large, red-bordered rectangle had appeared and flashed quickly. Inside of the rectangle, Will could read in large, red letters: '2-black-black—All Units Respond Immediately!'

'Oh dear!' said Contractus. 'That one's really bad.'

He pressed the confirmation button, swiftly picked up the reins, and jerked them abruptly. He barked a quick 'hold tight!' back at Will and Annabel, who did not really know what was happening, and took off at high speed. Only when they were high up in the air, moving fast, did he turn around to Will and Annabel, who were hanging on to their seats, rather bewildered by this sudden take-off.

'Sorry to frighten you. I don't suppose you know what a double black is, do you?' he asked. They both shook their heads, and Will was a bit surprised that even Annabel did not know. 'A double black is the worst that can happen on this particular day,' explained Contractus. 'It's a complete failure of Cloudy's Transportation network with a total disruption of the present distribution! I've never experienced that before, although there have been simulations and plans for this case. We've got to leave here immediately and head for the nearest distribution hub of Cloudy's.' He urged the reindeer on even faster.

Annabel clung to the railing of the sleigh. 'But wouldn't it be faster if we used the transfer system—you know, like via street lanterns?'

'Yes, normally it would,' replied Contractus, 'but with a double black, that system is also down.'

'Oh.'

'Yes, that sums it up pretty well,' replied Contractus dryly.

'But what about our work? What about the wrongly delivered presents? Are we going to leave them just lying about?' asked Will.

'They are not so important right now. The double black comes first. We'll have to take care of the presents after this is sorted out,' answered Contractus.

'And the code-red jobs?' pressed Will. 'I thought they must be dealt with at once, before anyone messes about with the presents.'

'Yes,' answered Contractus, 'they do need to be taken care of immediately. And for this reason not everybody gets called back, so one of the teams located in the adjacent areas is going to cover our area for the code red jobs.'

'Ah, I see,' replied Will.

By then they were high above the ground and nearing the clouds. Will looked at the screen in front of him. He saw that Contractus had entered their destination, and that they were getting closer fast. That was fine, for he had looked down a moment earlier, which had not been a terribly good idea, as his stomach was telling him quite pointedly. An enormous cloud loomed right in front of them.

Contractus turned slightly back to Will and Annabel. 'We're getting near to Cloudy's regional hub, but we have to pass through some clouds to get there. I'm afraid it might get a bit wet. Sorry.'

And he flew the sleigh right into the huge white cloud. Will held his breath and closed his eyes, as he did not quite know what to expect. But all he could feel was a slight cold mist on his face, so he opened his eyes carefully and saw—nothing. Only white fog that was wet on his face. It was so thick he could not even see Contractus on the seat before him, or Annabel at his side. He could only make out vague shapes.

'We'll soon be there, no need to worry,' Contractus called back to them, his voice slightly muffled by the fog.

Suddenly the mist parted, and they were flying into a large, open area that looked like a hangar. And in fact that was what it was: a hangar for sleighs, with a roof and walls made out of cloud. As Contractus flew their sleigh in, Will could make out about a dozen sleighs already standing there. Students and teachers hurried from them over to the main entrance on the far side of the hangar.

Contractus landed the sleigh quickly but smoothly in a free space near one of the walls. He grabbed his hand-held screen and turned around to Will and Annabel. 'Let's get inside quickly and see what's going on here!'

He jumped down from the sleigh and hurried over to the entrance where the others had already disappeared. Will and

Annabel followed right behind him. While they were running across the hangar, Will could see a few other students and teachers he knew from the school, but none of his immediate friends or classmates. They passed through the entrance and hurried down a corridor. The walls, floor, and ceiling were all made out of cloud. To Will it looked exactly like the facility he had passed through on his way to Snowfields less than a year earlier.

Contractus called to another teacher: 'Inventus! Do you know what's happening?'

'Not any more than you. We just received the double black and left immediately. Now we're here.'

'Well, I thought delivery was a bit slow this year. At least I remember having to do a lot more jobs in the last several years than I've had this year so far.'

'Hmm, yes, now that you mention it...I might have had fewer jobs this year too. But I'm sure we'll soon hear what the problem is.' He barked a short laugh. 'Not that Cloudy's ever was without a problem!'

Contractus laughed too. 'That's true for sure!'

Will and Annabel hurried along behind the two teachers, together with the two students who were working with Inventus. Will did not know them.

'Hi, I'm Will,' he said to the two boys, who were slightly older than he was. 'And this is Annabel.'

'Hi. I'm Peter,' said the boy beside Will.

'Justin,' said the other, and nodded to them.

'Your first year at Snowfields, isn't it?' Peter asked.

'Yes,' Will replied.

'Well, you're certainly getting right into it now. We've never experienced anything like this in our time here,' Justin offered.

218

'And I'm not quite sure I want to experience anything like this at all,' said Will.

Justin laughed easily. 'Ah, don't worry. The teachers are good at what they're doing. They'll sort it out.'

By then they had reached the end of the corridor and followed Contractus and Inventus into the central operations room of the distribution centre. About fifteen students and teachers had already gathered in there. Contractus and Inventus went straight up to the front. Annabel and Will, as well as Justin and Peter, stood right behind them. Then a member of the staff of Cloudy's Transportation Service climbed up onto one of the desks in front of them. He cleared his throat loudly.

'Ladies, gentlemen! For those of you who don't know me, I'm Lektrorus, your obedient va—sorry for that.' He grinned nervously. 'Unfortunately we had to call you in for an emergency. Our entire distribution system for this sector has broken down. We're still trying to find out what's happened. It looks to be something serious, not just some minor computer error or anything like that.'

Will saw that Contractus was nodding knowingly to himself, as if he had thought as much already. Will turned his concentration back to Lektrorus, who continued: 'We'll divide you up into several teams to help us investigate the source of this disruption. You'll be joined by members of my staff.'

He jumped down from the desk and hurried through the crowd. He assigned the tasks to the teachers, who immediately left with their students in tow.

Contractus turned around to Will and Annabel. 'Come on, follow me. We've been assigned to investigate one of the temporary storage rooms.'

Inventus stood right beside them and talked to Peter and Justin: 'And we've been assigned to another of those storage rooms.'

Contractus nodded. 'Let's go. We need to get this solved as fast as we can. The distribution has to continue as quickly as possible. As you know we've only got this one day.' And he led them down one of the corridors. In places, branches led off to other parts of the distribution centre. Will got the impression that Contractus had been there before, since he led the way so surely and quickly.

Finally they reached a large door. Contractus pulled it open and went inside. Will and Annabel followed him. Then Will stopped abruptly and stared: they were standing in a very big room, and it was nearly completely filled with presents. Some were stacked high against the walls, and there were lots of small, movable cloud platforms with parcels on them.

'Wow,' he said.

An employee of Cloudy's looked up from sorting through parcels. 'Thank the stars. Finally some help. Oh, it's you, Mr Contractus.' He smiled. 'It's good to see you again.' His smiled faded. 'Though it might have been under better circumstances.'

Contractus nodded in greeting. 'Hello, Lektroror, good to see you too. And good having you to help.' He pointed at Will and Annabel. 'These are Annabel and Will. Two very bright students of mine.'

The employee put down the box he had been holding in his hands, turned to Will and Annabel, and bowed: 'Nice to meet you both. I'm Lektroror, your obedi—' He interrupted himself with an embarrassed smile. 'Sorry, force of habit.' He looked back down at the packet in front of him. 'If you'd please join me over here, I'll show you what we are looking for.'

'Sure. If there's something here, we'll find it,' said Contractus. He led Will and Annabel through the maze of bundles over to Lektroror. There he joined the goblin behind a workbench that was also made out of cloud.

'Right then, this is what we know so far,' Lektroror said, and put a hand on the present. 'In one of the last batches we received, there was an unusual shipment. It didn't contain anything that was to be delivered for Christmas Eve, so its contents are likely to be illegal. What exactly could the contents be? We don't know. Our detectors just registered an unusual, unauthorized shipment and triggered the alert. But these detectors we've got are only there to detect major disruptions in the delivery system, and aren't sophisticated enough to show us what exactly is wrong, or which the faulty parcel is. That's why we had to call you all in. We have to sort through all the packages that have arrived in the last batches and find the faulty one. Fortunately all the delivery systems were shut down immediately by the alert, so no more presents have arrived and none were sent out. Therefore the parcel has still got to be in our centre somewhere.' He smiled wryly. 'That leaves only thousands of boxes to sort through!'

'Okay,' said Contractus, nodding slowly. 'I understand your problem. What exactly are we looking for? And how are we going to examine the parcels?'

'That's quite simple. We just have to examine each one with the transparency spell and see if it's a regular present or if it's something else. What that something might be? I don't know.' He smiled ruefully. 'And we'll have to do that just several thousand times. So we'd best get on with it.'

'Okay,' said Contractus, 'let's split up, then we should get through this faster. Lektroror and I will perform the transparency spell. Will, you'll fetch us new parcels to scan. Annabel, you'll put them back again. It would be best to store them over there on the empty shelves so we don't confuse them and scan them twice.'

He picked up the first package, put it down in front of him, pointed his wand at it, and performed the transparency spell.

The parcel turned partly transparent so they could look inside. Will could see a teddy bear lying there. Contractus swept his wand over the parcel again, performing a spell to detect irregularities. Nothing happened—at least nothing that Will could see—and the box turned non-transparent again.

Contractus nodded and motioned to Annabel, who picked up the present and placed it on a mobile cloud beside her. Will promptly placed a new one on the workbench in front of Contractus, who repeated the scanning spells. Meanwhile Lektroror had finished scanning his parcel and Annabel had already removed it, so Will put the next one in front of Lektroror. They continued this until the transporting cloud next to Will was empty. He gave it a shove, and it floated over to Annabel, who had just finished putting the last gift on the mobile cloud beside her. She pushed it over to the empty shelf, where she stored the presents away neatly.

Will hurried over to the heaps of boxes and carefully pushed another heavily loaded transportation cloud over to the examination desks. Then they continued scanning the presents. This went on for some time, and slowly—much too slowly, Will thought—the heaps waiting to be scanned grew smaller, while the shelves on the opposite side of the room filled with parcels that had cleared the process. At one time Will saw a movement at the entrance to the storage room out of the corner of his eye, and when he turned his head to have a look, he thought he saw Richard peering into the room. But he immediately dismissed this thought. He really had not seen much more than a shadow. And why should Richard be there? And why should he have looked into this specific room?

Will shook his head silently and concentrated on his task again. Annabel had already removed the last present after Contractus had scanned it, and Will belatedly placed the next parcel in front of his teacher. They continued this for another twenty parcels or so, until Contractus stopped and sighed.

'Whew, I think I need a break. This is exhausting!'

'Definitely a good idea,' agreed Lektroror.

Will pushed some empty transporter clouds towards the workbench: 'We could rest on these.'

'That's a good idea,' said Contractus. He pushed a smaller cloud into the middle and waved his wand in a complicated pattern over it. Four glasses, several bottles with juice and water, and a platter filled with sandwiches appeared on the cloud.

'Wow,' said Will.

Contractus grinned. 'Don't stare. Dig in!'

And that was what they did. Soon they had finished the sandwiches and the juice. Contractus got up and cleared the table with another spell. They went back to scanning the parcels. Will continued placing them in front of Contractus and Lektroror, and Annabel in turn removed them and stored them away again.

Then Contractus suddenly exclaimed, 'What's this?' He pointed at the present lying on the workbench in front of him. The others gathered around him. Lying there was a parcel that Contractus had already spelled, so its sides were transparent and Will could look inside it. He could see what appeared to be a gun. A gun as a Christmas present for a child? No wonder Contractus was surprised.

Lektroror looked at it. 'Hmm, let's see....' And he pointed his wand first at the object and then at the hand-held screen lying by his side. Will could see that a sort of code popped up on the screen. Then the code vanished, and a description took its place, but it was too small for Will to read.

Lektroror looked at the screen. 'Ah, yes, that's what I thought. That's a genuine-looking water gun. You know, like those water guns we had as children.'

'That's the first time I've seen one of those. I didn't even know that we produce anything like this.' Contractus eyed the gun. 'It looks awfully real to me.'

Lektroror just shrugged his shoulders and continued scanning the next parcel.

'Oh well,' said Contractus. 'Not the time or place to wonder about this.' And he handed the parcel to Annabel while motioning for Will to place the next one in front of him.

They continued this for a while with nothing spectacular happening. Will looked around and judged that they had sorted through about half of the presents that were lying in the room. He continued putting box after box in front of Contractus and Lektroror, and twice they thought they had found something. But when Lektroror compared it with the shipping information in the distribution system, they saw that the parcels contained exactly what was supposed to be in them. Once or twice Will glanced towards the open door, as he had the feeling somebody was looking into the room, but he never saw anybody apart from the instant when he thought he had seen Richard.

He was recalled from his musings when Contractus said again, 'Let's check this one! This certainly doesn't look right.'

Will looked up and saw Contractus give him a quick but very pointed look. At first he did not understand why, but then he looked at the present in front of Contractus, who had already performed the transparency spell on it so they could see its contents. Will could not quite believe what he saw: money—loads of money! There were several bundles of notes tied up neatly with paper bands—and they were twenty-pound notes! Now he could understand Contractus's look at him. This had to be a shipment by the forgers they had been hunting in Snowfields.

Lektroror was already consulting his hand-held screen. 'Hmm, I can't find anything about this parcel in the database. There's absolutely no information on it—no code, no contents, nothing. As far as I can see, this parcel shouldn't even exist!' He looked again at his hand-held, completely confused.

'Ay,' said Contractus under his breath, but loud enough for Will to hear, 'it certainly should not.'

Before Will could do anything, something strange happened: suddenly everything seemed to become very slow. The movements of Contractus and Lektroror, Will's own movements, even his thoughts seem to be getting slower and slower, seemingly coming to a complete stop. Then, just as suddenly, everything seemed to be normal again. Will could not remember what exactly he had been doing. He only knew that somehow his left side was hurting. He gingerly touched his stomach, and it felt as if he had a bruise there. He looked down and saw that he was holding a present in his other hand. So he put it in front of Contractus, who frowned at it and shook his head. He and Will looked at each other and Will shrugged his shoulders. Contractus motioned for him to be quiet, and turned round to Lektroror and Annabel.

He said to them, 'I've just thought of something. I'll have to go outside and check it. I'll need Will to help me. We won't be long. Just keep checking the presents, okay?'

He signalled for Will to follow him, turned round, and went out of the room. In the corridor he turned left and led Will only a few yards down until he reached a narrow door. He opened it and Will followed him into what turned out to be a small conference room that could hold a handful of people.

Contractus turned round to Will and looked at him gravely. 'Okay. You looked as if you felt something as well inside there.'

Will nodded.

'What did you feel?' asked Contractus.

'Well, I can't really say. I don't even know if I felt anything at all. It just seemed to me like everything was frozen for a moment, and then everything was back to normal again. Except I have the feeling that something happened during that moment.' Will hesitated. 'A lot, really. But I can't remember a thing. I can't really even remember what exactly I was doing the moment everything froze.' He glanced down and carefully touched his side, which felt very sore. 'And somehow I got a bruise on my side and stomach that was not there before.' He looked up at Contractus and was rather surprised by his reaction. Contractus looked quite intrigued, impressed, and even a bit taken aback.

'Will,' he finally said, 'I'm more than impressed. Most people wouldn't have felt anything at all. I'm sure Annabel and Lektroror didn't feel a thing and just kept on doing what they had been doing. And I've had special training to detect something like this. But to feel and to realise as much of it as you did is a rare talent. Extremely rare.'

Contractus looked at Will as if he wanted to add something, but then he just shook his head. 'We'll have to talk about this later. First we have to find out what this was about. What you felt there was a freezing spell. It freezes every person in the room and modifies their memories so they don't remember anything about it later. Quite often they can't even remember several moments before the spell. Now we have to find out what happened during that time and why the spell was used on us.'

'How can we find that out?' Will could not imagine how that might be possible.

'Fortunately,' Contractus said, and dramatically raised a finger into the air, 'there is a spell that replays this lost period of time, and that'll show us what this was all about. Come, sit down. It's a bit like watching a film. Want some popcorn?'

Will stared at Contractus, who grinned. 'No popcorn. That was a joke. But watch closely.'

And he took out his wand and used a spell Will had never seen before. In front of them, right on the wall, a picture appeared. It *was* like watching a film. Will could see inside the storage room where they had been working. He could see himself as he placed a new parcel in front of Contractus, Lektroror as he performed a spell on the parcel lying in front of him, and Annabel as she put some presents on the shelves.

'These are the last few minutes before the freezing spell was conjured. Just wait,' said Contractus. And Will continued to watch himself as he fetched new presents and placed them in front of Contractus and Lektroror in turn. Nothing unexpected was happening. Then Contractus suddenly said, 'Now!' and he pointed towards the entrance to the storage room.

Will could see a wand that was aimed into the room from outside. But he could not see the person holding the wand. The person was hidden by the door frame from this perspective. The wand moved in the pattern of a very complicated spell, and Will could see a blue shimmer emanating from the tip. The shimmer flooded the room, and finally reached Contractus, Lektroror, Annabel and himself, who had all stopped their work and were staring at the door and the person holding the wand. The Contractus in the film reached for his wand, but then the blue shimmer reached him, and his movements froze.

'Ah,' said Contractus, more to himself, 'too slow!' By then the shimmer had enclosed the others too, and they also froze in their tracks. 'Look, here he comes!'

Will looked intently at the scene. Then he caught his breath—for the person that walked into the room with a satisfied smile on his face was none other than Richard! So Will had in fact been right when he had thought he had seen Richard earlier. He felt quite angry with himself. He should have trusted his feelings and should have checked then. But he pushed the anger aside quickly. He had to watch the rest, to see what Richard had done.

Richard had strolled into the room. He stopped when he reached the frozen Will, the edges of his mouth curling up in a cruel grin. He kicked Will viciously in the side. Without taking his eyes off the 'film', Will's hand involuntarily touched the bruised and tender area. Richard moved forwards and stopped before Contractus. He looked down at the package that was lying on the workbench in front of the teacher—the one with the bundled notes inside. Richard smiled again, picked it up, and strolled out of the room, not really in a hurry. He reached the door and went out, so Will could not see him any more. He could just see that Richard pointed his wand back into the room and performed a short spell. Then Will could see himself and the others unfreeze, looking up in bewilderment for a moment, and then going back to work.

Contractus's spell stopped, and the projection on the wall disappeared. He raised his eyebrows and looked at Will. 'Well? What do you think?'

Will looked back and slowly said, 'I always thought there was something strange about Richard. He's always so arrogant, and he never does anything with the rest of us. He's always hanging out with Michelle. And they always stick together, talking in secret and turning really tight-lipped when anyone joins them. But I've never seen him actually do anything suspicious, or something that connects him directly to the forgery—at least until now.' Will thought for a moment. 'The only thing I can remember is when I found the forged note in the corridor, Richard was following close behind me. But I don't think he saw anything. I immediately hid the note.'

'Hmm,' Contractus said, stroking his beard, 'but now we've caught him red-handed. So what do we do about him now? He's certainly not the leading figure behind all this. This is a rather large case of forgery, and quite a few people must be involved in it.' He was still rubbing his beard, deep in thought. 'What to do now....'

Will jumped up from his chair, looked at Contractus, and asked, 'Shouldn't we follow Richard?'

Contractus shook his head. 'No, I don't think that would be a good idea. Firstly he'll be long gone by now. And secondly he wouldn't really be of much use to us. We'd only catch him, but not the others who are involved in this. No, that wouldn't help us at all.'

'And what do we do instead? What do we tell Annabel and Lektroror?' asked Will, slowly sitting down again.

Contractus looked at him. 'Good questions. Let's see.... We obviously can't tell them the whole story. But we've got to tell them something. We've got to finish this search and get back to our task at hand, the correct delivery of the presents. We mustn't forget that it's Christmas after all. And Cloudy's needs to start up operations again as soon as possible. We've lost enough time as it is!'

'Oh,' said Will, slightly embarrassed. 'I'd nearly forgotten with all this happening.'

Contractus smiled at him lopsidedly. 'We need to get back to the others.'

Will got up again. 'What do we tell them?'

'We'll tell them what happened. We'll say we were spelled and the present was stolen.'

'And what are you going to tell them if they ask what was in the parcel?' Will pressed on.

Contractus replied, 'That we don't know. That it was stolen before we could have a look inside. And that we've done all we can, and the security service has to take over.' He winked at Will. 'And who is the head of security?'

Will frowned. 'That's Mr Securitas, and...oh, now I understand, sir.' He looked at Mr Contractus 'He's part of the investigation team. He'll know what to do and can carry on the search in an appropriate manner.'

'Exactly,' confirmed Contractus. 'And we can carry on with the delivery of the presents. As I've already said, it's still Christmas after all.'

He led Will back into the storage room, where Annabel and Lektroror were still examining the presents.

Mr Contractus walked right over to them. 'You can stop it, you two.'

Lektroror looked up in surprise. 'Oh, did you find something?'

Annabel looked up as well.

'Yes. And no.' Contractus smiled grimly. 'I could detect that we were spelled with a freezing spell. We had obviously found the present we were looking for, but then someone used the freezing spell on us and took it.'

Lektroror looked worried. 'It was stolen? But you know who it was? And what was in the parcel?'

Will looked at Contractus, who pointedly ignored him.

'Unfortunately we don't know either. Will and I tried to follow him, but he was already gone. And he had taken the parcel before I could have a closer look at its contents.'

'But—' Lektroror continued. Contractus interrupted him at once and held up a hand towards Annabel as she started to say something as well.

'There's nothing more we can do here right now,' Contractus continued, 'and we need to get back to the delivery of the presents as quickly as possible. After all, it's still Christmas!'

Lektroror nodded and squared his shoulders. 'Of course you are right. We must get back to our actual work immediately—as you say, it *is* Christmas, and we've got to get things up and running as fast as possible. I'll go and inform my superiors.' He turned to leave. But then he turned back to them. 'Oh, I'm sorry.' He bowed deeply and smiled mischievously. 'Your obedient valet!'

Contractus groaned, and with a final laugh Lektroror turned around and quickly left the room.

Contractus looked at Will and Annabel. 'And we'll hurry back to our sleigh and return to our sector. Follow me!'

They followed him out of the storage room, back through the corridors, and into the hangar.

Contractus pointed to their sleigh. 'You two get over to the sleigh and get it ready so we can leave straight away. I'll just inform headquarters about what we were able to find out.' And he went over to a console on the wall of the hangar. Will and Annabel hurried over to the sleigh and were so busy preparing it for the take-off that, to Will's relief, Annabel had no time to question him more closely about the events in the storage room. Soon Contractus jumped up onto the sleigh and they were off again, flying back to their sector.

Once they were there, jobs came in immediately, and they were kept busy hurrying here and there, gathering up presents from all over the place and putting them under the right Christmas trees. Fortunately nothing else out of the ordinary happened, especially not another double black. The work went on the whole day, until in the evening their shift ended and they were relieved by the next team, which was going to continue throughout the night. Soon they were flying back towards Snowfields. To Will the return journey seemed much longer, but then he guessed this was just because he was tired, and in the morning there had been the excitement of going into the field for the first time. Finally Contractus landed the sleigh smoothly on the lawn behind the school.

He turned round to Will and Annabel. 'That was great work. Thank you very much, both of you.' He jumped off the sleigh. 'You know, we have a fine tradition here at Snowfields. You see the stall over there?'

They both looked where he was pointing. Next to the wall of the school, Will could see a wooden stall with Christmas decorations, fir branches, pretty red baubles, and thousands of small lights.

'Let's go over and see what they've got there,' Contractus said. He smiled and led the way.

Once there, Will could see Mr Worker and Miss Itaway behind the counter. They greeted Will and Annabel cheerfully and handed them steaming mugs.

'Merry Christmas to you.' Miss Itaway smiled at them.

Contractus took a mug and lifted it up to his face. 'Ah.' He sighed deeply as he breathed in the steam and the aroma. He turned to Will and Annabel. 'This is our famous Christmas tea. It's only made on this special day, and you only get it after your shift. Mr Worker here has a keen eye on that.'

Mr Worker heard this and gave Contractus a sly wink.

'Go on, try it,' Contractus encouraged them.

Will tasted the tea carefully, as it was still steaming. It was delicious, with lots of Christmas aromas. Will could especially taste cinnamon and a hint of marzipan.

'It's good,' he told Contractus. But Contractus just watched them. So Will added: 'Very good, with cinnamon.'

Contractus nodded, but still kept on watching them intently. Confused, Will took another sip. And his eyes widened in surprise. He looked at Contractus in amazement. 'But now... it tastes like baked apple.' He took another sip. 'And now it tastes like orange.' He stared at his mug, but could not see any change in its contents; there was still the same brownish-looking liquid in it.

Contractus laughed. 'Good, eh?' he said. 'That is our great Christmas tea! With every sip it tastes different. But it always tastes like Christmas.' And he took a sip himself. 'Ah.... Simply delicious.'

Again Will looked at his mug in amazement, and took another sip. It was the best tea he had ever tasted.

Chapter 13

Will had been thinking hard during the last hours. He had tried to figure out who could be behind the fraud, behind the forgery. Richard was certainly part of it—he had proven that when he had stolen the parcel at Cloudy's transportation hub. But he could only be a small cog in the wheel, as he had only come to the school recently, together with Will.

No, to pull off a fraud like this, there had to be persons on the higher levels involved, maybe even from the highest level— the directors, for example. They could most easily access the Bluerin. Will thought and thought about this. Finally he reached the most surprising but also most likely conclusion. When he considered the means, the necessary structures, and the logistics needed for such a fraud, everything pointed to only one possible solution. But this solution unfortunately also meant he could talk to no one about his suspicion, because if the person he was thinking about was really the head of everything, Will could trust no one, for he could not know who else might be involved.

Therefore he was now on his way to verify his conclusion in the only way he could think of: he would confront the person he suspected of being behind all this. He was on his way to Beltorec! Why Beltorec? He had all the means at his disposal. He could easily acquire the necessary personnel. He had most extensive connections with all departments. He could force students to do the dirty work by threatening their school careers. But then Richard, for one, probably had not needed much threatening. He had most likely been all too ready to go along. And then Will remembered the strange scene he and his friends had observed when they first visited the village—Richard and Michelle talking to the goblin holding the box of Bluerin, Beltorec's sudden angry appearance and rough treatment of the two students. So Richard had been tied to Beltorec and Bluerin right from the start. Will realised this made his theory all the more likely.

Will finally went around the last corner and was standing in front of the door to Beltorec's office. Taking a deep breath and trembling slightly, he finally opened the door. Interestingly, Crown did not react at all; the smooth square in the wood of the door remained that way. Will went inside the anteroom. It was empty—fortunately no Mrs Script he had to fight his way past—and so he walked straight towards the next door. Before he had even reached it, the door to Beltorec's office opened. Will went inside warily. Beltorec was sitting at his desk, smiling enigmatically.

'Ah, hello Will. I thought it might be you. Not a good idea to come here on your own, you know. But here you are, so time for you to meet my friends. Say hello to them, Will.'

Beltorec gestured towards the wall next to the door. Will turned his head—and was shocked. Beltorec had done the unthinkable, the ultimate forbidden! There, lined up neatly against the wall of the ornate office, were six huge figures, each with a slight blue glimmer. Beltorec had created Bluerorcs! Evil, mindless creatures made totally out of Bluerin—no life, no feelings, no conscience. And no restrictions. And invincible!

Will had learned about Bluerorcs in one of his lessons. However, since no one alive had ever actually seen one, they were sometimes regarded as myths, as nightmares to scare people with. It was believed that no one had the knowledge to create such a horror anymore, and even if they did it would be far too dangerous to call them into existence. Strangely enough, at the time Will had not made the connection between the mythical Bluerorcs and his dream so long ago—the dream he had had before he even knew anything about Snowfields or Bluerin. Only when he saw them standing before him right now did he feel a first flicker of fear.

'But...why?' he asked finally in a low voice.

'You mean why I did this? Why I created my dear friends here? Or why I forged the money?' Beltorec curled his lips in disdain.

Part of Will's mind shuddered at the look.

'Y-y...Yes, well, all of them really. You are headmaster here. You are one of the directors. What more could you want?'

Beltorec's countenance darkened. 'What more could I want?' His voice got louder. 'What more could I want?' He jumped to his feet. 'Being headmaster of a scruffy old school, always bothered by stupid students who think they are oh so clever? Being cut off from the world, being confined to this tiny village with nowhere to go?' His voice grew still louder. 'And you ask me what more I could want?'

Will ducked. 'Well...sir...you've achieved so much here, I would think. But if you don't like it here, why didn't you just leave to live somewhere else?' He was genuinely surprised.

'Why didn't I just leave?' Beltorec screamed madly. 'Because I've been stuck here the last fifty years, you idiot! How could I live in the normal world after such a long time? What job could I do? I'd just go to a firm and say, "Hello, I'm really experienced, and I can do a great job at your firm." And when they ask me about my references, I'd just tell them, "Oh, you know, I've worked with the White Christmas Organisation, which you have never heard about, and I've been headmaster of a school nobody knows exists, and, yes, in a place that's hidden and nobody has ever heard of. But I'm really good at it, right, just the best!"'

Will backed up until he was right against the wall. 'Okay, yes sir, I can see the problem now.'

'Ooooh, he can see the problem now, can he? Fancy that.' Beltorec pointed a trembling finger at Will. 'You know nothing!' he said slowly. Then his voice suddenly became very soft when he saw Will moving. 'Get him, my beauties. Go, my Bluerorcs, chase him down!' he purred at them.

Will, who had expected this the moment he had seen the Bluerorcs, inched towards the door. The moment Beltorec called them, the Bluerorcs started glowing blue and came to life. They opened their eyes, which were piercing blue, and started moving their limbs as if trying to get a feel for them. Will bolted through the door, running as fast as he could. Beltorec's mad laughter followed him.

'Run, Will, run! Give my friends a good chase. But don't you worry, they'll get you without doubt.'

Will raced onwards, and Beltorec's voice became fainter and fainter as he kept up his mad ravings, until Will could hear him no more.

But what he unfortunately could hear most clearly were the Bluerorcs lumbering after him, crashing and smashing through everything that was in their way, not even bothering to open the doors he had slammed shut behind him. They just crashed through the hard wood without missing a step. Will ran on, taking turns at random. He started to breathe more heavily. And still the Bluerorcs were behind him, though they were a bit slower than he was, and so he was able to put a bit of distance between him and them. But they followed him un- erringly. He slammed another door shut, ignoring the loud and angry protest of the door guardians:

'Oi, what do you think you are doing!'

'Alert! Berserker on the loose!'

'Who was't? Who was't?'

'OUCH! You idiot!'

'Who do you think you are? You daft or what?'

'What the...?'

They screamed after him. He ignored them, racing on-wards, starting to panic because he had lost all sense of direction. Suddenly he felt a presence beside him and he nearly jumped out of his skin as something touched his shoulder. They had got him! But his legs kept pumping and dragged him onwards. Then he only felt the pressure of a reassuring hand. 'Will. It's me. Calm down.'

Will knew this voice! He quickly glanced to his side and saw Conrad jogging next to him.

'What can I do? ' cried Will. 'Where can I hide? I can't last much longer with those things behind me.'

'This way,' said Conrad confidently. The security agent pushed Will down a couple of corridors and through a door.

'He'll help you and I'll try to divert the Bluerorcs.'

And he was gone.

Another figure stood in the doorway as Will came stumbling through it.

Will looked up. It was Contractus! He pushed Will to the side of the door. 'Was that Conrad? Good agent that one. You're lucky he was assigned to you. Watching over you even here in Snowfields. Not all the field agents would do that. Now, quick! Stand next to the wall on the other side. And take this!'

Contractus quickly shoved a brown bag into Will's hands.

Will looked at it and ripped it open. 'What is it?'

There were small, glass globes in the bag. They glittered bright blue, and Will could see small amounts of Bluerin in them.

'Bluerin?' he asked incredulously.

'Yeah, the only thing that is supposedly able to stop Bluer-orcs! Of course nobody has much experience with them, especially nowadays. Their last known appearance was around three hundred years ago. Luckily I read a bit about them once, and the only thing that was ever tried successfully against them is pure Bluerin!'

'But...how?' Will asked. 'That's what they're made of.'

'Well, don't ask me. Let's just hope it works. Perhaps it disturbs their structure or something. Now is not the time to question this. Here they come!' Contractus stood next to the other side of the door, opposite Will. 'Just throw the globes at them. The glass is thin and should break as soon as it hits them.'

Contractus pulled open his own bag and took a globe in his hand, gripping it firmly. Will took out a globe too, noting absently that it felt slightly warm. The crashing noises of the Bluerorcs were really close by now. They should be here any second. Then the door in front of them burst with a crash. Will ducked to avoid the flying splinters.

The first Bluerorc came crashing through the remains of the door and slowed when it saw Contractus and Will standing there. It swayed from side to side for a moment, as if wondering who to attack first. Then another one crashed into its back, but could not get through the door.

'Now!' shouted Contractus.

Will threw the globe at the first Bluerorc. It hit it at the same time that Contractus's globe hit on the other side. The Bluerorc stopped dead in its tracks.

'It works!' shouted Will. 'It really works!'

'Yes, it looks as if it does. But let's move away a bit, just in case,' Contractus replied.

They moved away from the Bluerorc, their backs to the walls. It was still not moving.

'Should we throw another one?' Will asked breathlessly.

'No, we should wait and see what happens. And there are still more of them.'

On cue the Bluerorc in front of them was pushed aside as the next one made its way into the room. This one went straight for Will.

'Throw!' Contractus shouted, and Will hurled a globe at the new Bluerorc. Contractus threw one from the other side. This Bluerorc also stopped dead in its tracks.

'Let's move on a bit,' said Contractus.

They edged along the walls towards the next door, still watching the Bluerorcs.

'It seems to freeze them,' said Will. Indeed the Bluerorcs seemed frozen in the positions they had been in when the globes hit them. Other Bluerorcs bumped into them from behind, trying to get through the door. They pushed harder until finally the two frozen Bluerorcs fell forwards. Two more Bluerorcs stepped mindlessly over them, not caring whether they trampled on their fellows.

Contractus and Will were ready. They threw another load of globes, which hit the Bluerorcs. These two also froze right away. But they again were immediately pushed over by the Bluerorcs following them. Will and Contractus threw globes at them. And again the Bluerorcs stopped.

'How many are there, do you know?' asked Contractus. 'I don't have many globes left.'

'There were six in Beltorec's office when I left. I haven't seen any others.'

'That's good! Then we've got them all for now,' answered Contractus, relaxing visibly.

'What will happen to them? Are they just going to stay frozen like that? Will Beltorec be able to bring them back to life?' asked Will, eyeing the frozen Bluerorcs.

'I have no idea,' replied Contractus. 'The book in which I read about this didn't say anything about what would happen to them after you throw the globes at them. But I'd expect that since he was able to create them, Beltorec will surely be able to revive them. He is, after all, very knowledgeable and very able. He knows a lot about Bluerin, and even some quite exotic spells. Nevertheless it's amazing that he was able to create the Bluerorcs—and six of them at that! So I guess no one suspected how much he really knows and what he's capable of. But let's get away from here while we can. It's not safe. We can ponder these questions later.'

They moved away from the Bluerorcs quickly and went to the door on the other side of the room.

'Where are we?' asked Will as they hurried through. 'I don't recognise these rooms. I just ran away without looking where I was going.'

'We're at the back of the school. These rooms aren't regularly used for students, but are sometimes used as offices or as project rooms—whatever the need is.'

'I see.'

They hastened through other rooms, and down several corridors and stairs without encountering anyone, or anything for that matter. They also heard nothing out of the ordinary, especially no crashing caused by Bluerorcs chasing them.

'Will Beltorec have already found out about what we've done to his Bluerorcs?' asked Will.

'Probably not. I'd guess we would have heard that,' Beltorec replied dryly.

They went down another corridor and round a corner.

'Ah, I recognise this one. Over there is one of our classrooms,' said Will.

'Fine. Hurry up!'

They took several turns, until Will again did not have the faintest idea where they were. Then Contractus led him down several flights of small stairs, and the corridors became barer. They were seldom used, judging by the puffs of dust that rose as Will and Contractus hurried along. Then the walls turned to rough stone, and the air became cold and musty. They still hurried on, through ancient passages, up and down worn stairs, and through rusty, creaking doors until Contractus led him up some stairs again and through doors that were in far better repair.

'Hey, I recognise this! I've been here before!' Will said. Then he clamped his mouth shut and coughed in embarrassment. They were in the forbidden house where the secret meetings about the investigation into the forgery had been. How could Contractus know about this? And now Will had told him that he was involved!

Contractus barked a short laugh as he saw Will's panic-stricken face. 'No need to worry, lad. I know about the meetings and the committee investigating the forgery. Just remember the situation at Cloudy's transportation hub—I knew about the forgery then!' He winked at Will. 'Though I'm not headmaster or somebody important in Snowfields, I still know my way around. I know the right people. So I know pretty much what's going on, if only indirectly. And I care for Snowfields! This is my life, my dream!' His face hardened. 'And I won't let it be destroyed by a self-centred bastard.'

Will suddenly felt very foolish. With all the excitement and the pain in his side it had never even occurred to him to question Contractus's knowledge of the forgery during that episode —or even afterwards. He was concentrating too hard on his job, and then on who could be responsible for the fraud. Somehow he trusted his teacher so much he had never once been suspicious of him. What a fine secret agent he had turned out to be!

They went on, right up to the door of the room where the meetings had taken place. Contractus opened it, and stepped inside. Will followed.

'Hello, Will,' said a warm voice that carried the hint of a smile.

Will looked up. He knew that voice. Sitting there, smiling at him, was Lektrarissima.

He quickly sat down at the table. It had again been turned into a huge computer display, with a map of Snowfields. Contractus moved his hand over the school building and tapped on it. Promptly the display shifted and changed so the school building turned transparent and grew in size and they could make out the details.

'Now, let's see,' he said slowly. 'Beltorec's office is here.... He's not in there. I met you over here.... Hmm...let's see.' He moved his hands and zoomed in on the area where they had fought the Bluerorcs. 'Ah, here they are. And there's Beltorec, see? He's there already.' He moved his fingers and touched one of the dots. A small box appeared next to it. 'Beltorec, vice chancellor of Snowfields School'. Hmm. Here are the Bluerorcs.' He tapped on one of the six larger, blue dots. Panels appeared beside them reading 'Bluerorc'. Contractus squinted at the scene. 'Looks like he's still trying to revive them. We must assume he can do that because we've obviously rather underestimated him so far.'

Lektrarissima nodded, not smiling anymore.

'You know, I don't know very much about Bluerorcs,' Contractus went on. 'It's, thank goodness, not a common topic, and for a long time there has been no reason to be concerned about them. There's hardly any literature about them, and there is surely nobody alive who's had to deal with them before.' Contractus stood up. 'I think we should visit Wonderock!'

Lektrarissima nodded, a faint trace of her characteristic smile reappearing. 'Yes, if there's anybody who'd know anything about them, he would. After he retired he positively drowned himself in studies about almost everything concerning our special business, and naturally especially everything dealing with Bluerin. He would know.'

'Then let's go, before Beltorec can get them revived and starts hunting us again!' Contractus got up and pulled his wand out of his pocket. Then, to Will's horror, he set fire to the table.

'What are you doing?' Will shouted. 'The table.... The computer!' He was at a loss for words, seeing the table engulfed in flames.

Contractus looked at him calmly. 'We can't let the table fall into Beltorec's hands. He would only use it against us, to locate us and to spy on us. He'd know exactly where we were and would hunt us down immediately!'

Lektrarissima nodded without a smile.

'But....' Will started again meekly, looking in horror at the table that was slowly being consumed by flames.

'I know,' said Contractus, 'but the wizards are quite capable, and I believe they'll be able to recreate such a table after this is over. Of course it won't be easy. But we have to deal with this problem first. And right now we just can't take the chance! Let's leave. We need to find Wonderock.'

By then the dry table had burned down to a miserable heap of ashes and molten metal. They quickly left the room. Contractus once again led the way, and Lektrarissima followed Will. They went down several flights of stairs until they were back in the bare passages down below Snowfields. Contractus again took a route Will did not know. They passed through grey and ill-lit tunnels with bare and crude stone walls, damp and musty, sometimes with water running across the ground or dripping from the ceiling.

'We'll head up here,' Contractus finally said, and opened a rusty, iron gate that squeaked in protest. He lead them up several flights of stairs, and down deserted corridors. Finally Contractus opened an iron grating. They went through and were standing outside in a street Will did not recognise. Contractus replaced the grate. Will looked back at it: from there it just looked like a totally harmless drainage tunnel, not at all like a door to hidden passages.

'Come on!' Contractus again led the way down the street: 'It isn't far.'

They passed several nondescript buildings, probably some staff homes. Then there were some rather larger and better-looking homes, with an even larger building at the end of the street just before an intersection. This building was also made of the red brick that was so common in Snowfields. It had beautiful, lattice windows with inlays of coloured lead glass and golden frames. Warm light filtered through the windows, illuminating the inlaid Christmas scenes.

'Here we are.' Contractus went to the ornate entrance and knocked, using an intriguingly-carved brass knocker. It took some time, but finally they heard steps inside. The door opened slowly.

'Yes? Who's there?' croaked an elderly voice.

'Good evening, Mr Wonderock,' Contractus greeted him respectfully. The door opened fully.

'Ah, Contractus. And Lady Lektrarissima, what a lovely surprise for an old man.' He smiled pleasantly at them. 'And who's this young man then?'

'Yes, sir, this is Will Burns, a student at our school,' replied Contractus.

'Nice to meet you, Will.'

'Thank you, sir!' replied Will.

'But please, do come in. It's unpleasant out here.' He looked up into the sky.' There's something....' Wonderock shook his head and stepped back into his house, motioning for them to follow him inside.

On the way in, Contractus muttered, 'It is indeed unpleasant out there!'

'What was that, Contractus?'

'Sir, we've got to talk,' Contractus replied shortly with a last glance outside, as if to make sure they had not been followed.

'Well, come into the living room and let's sit down then.' Wonderock went through a broad door, and Will and the others followed him into a large sitting room. It had comfortable furniture made out of warm woods, lots of lamps gleaming with a pleasant golden glow, bright wall hangings, and many bookcases. They settled down in upholstered chairs and couches that were clustered around a large table littered with books, scrolls, and pens.

'Now, my dear friends.' Wonderock smiled fondly at Contractus and Lektrarissima. 'And my new friend.' He winked at Will, who immediately felt that he liked this old man. 'What gives me the pleasure of your unexpected visit? I'm sure this isn't just a social visit.' His smile turned sly.

Contractus cleared his throat. 'Sir, our worst fears have come true. Beltorec has created Bluerorcs!'

'Great fir tree!' Wonderock exclaimed. 'That's a nasty surprise indeed. You're sure?' He looked sharply at Contractus.

Contractus nodded. 'Yes, I've seen them myself. In fact Beltorec had set them on Will, and they were hunting him when we were temporarily able to stop them with Bluerin globes. But even as we talk, Beltorec is trying to revive them.'

'Well, we've at least got some time then. Alas, I never thought I'd see these horrible creatures walk the earth.' He sighed heavily. 'But we've got no time to get sentimental—we've got to devise a plan to deal with them. Fortunately I've had a lot of time since my retirement to study Bluerin and everything connected to it, so I've also made a study of Bluer-orcs. But information about them is scarce. And, of course, I didn't have the real thing to study—not that I would have liked that, mark you. And nobody alive has ever seen Bluerorcs or had any experience with them. But I think I know most of the things that can be known about them.'

Contractus nodded. 'That's what I thought, so we came straight to you. We only passed by the secret observation room first, where we met Lektrarissima. And we checked where Beltorec was and what he was doing. Fortunately he was still stuck with his attempts to revive the Bluerorcs. After that we destroyed the table.'

Wonderock nodded gravely. 'Yes, that's rather a loss. But most unavoidable too. It wouldn't do us any good if he got that into his hands. Beltorec, you say? I can't say I'm surprised. Even as a student at school, when I was headmaster there, he seemed just a bit too ambitious. And there were always some strange things going on around him. But I never could track them down or prove his involvement. I could never find anything really wrong with him. He always did what he was told. And he did well, scored high marks. That alone is rather suspicious in a student, in my experience. Don't you think?'

He looked at Will, who smiled rather embarrassed. Wonderock looked back at Contractus. 'So you stopped them with Bluerin globes, eh? That was a rather good idea—where did you get that notion from?'

'Well, I also have a bit of knowledge about Bluerorcs, but not nearly as vast as yours must be. I just remembered suddenly that I read somewhere they could be stopped in such a way.'

'Yes.' Wonderock nodded. 'Extenboom described such a method of stopping them in his rather unpopular scrolls. Bah.' He looked rather disgusted. 'People are always so stupid. They think that just because they choose to ignore something unpleasant it will go away.'

'The globes did indeed stop them,' Contractus went on, 'but I fear that Beltorec is trying to revive them as we are talking. We have to do something! We have to stop him!'

Wonderock rubbed his beard and nodded. 'Hmm, revive them.... I guess that might be possible. Especially Beltorec might be able to do that—he has the capability, that he has.' He looked at Contractus. 'Yes, yes, we have to do something, or it will get far worse than it already is. Fortunately I didn't only read Extenboom, but also Sententee, one of his students. He wrote some very interesting scrolls about the possibilities of dealing with Bluerorcs. He especially expanded the theories of Extenboom and explored the possibilities of dealing permanently with Bluerorcs—methods to destroy them. Of course this is all just theoretical, as no Bluerorcs have been around for a long time. Luckily no one dared to create them after the havoc they caused in the past. That is, no one has dared until today!' He shook his head. 'Well, we'll have to deal with this mess now.'

He got up and went over to the bookcases where the books were piled up to the ceiling. Scrolls had been stuffed everywhere in between. Wonderock stood in front the shelves, muttering under his breath: 'Now where is.... I know I had it in my hands only the other day.... It was here somewhere....' He sorted through the scrolls and finally pulled out one that was rather battered, antique-looking.

'Aha!' he called. 'I knew it was here somewhere. That's what we need.' He came back to where Will and the others were sitting.

'What is it?' asked Contractus, looking curiously at the scroll in Wonderock's hands.

'What? Oh....' Wonderock looked up from the scroll he was unrolling. 'This is one of the works of Sententee, in which he explores a theory on how to disable Bluerorcs permanently.'

'Oh,' replied Contractus. 'How does it work? *Does* it work?'

Wonderock barked a short laugh. 'How should I know? Fortunately I never had to deal with Bluerorcs. And even Sententee, or Extenboom for that matter, had never even met one. They could only work out some theories. But those are sound!'

'And how does this theory work?' Contractus repeated, still looking rather sceptical.

'Ah,' said Wonderock, raising his long and slender finger high in the air. 'Sententee proposed a method that uses both Bluerin and Yellowrin combined in one wand, released together with a special spell devised by him.' Wonderock made a spiralling gesture with his hand while he said this.

Contractus looked even more sceptical when he heard this. 'Bluerin and Yellowrin together? What's the effect of that? Bluerin okay, but Yellowrin doesn't have any effect at all!'

'Well,' said Wonderock, putting his finger along the side of his nose. 'That's what everybody believes, but it is only in modern times that we use Yellowrin as if it has no effect, no power. And it is good that everybody believes that. For Yellowrin by itself really has no potency, but in combination with

Bluerin it is truly powerful. In fact so potent it could quite possibly be the only means that may be useful against Bluerorcs.'

'Very well,' said Contractus, 'if you say so. Can you teach us this spell?'

'Yes, I think so. The instructions are all in here,' said Wonderock, pointing at the scroll.

'But even if he can teach us the spell, it won't be of much use to us,' interjected Lektrarissima.

'And why might that be, my dear lady?' asked Wonderock.

'Well, I don't have a wand that can be charged with both Yellowrin and Bluerin at the same time. Do you?' She looked at Contractus.

'No,' he admitted, scratching his head. 'I hadn't thought about that. So what now? We have the method to strike back at them, but we don't have the means.' He shook his head. 'This is really frustrating!'

'But no, no,' Wonderock retorted, 'not at all, my friends. Trust old Wonderock! Hardly anybody knows this, but over the years I have collected quite a few old wands, odd wands, special wands, and some of them can be charged with Yellowrin and Bluerin at the same time.'

'Oh...all right,' said Contractus, rubbing his hands. 'Now then, for the spell?'

'Very well,' said Wonderock, 'please watch carefully.' And he took out his wand, stepped over to a desk on which a small container with Yellowrin stood, charged his wand, and stood in front of them. Then he showed them the spell, carefully teaching them the rather complex, spiralling motion. When the three of them could perform it adequately, he nodded. 'That's good enough. Let's get you the wands. Follow me.'

Will, Contractus, and Lektrarissima followed Wonderock into his cellar. There he opened a large cabinet and took out three narrow but long boxes which he laid out on a table. Will opened the box closest to him. Inside was a wand that looked rather old and was richly decorated. When he picked it up, he could feel the age and the power. The others picked up wands that looked to be of equal age.

'Beautiful!' said Contractus, admiring the wand he held in his hand.

While Will looked closely at his wand, he remembered something. 'Sorry, sir, but will these wands work for us? I was taught they have to be personalized to you before you can use them.'

'Ah,' replied Wonderock, 'I see you actually listen to your teachers.' He grinned at Will, who blushed slightly. 'And yes, you are right. Normally they have to be personalized. But these are old and well-used wands that belonged to powerful members of the organisation. They were specially created using Bluerin and Yellowrin in the process—something that is very laborious and only done in special cases. Your wands are really just wooden sticks, and thus need the personalization. But these special wands can be used by anyone who knows how to use them. Therefore they can be rather dangerous, and that is one of the reasons why they are so rare.'

Contractus interrupted. 'Sorry, sir, but this isn't the time for lectures. We have to hurry if we want to stop Beltorec and his Bluerorcs. Does anybody know the nearest place where Bluerin is stored?'

'Er,' said Wonderock, looking slightly embarrassed, 'actually I have a small amount here. Just for an emergency, you know.' He looked at them. 'This does not need to go beyond us four, now, agreed?'

Contractus winked at him. 'Why, you sly old fox. But I'd say this definitely is an emergency. Where have you got it?'

Wonderock gave him an amused look. 'In fact you are just standing on it. If you wouldn't mind taking a step backwards?'

'Oh, sure,' replied Contractus, hurriedly taking two steps backwards and looking at the ground where he had just been standing. Will also looked there, but the only thing he could see were some rough, grey tiles. Wonderock took out his wand again and pointed it at the tiles. He mumbled a spell and made a gesture with his wand, and a faint trace of Bluerin streaked towards the tiles. One of them slowly lifted from the ground, and underneath a small, glass tank appeared. It was filled with Bluerin.

'Let's charge the wands then,' Wonderock prompted.

'Go on, Will,' said Contractus.

Will took his new—or rather the very old—wand and inserted it into the opening of the Bluerin container. After his wand was charged, he stepped back. The others charged their wands in turn, and after Wonderock had completed the charging of his wand, he again performed the spell and the tile slowly sank back towards the ground, where it fitted seamlessly in with the others, forming an unbroken surface. Nobody would surmise anything was underneath it. Then the four went back upstairs into Wonderock's study. Wonderock fetched a container with Yellowrin from a shelf and put it on the desk, and they all charged their wands with it.

'Good,' said Contractus. 'What are we going to do now? I don't think we have much time. We don't know what Beltorec is doing with his Bluerorcs at the moment. They could come storming in here anytime.'

Lektrarissima nodded. 'That may very well be. But even if we have the means to fight them now, where should we look for them? And where should we confront them? We should choose the time and place so we have optimal conditions to fight them. We should not take any chances.'

Wonderock nodded but said nothing. He went to one of the bookshelves and came back with a scroll that he placed on the desk in front of them, putting some books on the edges to prevent it from rolling up again. Will could see it was a map of Snowfields on which not only the streets, but also every single building was depicted. It was beautiful, highly-detailed and colourful.

Wonderock peered at the map. 'Where did you say you disabled the Bluerorcs?' he asked Contractus.

'Right in the school. I encountered them and Will in some of the rarely-used rooms in the western wing.'

'Hmm, yes,' replied Wonderock, thinking. 'And after you went to the control room and destroyed the table, you came straight here?'

'Yes. I took the most direct way I knew.'

'Hopefully Beltorec hasn't something similar to the table he can use instead. But I fear he might have. However, it would not be nearly as effective or powerful as the table.' He straightened up and pointed to a building on the map. Will could see he was pointing directly at the abandoned building. 'So I'd guess that after he has successfully revived his Bluerorcs, he will be headed straight there, in order to use the table to find you. We should go there immediately. With luck we'll arrive before him, so we can set a trap!'

Will saw that Contractus and Lektrarissima nodded grimly in agreement, and he thought that this seemed to be the best they could do.

'Any objections? Or maybe better ideas?' Wonderock asked, and looked around. Nobody said anything. 'Right, let's go then.' He rubbed his hands eagerly. 'I have direct access to the underground tunnels in my cellar. Follow me!'

He led them back down into the cellar, a much more sprightly and vivid figure than when Will had first met him. There Wonderock opened a hidden door with a spell, and the others followed him into the passage that lay behind it. They hurried through the tunnels underneath Snowfields again. After a while Will began to recognise the tunnels, as they were getting near the abandoned building. Wonderock, who was in the lead, slowed down a bit.

'Careful now!' he whispered back to them. 'We don't know where they might be.' He slowly went on, looking ahead and checking the sides carefully. Will, Contractus, and Lektraris-sima followed close behind him, all with their wands out and at the ready. Suddenly Wonderock threw himself to the ground, and a bright, intertwined streak of Yellowrin and Bluerin passed over him, missing Will only by inches. Wonderock immediately threw a spell back towards the source of the streak. Will heard some swearing and thought that it sounded somehow familiar. Then it stopped.

'Who's there?' Wonderock called. 'Show yourself!'

This was greeted by silence.

'Wonderock?' A low voice finally came out of the direction where the swearing had come from. 'Is that you, sir?'

Wonderock called right at the same time, 'Stunt? Ethan Stunt?'

From behind a stone block rose the figure of Mr Stunt, wand out in front of him, held at the ready.

'Sir!' he said again to Wonderock as he walked up to them. 'Nice to meet you. But what are you doing here?' When he came nearer, he also saw the others. 'Contractus! Lektraris-sima! And Will? What an odd group. What are you all doing here?' he repeated.

'Beltorec is behind the fraud and the forgery,' Wonderock told Stunt grimly. 'Will has confronted him and discovered that he has created Bluerorcs. He immediately sent them after Will. Fortunately he and Contractus could disable them for the moment. But I believe Beltorec will be able to revive them. We came here because we hope to catch him and finish off the

255

Bluerorcs. But what are you doing here? And armed like that?' Wonderock looked almost accusingly at Stunt's double-charged wand.

While Wonderock had been talking, Stunt's expression had darkened noticeably, even compared to his normal scowl. 'I feared something like this. I was late in the school and checking the grounds when I heard something. Then I heard some noise and some crashing from inside the rarely-used rooms. So I went in there to investigate. First I saw only debris and broken-down doors, then I saw a Bluerorc! I hurried back until I reached some containers and could charge my wand. Then I followed the trail left by the Bluerorcs. I had just got here when I heard you coming, and took cover. Sorry for the attack.'

Wonderock looked at him sharply. 'How come you know how to fight Bluerorcs?'

'Sir!' replied Stunt sharply, drawing himself up. 'As commanding officer of the security forces, that is my job!'

'Yes, yes,' said Wonderock impatiently, 'but how do you know? Certainly not from some standard manuals.'

'Well, sir, when I was made officer in the security forces, one of the older officers took me aside one day and told me about this theory. He said I would make my way in the security forces and someday I might need this knowledge. He had never seen a Bluerorc in his life, but he was sure the day would come that we would see them again. And that it was his duty to pass the knowledge on before his retirement. Didn't believe him back then, of course, but then I also didn't forget. And today proved him right after all.'

'Hmm, that officer, that wouldn't have been old Stoneface, would it?' Wonderock asked with a wry grin.

'Yes, sir, it was.'

Wonderock nodded. 'Good. Now, here is what we intend to do.' He quickly explained their plan. Then he asked, 'Do you know a good place for an ambush down here?'

'Of course, sir!' Stunt drew himself up straight. 'Follow me.'

'Let's go then!' Wonderock called to the others. Will went after Stunt, immediately followed by Contractus and Lektrarissima, with Wonderock bringing up the rear. They hurried through the corridor until they reached an intersection. Will knew this place. The corridor to the right led directly into the abandoned building.

Stunt stopped and conferred quickly with Wonderock. Then he placed Will and Contractus on one side of the entrance behind a column, Lektrarissima and Wonderock behind a column on the other side. He himself took cover behind a boulder directly opposite the opening to the corridor. Then they waited. Will tried to stay calm and not think too much about what he had got himself into.

Contractus very quietly said, 'Will?' He laid a calming hand on Will's shoulder. 'Everything all right?'

Will tried to nod calmly and whispered back, 'Yes, sir.'

Then he stiffened. Had he heard something? He listened intently, but nothing happened. He tried to relax again, but held his wand at the ready. Then he definitely heard something! The noise was getting louder, and something was coming down the corridor. It was coming nearer and nearer. It was the heavy and partly grinding sound he remembered all too well from earlier, when he had been chased by the Bluerorcs.

Will pointed his wand directly at the opening. Suddenly he felt a wave of panic! He had forgotten the new spell Wonderock had taught him against the Bluerorcs. Was it a sweep to the left or the right? And then the helix or the circle? He could not remember. Then he felt Contractus's hand on his shoulder, squeezing him.

'You can do it, Will!' Contractus whispered, 'Just be sure to stay covered.'

Will could see Contractus's wand beside his own, and suddenly he could remember the spell. Then the Bluerorc came crashing out of the tunnel and into the opening between them, directly where they had prepared the trap. Immediately it was hit by five intertwined beams of Yellowrin and Bluerin. It was working! Under the combined power, the Bluerorc started to dissolve. It looked as if it were melting. And quickly it dissolved completely, until only a blue puddle was left on the floor.

Will punched the air and grinned excitedly: they'd done it! The spell had worked! But then he again heard a noise coming from the corridor. He calmed down quickly and concentrated again. He ducked back behind the column and held his wand at the ready, pointing it towards the opening once more. The noise in the tunnel was coming nearer quickly. And it was much louder than the first time.

Will held his breath. He once more felt Contractus squeeze his shoulder in reassurance. Then, with a loud crash, two Bluerorcs stomped out of the tunnel. Will did not have time to think, but just reacted—and that was what saved him and the others. For one of the Bluerorcs was hit by four combined beams of Yellowrin and Bluerin, but the other one was hit by only one—Will's beam. It worked nevertheless. Both Bluerorcs started to dissolve and seemed to be melting, until only two blue puddles were left on the floor. Again Will relaxed a bit.

Contractus looked at him gravely and whispered, 'Well done, Will. That could really have gone wrong if it hadn't been for you!'

Will just nodded, but felt immensely proud. Before he could dwell on it, he started to hear a noise coming from the corridor yet again—and it was coming nearer and getting louder quickly. Will straightened up and braced himself again. He took a firm grip on his wand. Stunt raised himself slightly from the boulder he was hiding behind and gave a low whistle. When they were all looking at him, he made several fast gestures to instruct them that they should all engage the Bluerorcs on their sides, and he would deal with the ones in the centre. Will and the others gestured back that they had understood and would follow the instructions.

The sound out of the tunnel was getting really loud. Will took a deep breath and prepared himself. And with a loud crash, three Bluerorcs broke free of the tunnel, the outermost mindlessly tearing down the sides of the entrance and the nearest pillars. Will fired off the spell, hitting the Bluerorc that was nearest to him. The Bluerorc had such a momentum Will nearly missed it, but fortunately the beam hit it in the side, and the Bluerorc began to dissolve immediately. Will looked around to see how the others were faring. He saw that each of them had engaged one of the Bluerorcs, so they all were sinking slowly to the ground.

Will was surprised to see that only Stunt had not used a spell, but instead was staring intently at something right in front of him. Will followed his glance—and froze. Behind the Bluerorcs he saw Beltorec. The headmaster stood in the entrance of the tunnel, his eyes glittering dangerously and locked on Stunt. He had his wand out in front of him and was pointing it at his opponent. For Will, time seemed to freeze. He looked at Beltorec's face and was appalled by the expression he saw. There was nothing of the friendly and understanding headmaster he had trusted. Instead Beltorec's face was a mask of pure hatred and disgust as he looked at Stunt.

259

For a split second, Beltorec turned his head and looked directly at Will, who involuntarily shied away, for there was so much hatred and abhorrence in the glance. Stunt took advantage of this small instant when Beltorec was not focused on him, and fired a spell directly at him. But Beltorec's attention was already completely back on Stunt, and he blocked the spell with an easy, almost lazy flick of his wand.

By then the Bluerorcs had dissolved completely, and the way was free so Wonderock and Lektrarissima were hit by parts of the deflected spell. To Will's horror they both sank to the ground unconscious. Beltorec smiled brightly as Stunt fired another spell at him, and again deflected it easily. Again fragments of the spell ricocheted off the walls and flew through the corridor.

Will ducked instinctively. Then he heard a grunt beside him and was hit hard in the side. His first thought was that he had been hit by part of the spell, but then he looked down and realised, to his great dismay, that Contractus had fallen to the ground beside him unconscious. He ducked farther behind the column in fear as Stunt fired another a spell at Beltorec. But again it did not reach Beltorec as he brushed it aside with a flick of his wand, laughing cruelly, madly.

Will tried to overcome his fear. He had to do something! Otherwise Beltorec was surely going to kill them. He feverishly hoped Stunt would be able to disarm the vice chancellor, but again he had to watch as another spell did no harm to Beltorec at all. And he saw that Stunt was beginning to tire. The hand with which he held the wand was starting to shake as he fired yet another desperate spell at Beltorec, who again deflected it. Will sighed in frustration. What could he do? How could he help Stunt? He knew nothing about fighting with magic or the necessary spells, especially compared to a master and member of the security forces like Stunt. He only knew some basic spells he had been taught for the delivery of the presents. But he had to do something! Anything!

'Use the freezing spell,' said Conrad.

Will looked up in shock. The security agent was crouching next to him again.

'I can't,' moaned Will. 'I don't know how.'

The agent glanced at Will in surprise. Beltorec had recovered faster than Will and used this moment to fire a spell that hit Conrad's wand which burst in flame.

Conrad swore heftily and immediately dropped it.

'Quickly, give me your hand, I'll help you,' he turned to Will.

Will saw Beltorec fire a spell back at Stunt, who barely ducked in time. He concentrated and waited until Beltorec was engaged with firing another spell. Then, Conrad guiding his hand, he performed the freezing spell. He released it at Beltorec, but the vice chancellor was quick! He spun around towards Will and raised his wand quick as lightning to deflect Will's spell back. Will tried to duck, but part of it hit his right arm. An ice-cold shock ran up his arm. It started to tingle, and then turned numb.

Will quickly grabbed his wand with his left hand before his right hand was so numb that the wand would fall down. Then he just reacted without thinking: with Conrad still guiding his hand, he immediately fired another freezing spell at Beltorec and caught him by surprise. But because he was using his left hand, his aim was so bad he barely hit Beltorec at all. Nevertheless, he was lucky: the spell hit Beltorec's right hand and froze it, so his wand fell uselessly to the floor and rolled away from him.

Beltorec looked startled, and gazed at the wand. Then he stared at Stunt, who seized the chance and started another spell. Beltorec swore heavily, spun around, and ran back down the corridor from which he had appeared so suddenly. He was so quick that Stunt's spell missed him completely. Then he was gone.

Will looked over to Stunt, who was slumped against the boulder in exhaustion. Their eyes met, and Stunt gave Will an appreciative nod. Will relaxed a bit and looked around. He saw Wonderock, Lektrarissima, and Contractus still lying unconscious on the ground. He knelt down beside Contractus and nudged him, but nothing happened. Contractus did not react at all.

Stunt looked over at him. 'Leave them, Will,' he said tiredly, taking deep breaths. 'There's nothing we can do for them right now. But they'll probably come round in an hour or two.'

Will nodded. He touched his right hand with his left hand. His right arm was just hanging limply down his side, and as he touched his right hand he felt nothing. He could not even move his fingers.

Stunt limped over and picked up Beltorec's wand. 'Don't worry about your arm. It may take a few hours, but then it will be alright again.' He slowly walked over to Will. 'Can you walk?' Will nodded. 'Good. We have to follow Beltorec before he can recover and create more havoc. Conrad, you're coming with us? Let's go.'

Conrad prodded the charred remains of his wand with a foot, while he held his right hand.

He looked up: 'Injured and without my wand? No. I can't help you like this.'

Stunt nodded gravely, straightened up, held his wand in front of him, and led Will down the corridor after Beltorec. Will followed him a bit reluctantly, because he had a bad feeling about leaving the others lying there. But Stunt was right—

they had to stop Beltorec as soon as possible. They went up the stairs.

Will was thinking about what Stunt had said, and then he suddenly remembered something. He whispered, 'Sir, did Mr Contractus tell you he destroyed the table earlier on?'

Stunt stopped. 'Wonderock mentioned it. But that doesn't really make much difference,' he whispered back. 'The room with the table is the only one that has any use for Beltorec in this building. So he'll head there. Let's go.'

He led Will onwards again. They passed through several more corridors and went up some stairs until Will recognised the surroundings and knew they were near the room that had contained the table. Stunt cautioned Will with a signal of his hand and slowly inched towards the door, with his wand out in front of him and at the ready. He cautiously opened the door with Will close behind him, also with his wand at the ready. As the door opened farther, Will could see no one in the room. Stunt slipped through the door without any noise, and then Will heard him call, 'Come on inside, Will, he isn't here. There's nobody in here.'

Will hurried into the room. There he saw the blackened remains of the table.

Stunt was looking closely at it. 'Good,' he said. 'Beltorec could not use this anymore, that's for sure.'

Will looked around. Besides the table there had only been some chairs and an empty bookcase in the room. Nothing else that could have been useful to Beltorec. Stunt followed his glance as he looked at the bookcase.

'Watch,' he said to Will, and went over to it. There he pulled on the second shelf from the ground. Will watched in astonishment as the bookcase swung silently away from the wall and revealed a secret opening behind it. Stunt went inside, and Will followed him, stopping in the doorway. Behind the bookcase was some sort of office—a windowless, small, and cramped room with a desk and some shelves. It was in a complete mess. Papers had been scattered all over the desk and on the floor. Books had been ripped off the shelves and thrown onto the ground, some with torn pages or facedown.

Stunt gave the mess a cursory glance, shook his head, and turned round again. He said to Will, 'Let's go. There's nothing we can do here. Thankfully Beltorec was in a hurry, so I don't think he found anything useful.'

Will nodded. 'But where is he now? Where should we look for him?'

Stunt walked over to the charred remains of the table. 'Watch and learn.' he told Will cryptically.

And Will watched as Stunt took his wand and pointed it towards the floor next to the table. Will could see ash lying there, and then he saw that in the ash was the imprint of a shoe. Stunt pointed his wand right at the imprint and performed a spell Will had never heard of. The imprint started to glow faintly blue, like Bluerin. Then Will saw that several other imprints started to glow blue all over the floor.

Stunt gave Will a quick look. 'Luckily Beltorec has stepped into the ashes, so we have this imprint and can follow his steps. Come.'

He led Will out of the room, tracing the imprints that continued to glow faintly on the floor. They followed them towards a staircase and upwards. Will and Stunt cautiously went upstairs, but still did not see Beltorec or anything unusual. They were nearly at the top of the building when Stunt went past a window and stopped so abruptly that Will nearly bumped into him.

'Dammit!' Stunt said.

'What is it?' Will asked.

'Look!' said Stunt, and pointed out of the window.

Will stood next to him. Then he saw it too: a sleigh with reindeer was flying away from the building—and Beltorec was on it.

'What are we going to do now?' Will asked.

Stunt shrugged his shoulders and sighed. 'There isn't much we can do. Let's go back and see how the others are doing.'

They hurried back through the building, into the cellar, and out into the corridor where they had left the others. When they reached the scene of the fight, Will was relieved to see that Wonderock had recovered already and was helping the others, who were just coming round.

Wonderock looked up when he heard them coming. 'Stunt! What did you find? Did you catch Beltorec?'

Stunt made a face. 'No, sir, I'm afraid not. We were on his trail. He had broken into the hidden study in the table room, but it didn't look as if he had the time to take anything valuable. We followed his tracks up near the roof, but then we saw him through a window as he was flying away with a sleigh. Sorry I failed you, sir.'

Wonderock shook his head grimly. 'No, that's not your fault. We have all failed. Now we need to get back to the school as fast as possible. That's most likely the place he'll go. Can you two walk?' he asked Lektrarissima and Contractus, who were just standing up.

Contractus nodded stiffly, and Lektrarissima replied, 'Yes,' although she looked rather white and her voice was husky.

'Good.' Wonderock nodded. 'You'll lead the way,' he told Stunt. 'Let's go!'

'Where's Conrad?' Will asked quickly.

'Oh, he helped me come round, then he had to leave for his headquarters to seek medical attention. Nasty magical burn there. But don't worry, he's tough, he'll be fine.'

Stunt led them along the corridors towards the school—the same corridors Will had walked down with Beltorec not so long ago, not knowing that the vice chancellor was the real enemy. Finally they reached the school and stood in front of Beltorec's office.

Stunt turned to Wonderock. 'Sir, you should lead the way from here. You can easily take us past the door, past Crown.'

'Right,' said Wonderock, and walked towards Beltorec's office. He thumbed the smooth plate on the door. A face melted out of the wood, and Will recognised Crown. He looked rather annoyed.

'Who...?' Crown started to speak even before his face had formed completely. Then he recognised his old master.

'Sir! What are you doing.... Oh, sorry,... I mean... welcome back, sir. It's good to see you.'

'Open the door, Crown,' Wonderock told him brusquely. 'Is Beltorec in?'

'No, sir,' Crown replied quickly as the door swung open.

They went inside. The desk of Beltorec's secretary was empty, and the door to his office stood open. They entered carefully. There was no one in there. In fact there was not much of anything in there. Beltorec had beaten them to it and had taken most of his belongings away.

Stunt poked through the meagre remains. 'Not much left here. He seems to have planned his disappearance well in advance. What are we going to do now?' He looked at the others.

In turn they looked at Wonderock. Nobody volunteered anything. He thought for a moment.

'Well, nothing we can really do about it now. He's gone for good... or bad. Hopefully he won't come back—but I fear this won't be the last time we've heard from him. No, I fear it won't.' He sighed and slowly shook his head.

'I could try to follow him, sir, to catch him. If I use a fast sleigh...' Stunt said, already heading towards the door.

Wonderock moved fast and blocked his way. 'No, Stunt, no! You won't be able to catch him. His head start is much too great, and he's too cunning and powerful for you to catch him like that. Look how easily he could create his Bluerorcs without anyone suspecting him. No, we'll have to let him go for now.' Wonderock seemed to shrink with his words; he looked more the retired teacher again than the cunning magician and fighter for justice Will had seen during the last few hours.

'Well, what are we going to do then? Just act as if nothing has happened?' Stunt demanded.

'No, no, of course not,' replied Wonderock. 'Sadly that won't be possible. A new vice chancellor needs to be appointed, Beltorec's disappearance will have to be explained, the damage caused by the Bluerorcs will have to be repaired, and anyone who might have encountered them will have to be treated. But the extent and details of the fraud should remain confidential, for misuse of Bluerin is always a great danger, and this should not become known as an almost successful example.'

Lektrarissima nodded and added, 'You're right sir, but if I may suggest this, we'll need someone with authority who can take the necessary actions, and there is nobody here with much knowledge about how to handle such a situation—nobody except you, sir. Would you please consider stepping in and doing what is necessary?' She looked steadily at Wonderock. The others nodded or voiced their agreement.

Wonderock looked hard at them and finally shook his head in resignation. 'Yes, yes. I fear you are right. I'll help you do what is necessary. But'—he held up his finger—'as soon as this is sorted out, I'll return to my well-earned retirement.'

'That would be acceptable, sir,' Lektrarissima said, and grinned.

Contractus cleared his throat. 'Yes, except for one thing. I'd strongly suggest we retain a secret group to prepare for the eventuality that Beltorec will reappear. And that you'll be part of that group, sir.'

Wonderock nodded. 'Yes, that would be prudent. We are agreed then?' He looked sharply at everyone in their round, and they all nodded. 'Good then, let's do what's necessary. Stunt, you will come with me. We will first deal with the damage the Bluerorcs have caused and make sure they have all been destroyed or disabled. Lektrarissima, you will use your organisation and try to find out where Beltorec has gone, and whether there is anything of the fraud left in the systems. Contractus, please take care of Will and then make sure all the Bluerin is accounted for and no more workrooms from the forgery remain. I will contact you again for another meeting. Now go and deal with your tasks!'

They nodded and started to leave. Contractus turned to Will and looked at him gravely 'Come with me, Will.'

And Will followed Contractus to his office.

'Will.' Contractus turned to him, looking concerned. 'Are you alright? Nothing happened to you? No injuries?'

Will shook his head: 'No, sir. Everything's fine.'

Contractus still looked dubious.

'Really, sir, I'm fine. Part of Beltorec's spell hit my arm, but it's completely normal again.' He waved his arm around in order to convince Contractus.

'Okay, if you say so.' Contractus smiled. 'But if there is something—anything—wrong during the next few days, if you feel ill or there is anything you want to talk about... my door's always open.'

Will nodded. 'Thank you, sir.'

***

During the next few days and weeks, everybody was busy repairing the damage Beltorec and his Bluerorcs had caused. Miss Dustfall took over as interim headmistress, aided by Wonderock, though he stayed in the background as much as possible. Finally everything settled down again, and things were nearly as they had been before.

But for Will it was not quite like it had been when he had started at Snowfields. He still had to think about the fraud and the forgery. Because although they had exposed Beltorec, he still had to have had helpers. And they were still in Snowfields. Certainly Richard was. Will had talked with Contractus about Richard, but apart from what the two of them had seen during the spell on Cloudy's platform, they had nothing, and especially no proof against him. So there was not much they could do about him. And Richard knew this all too well. Every time he saw Will, he gave him a knowing and impertinent smile. But Will swore to himself he would continue to watch Richard and try to find proof of his involvement.

Three weeks after Christmas, everything had been restored, and life in Snowfields was back to normal. Will and all the other students gathered in the Ferum for the traditional feast after Christmas. After they had had a delicious meal, Miss Dustfall stood up.

'Students,' she began. 'Although we have kept it secret, I have no illusions that you all know perfectly well what has happened here this term. But now we have repaired everything, and school can go on as usual. And I can only now thank you all for your great work and your diligence on Christmas Eve. Every parcel was delivered on time. On Christmas Day there were no errors, and everybody got the presents that were designed for them. Thank you very much, all of you.' She bowed deeply.

There was a huge cheer and applause from the students.

'And now....' She took out her wand and performed a spell. 'I have the great honour to present someone who wants to talk to you himself.'

While she had been talking, Will had seen that some sort of white mist had been forming on the raised platform next to her. Now this mist became more solid, and the form of a person became visible. And in the next moment—Will jumped to his feet as all the others around him did in surprise—Father Christmas stood there. Or at least his image.

'Ho, ho, ho, my dear friends.' He looked around the room as if he could see them. 'My warmest greetings to all of you. And to you as well.' He nodded towards the teachers. 'I want to thank you very, very much for your excellent work on Christmas Eve. You all did extraordinarily well. All the presents were delivered safely, and you made a lot of children —and adults of course—very happy. You helped to provide a wonderful Christmas for them all, with wonderful presents.

'And some of you did even more. But those problems have also been sorted out. Well, nearly all of them. Because this school is missing its headmaster. So it needs a new one. I've heard—and when I look around here, I see for myself—that Miss Dustfall has done a great job as interim headmistress.' He turned slightly so that he could look at Miss Dustfall. 'Therefore it's a great pleasure for me to introduce you to your new headmaster—or better your new headmistress. Miss Dustfall!'

There was a great round of applause from the students, as Miss Dustfall was a good, fair teacher, and she was quite liked among them.

She looked surprised as well as pleased. 'Thank you very much, sir,' she said modestly, and curtseyed towards Father

Christmas. 'This is a great honour for me, and I hope I'll be able to fulfil your expectations.'

Father Christmas smiled at her. 'Of that I am sure, my dear.' He looked around the Ferum again and rubbed his hands. 'Now that all the work is behind us, I don't want to keep you from your holidays any longer. Once again, thank you very much, enjoy your well-earned holidays, and I am looking forward to seeing you again next term. Farewell.'

While he waved his hand, his figure turned transparent, and then there was only a shimmering mist that cleared away quickly. There was applause from the students again.

'Very well, everything is settled for now, and I hope the next term will be rather less disturbing than this one was at the end,' Miss Dustfall said.

Just at that moment, Will looked around and his eyes fell on Richard, who caught his look and gave him a nasty grin. Will tried to look away without acknowledging that he had seen this. He did not want to give Richard that satisfaction. But inside he feared that the next term would not be as uneventful as Miss Dustfall had wished, and that he would have to keep watching Richard.

Miss Dustfall continued, 'I think there have been enough thank yous and I'm sure you're all anxious to get home to your families. So I wish you all a great holiday.'

And with this the term was over. Everybody stormed from the Ferum and hurried to their rooms to pack their belongings. Will quickly packed his suitcase and bid his friends goodbye. He left his room, ran down a staircase, and was just passing by a dark corner in the corridor when he heard a deep but some-how familiar voice: 'Will? If you have a moment, please?'

He stopped and turned towards the dark corner. Instantly it brightened and Will could see Father Christmas standing there in front of him!

271

'Will Burns, although you think we haven't met before, I know what great service you have done this term. Not only for the White Christmas Organisation, but also for me. Without your help and your courage, Beltorec would have been able to do much more damage to Snowfields and to the whole organisation. But you have stopped him and his Bluerorcs. That was just amazing. I want to thank you personally.'

And to Will's utter amazement, Father Christmas bowed deeply to him. 'I...' Will floundered. 'Sir, thank you very much. But I only did what I felt was right. And Beltorec escaped! And—'

But Father Christmas held up his hand and interrupted Will. 'No, my friend, no!' he said softly. 'You did a superb job, and you've earned my deep gratitude. Here.' He put out his hands and pulled a beautifully-wrapped parcel out of thin air. 'This is my Christmas present for you.' He handed Will the parcel. 'And now, enjoy your holidays. I'll see you next term.'

And with that he was gone. Will stood in the dark corner, clutching the present. He had not even been able to thank Father Christmas for the gift. He shook his head: nothing he could do about it now. Then he heard others coming down the stairs. The last thing he wanted to do was to explain this to anybody. He would wait until he was home before he unpacked the present.

He quickly pushed it into his suitcase and hurried onwards, and soon was on his way home via Cloudy's Transportation Service. It did not take long, and then he was standing again under the street lantern next to his parents' house. He was glad to be home again.

Made in the USA
San Bernardino, CA
05 December 2013